The door began to shake and the hinges jingled.

Latonya didn't have the energy to get up from her bed and answer it. Then she realized that if she was going to make any headway against the flu that had her flat on her back for two days, she was going to have to muster the strength.

She draped the sweat-soaked sheet around herself and walked the few steps from her bedroom to her front door.

"One second." Her sore throat was tested by even those two words. Leaning against the door for rest, Latonya realized she would be lucky to tell the irritating person on the other side that they had the wrong apartment. Her illness and annoyance blocked her normal caution of looking through the peephole and putting the chain lock in place.

She angrily snatched open the door and immediately regretted her haste. A cold chill washed over her as her worst fear materialized.

Her husband and his grandfather had found her.

GWYNETH BOLTON

became an avid romance fan after sneak-reading her mother's romance novels. In the nineties, she was introduced to African-American romance novels and her life hasn't been the same since. She has an M.A. in creative writing and a Ph.D. in English. She teaches writing and women's studies at the college level. When she is not writing African-American romance novels, she is curled up with a cup of herbal tea, a warm quilt and a good book. She currently lives in Syracuse, New York, with her husband, Cedric. Readers can contact her via e-mail, gwynethbolton@prodigy.net or visit her Web site www.gwynethbolton.com

IF
ONLY
YOU
KNEW

GWYNETH BOLTON

Bolton E.

My mother Donna Pough

My sisters Jennifer, Sandy, Michelle and Tashina

 KIMANI PRESS™

ISBN-13: 978-1-58314-773-3
ISBN-10: 1-58314-773-X

IF ONLY YOU KNEW

www.kimanipress.com

Printed in U.S.A.

5.99
7/19/06
NRN
6/24396666

Dear Reader,

I hope you enjoy reading Latonya and Carlton's story as much as I enjoyed writing it. A major theme of the novel is the issue of intercultural relationships between people of African descent. As an African-American woman with friends and ties across the African diaspora, this theme is near and dear to my heart. I like to believe that for the most part people in general have more similarities than differences. So the way certain black-on-black biases and prejudices play out as we relate to one another has always intrigued me. I think that Latonya and Carlton show us that love finds its way past the obstacles of cultural and class difference. Their love story provides inspiration for us all to move past the things that stop us from connecting more fully. I'd love to hear what you think!

Gwyneth Bolton

Chapter 1

"Hey, beautiful."

Latonya Stevens glanced up from the papers on her desk. Smiling, she tilted her head and batted her eyes playfully at her coworker.

Jeff Weatherby leaned against the entryway to her office wearing a designer suit and a smile that could best be described as sexy with a little mischief thrown in for good measure. His tall, lean, muscular build, along with his Hollywood heartthrob looks and boyish charm, made him *almost* irresistible. And he knew it. Observing the player-on-the-prowl gleam in his eyes, Latonya thanked God she had developed immunity to smooth-talking playboys ever since the first one, her father, broke her heart.

Jeff loosened his tie as he stepped into the office and

took a seat. "So, beautiful, how about you come to Soka's with us for happy hour. It's Friday and it's time to get ready for the weekend." His piercing cobalt-blue eyes glimmered as he spoke. He casually leaned back in the chair.

Watching as he made himself comfortable, Latonya admired his easy, laid-back nature. She figured that it must have been nice to let go and not have to worry about anything but working and partying hard, *sometimes* in that order.

Unfortunately, she had too many responsibilities to test the lifestyle Jeff seemed to promote so whole-heartedly.

"Thanks for the invite, but I have to get a head start on next week's projects." She stood up and stretched, moving her neck and head in a circular motion.

"You know what they say about all work…" Jeff ran his fingers through black hair that would put male-shampoo-commercial models out of business and let his words linger.

"I know. I'm dull," Latonya admitted as she sat back down in her seat. She didn't need anyone to tell her that she didn't have a social life. She couldn't remember ever having one. And given the amount of responsibilities she now had, she doubted she'd be getting one anytime soon.

She'd started working for Harrington Enterprise's Miami offices fresh out of her MBA program full of energy and hope. The company exported cement and refined petroleum products from the Bahamas and imported crude oil from the States into the Bahamas. At twenty-four years old, the job with the Fortune 500-company allowed her to remain at home and help out her family in a stressful time: her grandmother—who had single-handedly raised Latonya and her sister—had just had a stroke.

She'd needed a job that would allow her to take over the mortgage payments on the small two-bedroom home where she'd spent most of her life and pay the part of her sister's tuition that wasn't covered by scholarships. The entry-level position at Harrington had barely allowed her to make ends meet when she combined those responsibilities with her own student-loan debt, but she was getting by.

Jeff smiled as he stood up, slinging his suit jacket over his shoulder. "You're not dull, beautiful. Just a little uptight, that's all. But I intend to make it my business to loosen you up. You work too hard. You need to learn how to relax, and I'm just the man to show you how." He winked at her.

Tilting her head, Latonya squinted and pursed her lips. "I'll tell you what, when I have time for a social life you will be the first person I call. How about that?" She knew she would never take him up on his offer. Flirting was fun, but it didn't pay the bills.

"That sounds like a plan to me, beautiful. I'll see you on Monday. That is, unless you want to give me a call later and hang out this weekend. Let's say Saturday night. You, me, a little dinner—"

"I'll see you on Monday, Weatherby. Now, go and

party or whatever it is you guys do on a Friday night.
I have work to do."

"Right. Catch you later, beautiful." Jeff gave her one
last wink as he strolled from the office.

*I'll tell you what, when I have time for a social life
you will be the first person I call. How about that?*

Carlton Harrington III let the words linger in his
mind as he continued down the hallway. He hadn't
meant to listen in on the conversation between Jeff and
Latonya. He'd simply been walking by her office when
he heard a sound that he seldom had the pleasure of
hearing from her. Laughter.

Had he known that he would become automatically irritated by what he heard, maybe he would
have kept walking.

As he made his way through the fairly empty cor-
ridors of Harrington Enterprise, two of his employees
stopped him.

"Hey, Mr. Harrington, do you want to come to
Soka's with us? A few of us hang out there on Fridays
to unwind after a long week."

Carlton glanced up and noticed Stan Carter and
Juan Esperanzo standing in front of the elevator.
Before he could answer Stan's inquiry, Juan spoke.

"Hey, Jeff, is she coming?"

Carlton turned and saw Jeff Weatherby trotting
down the hall.

"No, she says she has work to do," Jeff responded.

Carlton expelled a breath of air he didn't even know
he was holding as he moved to face Stan and Juan.

"I told you she wasn't going to come. Face it, man, your skills are lost on this one. That's a serious sistah and she is not checking for you, Jeff. Give it up." Stan let out a chuckle as he pressed the button for the elevator. He glanced over at Carlton. "So, would you like to come hang out?"

Carlton considered it briefly and decided to decline the outing with his employees. He already had plans to meet up with friends at Soka's later. "No, I'll take a rain check this time."

The elevator came and the trio of men stepped on.

"Just so you know, Ms. Latonya Stevens will be mine by the end of the year. I'm wearing her down. She won't be able to resist much longer. I can already see that she is falling for me—" Jeff's words and Stan and Juan's laughter were cut off by the elevator.

Like hell! Carlton thought as he listened to Jeff's boasting. Shocked that he even cared what went on between Jeff and Latonya Stevens, he continued on to the copy room. He had to make a copy of some paperwork from the Biltmore account and mail it to the Bahamas office.

It was hard to imagine that the small storefront business his great-great-grandfather had started back when he'd first moved to Miami from the Bahamas had become a huge import-export business. The company dealt mostly in cement and oil refining. Harrington Enterprise had two large main offices: one in Miami and the other in the city of Nassau in the Bahamas. They had several more satellite offices throughout the Caribbean.

As the sheets filtered though the copy machine, Carlton noticed that several key pieces of information were missing. He would have to go back to his office and add the information before sending the report. This meant he would be late meeting his friends.

On his way back down the hall, he stopped at Latonya Stevens's door. He couldn't figure out what it was about the woman that triggered the uneasy feeling in the pit of his stomach, but he hoped he knew enough to stay away from her. He realized that if he had any sense he wouldn't have been standing in front of her door.

He was about to turn away when she looked up from the paperwork on her desk. His stomach turned over and he almost smiled. However, the look on her face turned quickly into a frown when she saw him standing there. Before he could talk any sense into himself, his feet were heading directly into her office.

Latonya gritted her teeth. After weeks of managing to avoid prolonged contact with Carlton Harrington III, he'd just come barging into her office. When she heard footsteps in the hallway, she thought it might have been Jeff coming back to try to convince her to come with them to Soka's again. Flirting playboys, she could handle. Brooding, sexy bosses, she needed help with. Her immunity to men didn't seem to work at all with Carlton.

She had been with Harrington Enterprise for almost a year when the boss's grandson, Carlton Harrington III, had temporarily taken over her division. He had just returned from heading up an expansion project that pushed the Bahamas and Miami-based company farther into the Caribbean and seemed intent on making changes and making his mark.

The first Monday that she worked with Carlton she realized that she had several reasons to be nervous. The most unsettling were his ruggedly handsome looks and the powerful sensuality that she swore dripped from his pores. She had never seen a man so fine in all her life. His custom-made business suits, starched-shirts and silk ties draped his perfect form in a manner that proved the man made the clothes. She couldn't imagine any other man exuding a tenth of the cool, suave confidence he did in those suits.

The perfect combination of smooth dark chocolate with just barely a hint of milk, he had broad shoulders and well-defined muscles. His lush lips appeared soft to the touch. Although he never smiled at her, when she saw him smile at others, she had to admit that the perfect teeth along with those lips made for one delightful grin.

His eyes called to mind deep, dark pools of water; they were liquid fire and full of expression. The only problem was, from the time he first laid eyes on her, she felt as if all his eyes could express were irritation and dissatisfaction. His perfectly squared jaw-line and sweet lips were always set in a frown whenever Latonya entered the room.

She couldn't seem to do anything right for the grumpy man. He never managed more than grunts toward her, but with others he seemed cordial, even friendly. She told herself by the end of their first week working together that she really could *not* stand the man, no matter how handsome he was.

If only that were true. Honestly, for the first time in her young life she was finding herself intensely attracted to a man. She got heart palpitations whenever she was in the same room with him. She had to think of increasingly creative ways to maintain a façade of calm.

Finishing up a report that wasn't due until the following week, she tried to still her rapidly beating heart at the sight of Carlton. Everyone else had long since clocked out, but she was staying late as she usually did, going above and beyond the call of duty because she needed to get a promotion.

"What the hell do you call this?" Carlton threw several pages held together by a gold paper clip onto her desk.

She watched the papers fall and took several breaths to compose herself before she picked them up. Before responding to the rude and insufferable man, Latonya noted that it wasn't even her report. She peered up at him and blinked, startled by how handsome he managed to look even when brooding. She squinted, took a deep breath, and reminded herself that the man was her boss.

She pursed her lips a moment and then spoke, trying to keep the sarcasm out of her voice. "This is Jeff Weatherby's report on the Biltmore project."

The scowl on his face told her right away that she'd sounded sarcastic, anyway. Sighing, she reasoned her long week—the younger Harrington being the biggest contributor to its length—was almost over.

His eyes narrowed in on her. "No kidding! I know what it is. I want to know why it's incomplete!"

"Did you ask Jeff?" Latonya's sarcasm refused to be contained.

"I'm asking you."

"Well, I don't know." *Shut up while you still have a job, girl!* She never listened to her inner voice when she should.

"Get him on the phone and ask him."

She took a deep breath, rolled her eyes and picked up the phone. She knew Jeff wasn't home. Rather than telling Harrington, she looked up the number and dialed it, anyway. When Jeff didn't answer, she left a detailed message, and then turned to face Carlton. Her pleasant smile dropped as soon as she noticed him glaring at her as if she were the bane of his existence.

His right eyebrow slanted and a smirk spread across his face. "Since you can't get in touch with Weatherby, you can fill in the missing facts. I need this before the end of the evening."

"What? It's not my report! Why should I have to spend my Friday night finishing Jeff's work?" All false pleasantries fell from her face and her voice.

"It shouldn't be that much of a problem. You are familiar with the ins and outs of the project, aren't you? You should be. There is no reason why you can't go through the files and data and finish this report within a few hours."

"What if I have plans, Mr. Harrington?" She had no

personal plans, but she did need to relieve her grand-mother's home health aide.

"Cancel them. I'd like that report before you leave." Turning, he walked briskly away.

Watching his retreating back, she cursed herself for noticing how his muscles filled out the shirt he wore. To her, Carlton was simply an insensitive jerk—albeit an extremely fine insensitive jerk—that she would have to learn how to work with until, God willing, he got sent off on some other plush assignment. He wasn't even her *real* boss. He was just filling in until the company decided on a replacement for the former head of the marketing department. Latonya hoped, perhaps unre-alistically, that even though she hadn't been with the company long, she would be considered for the position. However, her on-going battle with the younger Harrington, made that seem less and less like an attain-able dream.

Latonya angrily added the missing information and printed out a new report within an hour. Because of her desire and pressing needs to rise quickly in the company, she was on top of all of her projects *and* the projects of her coworkers.

Without bothering to knock, she walked into Carl-ton's office, dropped the report on his desk and didn't wait for his response. The ogre looked up from his computer and his gaze narrowed in on her, but she refused to acknowledge his glare. With briefcase and purse in hand, she headed to the elevator and left the building before saying or doing anything that would put her job in further jeopardy.

Instead of heading straight home, she stopped at Soka's. She had a few choice words for Jeff Weatherby and she planned on giving them to him straight away. *He* would get the telling off she'd had to hold back from their temporary boss.

Filled to capacity, the bustling brewery was a vibrant melting pot, filled with people from various races and ethnicities all laughing, drinking and partying together. Decorated in bright blues, subtle greens and warm tans, the inside of the brewery captured the colors of the water, sand and palm trees that surrounded the city. The deejay played a mixture of salsa, reggae and popular American music, and people had already taken to the dance floor.

"Hey, look who decided to grace us with her company. It's Stevens. What are you drinking, beautiful?" Always charming, Jeff gave Latonya his best dazzling smile. He'd removed his tie and rolled up his sleeves.

Jeff stood to greet her and gave her a hug. Latonya smiled in spite of the fact that she was there to tell him off and thanked God she considered herself playa-proof.

Latonya leaned into his embrace and the perpetual flirt pecked her on the cheek. "Don't 'beautiful' me. I just got reamed out by the boss because of your half-finished report. He made *me* finish it."

Jeff gave a shocked expression and opened his mouth to respond, but Stan chimed in first.

"No shit?" Stan rubbed his chin. "Wow, the boss

really seems to have it in for you. It's crazy, because you're like the hardest worker out of all of us."

Latonya cut Jeff a nasty look. "Well, at least *you* know it, Stan. And, Jeff, if you're going to hand in incomplete reports, let a sistah know so she can get out of the line of fire."

"That report would have been just fine for the old boss," Jeff countered playfully. "I'll tell you, I think Carlton Harrington III just has something to prove because he's the boss's grandkid. I say we all keep doing the caliber of work we did for Samuels and let him get used to *our* way of doing things."

Jeff was using his charm to try to incite insurrection, but Latonya wasn't having it.

"Well, I always make sure my reports are thorough. And since he didn't have me finish anyone else's report but yours, why don't you step it up a notch?"

Pouting, Jeff shrugged before breaking out a sulking frown. "Oh, come on, beautiful. You're bringing me down. It's Friday. Let me buy you a drink and let's just forget this. Come on. Sit down and take a load off. White wine, right?" The consummate charmer, Jeff knew when to give up a losing battle.

"Make that a gin and tonic with lime." After her run-in with the sexy ogre, something stronger was in order. Sliding into the booth, she occupied the spot Jeff vacated when he went to get her drink.

She moved over when he came back with her drink in hand and a mouth full of apologies. Deciding to forgive and forget, she slowly sipped her drink. Jeff rested his arm on the seat behind her.

"So, I guess we can thank good old *Harried Tres* for your presence tonight. If he hadn't made you angry you would probably still be in your office working before you headed home, not to be seen again until bright and early Monday morning," Jeff teased.

"It's called having a work ethic. You should try it sometime." She gave Jeff a sarcastic smirk before breaking into a smile at his nickname for the boss. Jeff had made up a funny way of referring to the Harrington men. While he alternated between *Harry* and *Harried* as a pseudonym for Harrington, it was always followed by *Uno* for the big boss and *Tres* for Latonya's nemesis.

"There is nothing wrong with my work ethic. It's workaholics like you and Harried Tres that need to re-evaluate themselves. I believe in having a balanced life." Jeff took a swig of his beer and bobbed his head to the salsa music playing in the background.

"Whatever. Some of us really need our jobs and some of us have to work twice as hard to make up for not being the right race or gender." She didn't have the privilege to buck the system like Jeff might.

Jeff feigned outrage. "Was that a white-male crack? Because some would say that as a white man working for a large black-owned company, I would face more than my share of discrimination. In fact, I *may* have it worse than you," he joked.

"Well, as the *only* woman in a department full of men of all races, colors and creeds and with a temporary boss who can't seem to stand me, I think I have it the worst. And I don't have the luxury of being able to quit my job at any time and go work for my dad at the family empire." She took a sip of her drink and gave Jeff a pointed look. His old money family hadn't taken it well when he'd declined to join the family business and set out on his own. They were always trying to get him to change his mind.

"You know you could always quit this job and let me take care of you. I have a sizable trust fund. You'd never have to work again. All you have to do is say the word." Jeff, the flirt, couldn't go for five minutes without making a pass.

Juan saw that as his opportunity to jump in. "Hey, *mamacita,* you know I don't have a trust fund. But if you're taking offers, I'll put my bid in. I'll work ten jobs for you, *bonita.*" Juan was tall and slender and of Afro-Cuban origin. He had a face that could only be described as beautiful. His eyes were warm and expressive, and the longest lashes she had ever seen on a man framed them.

Stan snorted before adding playfully, "The sistah isn't interested in either one of you. When she's ready to stop working so hard she'll coming looking for an African-American brother like myself."

Latonya smiled sweetly before she lit into the three flirtatious devils. In their own way they were just trying to cheer her up because of her constant run-ins with their new boss. A girl could have worse things happen than a multicultural alliance of handsome men working together to lift her spirits.

"You know what I think?" She spoke in a sexy, sultry whisper before moving in for the kill. "I think that when I am ready to leave Harrington Enterprise, my sexual-harassment case is going to be so airtight against this department, I won't have to work."

"She's playing the sex card! Okay, *mamacita.*" Juan laughed as he threw up his hands in mock defeat. "You know we're just playing with you. Lighten up, *bonita.*"

"Yeah, girl! How are you going to do a brotha like Anita did Clarence? You know I was just joking with you," Stan teased.

"Mmm-hmm, ha, ha, ha." Taking another sip of her drink, she felt the stress from the work week slowly leave her.

Jeff let his arm drop from the seat to her shoulder and smiled. "I'm not playing. You just let me know when and I've got you, darling."

"Please, stop playing. You know the company frowns on hanky-panky between employees." She smiled at him as she took another sip of her drink, musing that the risk of censure hadn't stopped Jeff from making his way through the other women on the staff. It would, however, stop her from even remotely considering the Ben Affleck look-alike and his offer.

"Who's talking hanky-panky? I'm talking you and me forever, till death do us part. And you won't even give me a chance. Tell the truth—it's because I'm white, right? That's discrimination. You won't give a man a chance because he's a little melanin challenged. That's cold."

Breaking into a fit of laughter, she playfully popped Jeff upside his head.

"Good, you're laughing. I knew we could get you to smile sooner or later." Jeff let his hand touch her cheek.

Just then, the sound of the younger Harrington's deep voice interrupted her laughter. "It's good to see my department getting along so well." His eyes fell on Jeff's arm draped lazily around Latonya's shoulder and the hand that softly stroked her cheek. It became obvious what Carlton meant to imply. She almost shoved Jeff's arm off of her. But against her better judgment she simply sat there and gave Carlton her best interpretation of a polite smile.

It wasn't as if the company actually stated it was against office dating, but it certainly didn't encourage it. People got skipped over for promotions when they didn't adhere to the unwritten codes of protocol. The last thing Latonya needed to do was to give Carlton Harrington III another reason not to like her.

"Hey, boss, you came to join us?" Jeff queried, breaking the ice.

"No, that's all right. Thanks for the invitation. I'm meeting some people here and I would hate to interrupt your *cozy* situation." Carlton gave Latonya a pointed stare as he emphasized the word *cozy*.

What does he mean by that? What was he implying about her with those snide comments and veiled looks? She mentally counted to ten in an effort not to blast the man where he stood. *How dare he!*

"Well maybe next time, boss." Juan smiled, clearly trying to diffuse the growing tension.

"Yes, maybe. Oh, and Stevens, I'll need you to come into the office tomorrow and work with me on the Biltmore project." Carlton's voice sent a shiver through her in spite of the hot Miami air.

She tried to keep her tone even and polite, but she was fighting a losing battle. "It's not my project. It's Jeff's," she spat before she could catch herself.

"It's yours now. I'll see you tomorrow bright and early." He nodded briefly to everyone in the booth before walking away to meet his party.

Latonya didn't waste her time being shocked. The man's obnoxious attitude and complete disregard for her was par for the course. If he were *not* rude to her *then* she would have been surprised.

Even though she'd come to expect Carlton's attitude and his treatment of her had become the running joke of the department, it didn't take away the sting. The way things appeared the younger Harrington had it in for her. She would've quit, but Latonya really needed her job.

Her colleagues were hell-bent on consoling her. Instead, she insisted she was okay, put on her brightest smile and let them know that she had to leave and get some rest so that she was ready for whatever Carlton Harrington III felt like dishing out in the morning.

Chapter 2

Sitting across from Carlton in the department's conference room, Latonya found herself sweating even with the air-conditioning on full blast. Once again, she cursed her intense reaction to a man who, for all intents and purposes, thought of her as a walking, talking idiot.

So far, she'd done a halfway decent job maintaining her composure while they were in the room together. She even managed to get a lot of work done. Every once in a while she would literally feel herself getting hotter and look up to find Carlton staring at her. His perplexed expression would always turn into a glare when she caught him. She tried not to wonder about what her workdays would be like if he *could* stand the sight of her or if he brushed those soft thick lips across her own.

Snap out of it, Latonya silently chastised as she shook her head to clear out the visions of kissing Carlton. Getting up from her seat and picking up her laptop, she walked over to where he sat on the other side of the conference room. As she walked toward him, she wondered why he sat so far away.

"I think I found the problem here." She pushed his laptop aside along with a stack of papers and placed her computer in front of him. Leaning over Carlton, she pointed at the spreadsheet she'd created.

She waited for him to respond, but he just sat there still and silent. He almost seemed to be holding his breath.

Latonya was tempted to check herself for body odor. She knew she'd perspired a little due to her nervousness, but she didn't think that she stunk or anything.

Taking a deep breath, she continued, "See, there are just some small inconsistencies where someone mistakenly put in the wrong averages. It looks like they actually doubled March and skipped April. Probably just a typing error. That's why—"

She stopped talking when Carlton hurriedly pushed away from the table and jumped out of his seat. He backed away from the table and her with such speed she swore he was running for his life.

"That's fine. I have some things to take care of in my office. Continue to fix those errors." He jetted out the door before she could say another word.

Latonya lifted her arm and sniffed just to be sure before picking up her laptop and going back to her seat. With each second that passed, she became more resentful.

She glanced at her watch with irritation. It was five in the evening on a Saturday and she had been in the office since seven-thirty that morning. If she didn't need the job so badly she would have told him exactly where he could go. She didn't expect high praise or kudos, but she felt that he could have at least managed not to bark and grunt at her. Then he had the nerve to run from the room as if she had the cooties just because she stood by him! If she didn't already have a thick skin, she would no doubt have one by the time he was done with her.

Brushing her hair back from her face, she wished that she had pinned it up in the French twist that she normally wore to work. She'd worn it down in a silent form of rebellion, along with wearing her navy slacks and a white short-sleeve shirt that she normally would have worn under her business suit. She'd been tempted to come in jeans and a T-shirt but thought that might have been going a little too far. If the ogre wanted her to come in on a Saturday, she would at least come in her casual clothing. Letting her hair down might not have been the equivalent of burning her bra, and maybe she wouldn't be compared to Norma Rae, but seeing him dressed in his usual perfectly styled business suit, she felt like she'd bucked the system in a small way.

Carlton came back and threw another stack of papers in front of her without saying a word. That simple act was her breaking point. Turning off her laptop, she shut it and placed the machine in its case before picking up her purse and briefcase.

"Where do you think you're going?"

"Home."

"We're not done here."

"*I'm* done. I'll see you on Monday, Mr. Harrington," she said as professionally as she could manage.

"We're not done, Ms. Stevens." His hard-edged voice matched his glare.

She couldn't take it anymore. "What is your problem? What do you have against me? What have I done to offend you? Can you please tell me that? Because I need to decide if it's worth it for me to remain in this department."

"Do you think you can transfer?" His tone took on a mocking edge.

"I think you leave me no choice."

His gaze narrowed and his lips took on a slight smirk. "I'll block it. If you can't withstand a little hard work, then maybe you're not cut out to be an employee of Harrington Enterprise."

"I don't believe this! I have a stellar record. I always give my best and you do nothing but insult me with your little snipes and condescension."

He walked over to her. Invading any semblance of personal space, he was close enough for her to smell his cologne, and what a cologne it was. The mixture of musk and pine along with the force of his manliness nearly took her breath away.

"Get back to work, Latonya. I'll let you know when it's time to leave." His voice was eerily calm as his mouth still held its daring expression.

"Go to hell, Mr. Harrington." She forced a pleasant

smile. "I have a life. I'll see you on Monday." She tried to walk around him but he grabbed her arm and pulled her back.

"What do you have to do? Go out with Weatherby?"

"That is none of your business. You're treading on thin ice, Mr. Harrington. I suggest you let go of me." She tried to snatch her arm away, but his grip remained strong. He pulled her closer.

He paused and shook his head as if clearing it. "You're right. It isn't any of my business." He folded his arms and stood silently for a moment, just looking at her. His smoky, searing, hooded gaze was flooded with determination. His eyes made physical promises that she had a feeling he fully intended to keep.

Despite herself, Latonya couldn't help being caught up in the intensity of it all. His eyes exuded seduction! And every playa-proof instinct in her body seemed to be on strike. No man had ever looked at her like that before. Men had desired her, sure, but this *felt* different.

"I think we have been going about this all wrong." He lifted his hand and caressed her cheek.

Taking a step back on legs shakier than she felt comfortable with, she said, "I think we have been fine. You could just try being nicer and showing a little appreciation and we should get along just fine."

"Nicer. A little appreciation. I think I can do that. In fact, that's exactly what I had in mind." He smiled and took another step forward, standing right in front of her and too close for comfort again. He bent his head and suddenly his lips connected with hers.

She opened her mouth in shock and his tongue darted in. She couldn't believe that he was kissing her. And though it was the last thing her *body* wanted to do, she tried to pull away from him. But he held her in a tight embrace.

Carlton's lips were a cross between punishing and tender. She resisted her desire for him as much as she could, but he wouldn't allow it. He pulled her closer and his mouth became a hot branding iron. She swore that every place he touched, he owned, and she soon knew what it meant to be putty in someone's hands.

His hands started to explore her body and she felt things she had never felt before. Her legs went weak, and she realized that Harrington wasn't the only one moaning and enjoying the kiss.

What am I thinking?

He was the last man she needed to be kissing. His hand roamed down to her behind and he pulled her so close, she swore she could feel his every pulse. Moving her hands up to his chest and resisting the urge to explore his fabulous pecs, she pushed back with all her might, finally breaking the kiss.

She tried to catch her breath, but it was next to impossible. Her heart raced. They stood there for a full minute panting and glaring at each other. Taking a step back, she reached for her purse and briefcase. She had to get away from the man in order to think.

One minute he was barking orders at her and the next he was kissing her. *Well, he had better okay my transfer, because there is no way I can work in the same department with him now.*

"Where do you think you're going?"

"I told you I'm going home. And I expect you to have me transferred to another department. What you just did was highly inappropriate!"

"Sit down, Latonya."

She began to back away. "No, I will not. I'm leaving."

"Please, sit down." His tone was soft, almost endearing.

Making the mistake of looking him in the eyes, Latonya noticed the slightest bit of vulnerability there. She'd never seen him even remotely unsure of himself. The small crack in his cocksure personality was enough to make her at least listen to what he had to say.

She sat in spite of herself. He dragged another chair up and sat right in front of her, running his hand over his face in a frustrated gesture.

"That shouldn't have happened."

"You bet it shouldn't have happened," she said, crossing her arms defensively. "You are way out of line, Mr. Harrington. However, if you'll just transfer me to another department—"

"Is that what you really want, Latonya?"

She nodded. "Yes, it is. I think it's best."

"We're clearly attracted to each other. What would you have us do with that?" His eyes narrowed and his voice took on a slightly suggestive edge.

"Transfer me to another department," she snapped in retort.

"That won't work. The company is not *that* big. Besides, I'd much rather examine our attraction. I'm tired of ignoring it. I think it's time we did something about it."

Swallowing, she stared at him and her eyes widened as she realized what he was insinuating. "How do you intend us to do that?"

"Spend the night with me."

The way he nonchalantly dropped the suggestion almost made her fall out of her seat. "You must be crazy! There is no way I will have sex with you, Mr. Harrington!" She started to get up and he placed his hand on her knee, staying her.

"Given the way you kissed me just now, Latonya, it's obvious that you are attracted to me, too. Why are you being so difficult?" he asked with a chuckle.

I kissed you? What play are you in? In her script she was the one who had a right to be irritated. She was the one who just had all of her senses attacked by a moody, but oh-so-fine man. She should be upset just because he'd had her body at war with her mind from the moment she met him.

"I'm being difficult, as you state, because I'm not accustomed to thinking that I can go around scratching each and every one of my annoying itches. No, Mr. Harrington, I won't do it. Now, either you transfer me to another department or I'll have to take other avenues." Latonya slanted her eyes just a little to let him know that she wasn't playing.

The only other avenue she could take if he refused to transfer her would be to file a sexual-harassment charge. Since his grandfather owned the company, she doubted it would do much good.

Carlton leaned forward and kissed her again, a softer, sweeter kiss. Her lips opened as if they had a mind of their own, and her tongue darted into his mouth as if on a mission of destiny. She felt a tingling sensation in the pit of her stomach.

This. Is. So. Wrong.

He pulled away, his gaze intense and seductive. "I'll tell you what. It is rather late and you're right that we should wrap things up here. How about I treat you to dinner for working so hard on the Biltmore project?"

She stared at him. And even though a small part of her mind screamed *do not* go to dinner with this man, other parts whispered seductively how gorgeous he was and how attracted she was to him. When the words reached her mouth, she was startled to hear her own traitorous voice say, "Okay, I'll go to dinner with you. But that's it."

He smiled and his hand brushed her cheek. "Fine, let's go. I'll have my driver take us to Manny's. It's a small Cuban restaurant I think you'll like."

She never thought she would see the day when Carlton Harrington III actually smiled at her. Her mouth almost went dry. Gathering her things, she followed him out of the conference room.

Chapter 3

She looked like a woman riding to her death sentence, Carlton thought wryly as he eyed Latonya in the back seat of his limousine. It almost seemed as if the warm, vibrant woman who had been in his arms fifteen minutes ago had been a mirage. The expression on her face showed a woman not too happy about the prospect of having dinner with him.

After crossing the line and kissing her, he knew that he wanted to kiss her again. He wanted to have her more than he'd ever wanted anything else in his entire thirty-five years of life. But if he were honest, he'd admit he'd known that before he kissed her. He'd tried to ignore his feelings. Hell, he even tried to be extra harsh on Latonya, hoping it would force her to stay clear of him. However, when he found she could gladly stay away from him, he'd started coming up with reasons to make sure he could be around her.

He wondered if working on the Biltmore project had caused a wrinkle in whatever relationship she had with Jeff Weatherby. The two of them were always flirting. Hell, Latonya always playfully flirted with the rest of the guys in the department—everyone except for him. What he wouldn't have done to have her bat those sparkling eyes at him.

In the short time that he had known her, she had managed to get under his skin in a big way. The way she kissed him once she had loosened up suggested that sex with her would be a delightful encounter. Passion leaped from her at his touch. When he kissed her, he swore he felt electric currents shoot through his system. He needed to find a way to get her out of his system and—after kissing her—he figured a more intimate arrangement might just do the trick. If they had sex, he'd be over his infatuation and they would be able to continue working together. He usually didn't hold any woman in his mind very long after he'd been inside her.

Permanent relationships just weren't his style. He'd learned early in life that love and commitment never came to a good end. The things he'd witnessed with his own parents made him more than a little gun-shy when it came to long-term relationships. Love wasn't something he was looking for.

Carlton glanced at Latonya again. Calling her a very beautiful woman felt like a huge understatement. Her flawless face was the color of rich toffee. And when she was happy, her brown eyes danced with passion and vibrancy. Her auburn hair fell in soft waves around her shoulders. He'd always imagined what her hair would look like when it wasn't pinned up. When she'd come into the office with it down, she looked prettier than he ever could have imagined. She wore a pair of drab navy-blue slacks, and even they were sexy on her. Her body had such delicious curves that he salivated just thinking about them. She made those boring nondescript business suits she wore look like something that could be found in a lingerie shop.

He'd been struggling to keep his eyes off her all day. When she'd come and stood by him, it was all he could do not to pull her onto his lap and kiss her senseless. He barely made it out of the office to catch his breath. No woman had ever had such an impact on him.

It was a good thing she'd been able to work, because he could barely focus on anything but her. It wouldn't have been so bad if she hadn't kept catching him while he stared at her. Always in control of his emotions, he felt thrown off balance by the woman.

That's why he'd made up his mind to face whatever attraction there was between them head-on. He was tired of running from it. It was out of character for him to run from anything or to deny himself something he wanted. He decided that must have been the reason Latonya was causing such strange feelings in him. Once he faced the feelings and they explored them, he would be fine.

Sitting as far away from him as she could possibly get, Latonya twisted her hands nervously in her lap as she gazed out the window. If he didn't know better, he would think she was running scared.

He pulled out a bottle of wine from the minifridge, hoping if she had something to drink that she would loosen up a bit more.

Clearing his throat, he implored, "Latonya, look at me."

She turned slightly and glared at him.

Well, that's progress, he reasoned. At least she showed some emotion. He handed her a glass of wine and she took it hesitantly.

"You can drink it. It's not poisoned."

Rolling her eyes, she turned to face the window again. Her hand shook as she sipped the wine.

Her jittery nervousness sparked a deep desire in him to ease some of her discomfort. Sliding closer to her in the seat, he placed his arm around her. She jumped and spilled the glass of wine.

"Why are you so jumpy? Relax," he whispered softly, picking up the glass and placing it in a holder.

He bent his head to kiss her. Her lips were soft and inviting. She tasted like the sweet wine and a hint of peppermint. Once he worked his tongue into her mouth, he felt any thirst he had ever had being quenched. She sighed just before she relaxed into his embrace and a sharp jolt raced through him at the sound. Suddenly he was struck with so much need he almost couldn't concentrate.

She was intoxicating and addictive, and he couldn't pull away from her if he wanted to. He allowed his hands to explore her luscious body. He pulled her closer until he almost had her on his lap. Still it didn't seem close enough. If he could have inhaled her, injected her into his veins somehow, he would have done it.

He pulled away and took a ragged breath. If he didn't stop kissing her, he would wind up quickly taking her in the back of the limo, and he didn't want that to happen. He wanted to savor every moment. The woman had wreaked havoc with his libido and his emotions and he fully intended to take his time to see if she offered all he'd imagined.

"We should probably stop," he managed to mutter as he tried without success to catch his breath and calm himself down.

A red stain flushed her toffee cheeks and her eyes fluttered. Her face became the picture of embarrassment as she put some distance between them. Clearing her throat, she took a deep breath.

"Mr. Harrington, I really would like you to reconsider this…dinner. I'm really not comfortable with it. I realize that there is some attraction. But this is not the best way to deal with it." She cleared her throat again as she ran her hand across her navy slacks, picking off nonexistent lint. "I think it would be best if you just have your driver take me home."

"Do you really? Because now that I've kissed you, Latonya, I can honestly say that wouldn't work for me at all."

She sighed and looked away, seeming emotionally torn.

He ran his fingers over her long auburn tresses.

"Tell me that you're not attracted to me. Tell me that you don't want this as much as I do."

With a face full of anger and passion, fueled no doubt by stilted desire, she turned to face him again. Instead of responding in words, she simply pursed her lips.

The sight of her luscious lips closed so defiantly made him want to kiss her again. At least she didn't deny she wanted him. He took a small relief in that as he continued to toy with her hair. Pulling her closer, Carlton whispered, "I'll tell you what, you let me treat you to dinner since you worked so hard today. And we'll just see how the night goes. Who knows, you might even have fun."

Her lips formed a smirk and Carlton couldn't resist. He had to touch them. Letting his hand trail down her cheek, he traced her lips with his thumb. He could feel the steady beat of her heart as she took a deep breath.

Even though it was the last thing he wanted to do, he moved his hand. "So, do we have a deal?"

"Fine, I'll let you buy me dinner."

Latonya smiled and Carlton could have sworn her eyes danced just for him. He had no idea the woman's smile could make his heartbeat skip. Not wanting to lose the closeness he was starting to feel, he let his hand rest on her shoulder and held her close.

The rest of the ride passed in silence. Carlton enjoyed the drive from downtown Miami to the restaurant near his home in Coconut Grove. The lush green foliage and the blue waters calmed him as he looked out of the window. Once they were in view of Biscayne

Bay he could almost feel himself relaxing a bit. Gazing at the blue water that surrounded the freeway offered a cathartic release of tension.

Although not as beautiful as his island home in the Bahamas, Miami held a beauty special to him as well. Ever since he was a child he'd split his time between the Bahamas and the almost tropical Florida city. A Bahamian native by birth, he considered Miami home while in the States.

Coconut Grove, the place of Miami's earliest black settlers, was also the spot his Bahamian-born great-great-grandfather decided to make his home. In the years since the first Harrington resided in Coconut Grove, the Harringtons maintained their Bahamian citizenship and heritage, keeping homes in both places. Carlton's home on Millionaire's Row had been in the family for several generations and he lived there by himself part of the year with a small number of servants.

When the limo pulled up in front of the small restaurant, he almost let out a sigh of relief. Out of the close confines of the limo, at least he didn't have to worry about trying to maul the poor woman anymore. He did have some sense of decorum about public behavior. Yet one look at her sweetly rounded bottom and long legs as she stepped out of the vehicle before him made Carlton realize that he'd better request the corner table in the back just in case he forgot all his home training.

Latonya looked around the small and sophisticated restaurant and tried to catch her breath. The white linen tablecloths gave the place a *Lifestyles of the Rich and*

Famous aura, and one look at the menu prices confirmed her observation.

She tried to wrap her mind around all that had happened between herself and Carlton. She'd felt an attraction to him from the first moment she'd seen him and that scared her. She'd never experienced such overwhelming desire before. Her grandmother, a strict, church-going woman, had a mantra that she preached to her granddaughters daily: *books before boys.* For the most part, Latonya had listened. She'd never wanted to disappoint her grandmother so she'd stayed clear of boys in high school and college. She often thought about what it would be like to have sex. She found herself thinking about it a *whole lot more* whenever Carlton was around. Those thoughts were not *safe* or *good.*

She looked up from the menu to find him gazing at her, and the heat traveled from the pit of her stomach to the tips of her toes.

Latonya was so caught up in Carlton's gaze that she barely heard the waiter as he spouted off the list of specials in a sultry Spanish accent.

"Do you like *mojitos,* Tonya? I think a cocktail is in order after all our hard work today." Carlton smiled and then ordered a pitcher full of the wonderful Cuban drink.

She took a deep breath. If a little rum, mint, sugar and lime didn't help her get over her nervousness, nothing would. She gladly took the glass the waiter poured for her when he returned with the pitcher.

Carlton proceeded to order their meal in flawless Spanish and she bit back the urge to tell him that she had been deciding her own meals since she was twelve years old. Before her mother died she took care of preparing meals for her younger sister and herself, and after that, because of the long hours her grandmother put in cleaning the homes of others, she had to prepare meals for the entire family. The *last* thing she needed was some guy thinking he could just decide what she wanted or needed.

He turned to her and smiled in spite of the daggers she was shooting at him with her eyes. "I know you can order your own food. But I come here a lot and I know what's good and what's truly superb."

Carlton proceeded to tell her what he'd ordered. Everything from the *croquetas* as an appetizer to the flan for dessert.

"The meal you've picked out sounds scrumptious. I can't wait. I'm famished." She smiled in spite of herself. It became increasingly harder to maintain an attitude with Carlton when he looked at her with that sexy glint in his eyes. She cleared her throat instead of reprimanding him and finished off her *mojito*.

He reached for the pitcher and refilled her glass as soon as she put it down.

"So, tell me about yourself."

Carlton appeared sincere, but she didn't know how much of her life she wanted to share with him. She squinted her eyes as she tried to decide. "What do you want to know?"

"I don't know, tell me everything, anything." He seemed genuinely interested.

"Well, let's see. I grew up in Overtown. My grandmother practically raised me. She had a stroke about a year ago and she needs constant care until she is fully rehabilitated. She's coming along well, though." Looking up, she found him staring at her intently.

"Is that why you took a job with the Miami office of Harrington Enterprise? So you can be with her while she's recovering?"

"Sort of. My grandmother took my little sister and me in when my mom died. She helped me out when I was in school, and it was understood that I would help her to send my little sister to college." Smiling with relief when the waiter brought their food, she figured they could start eating and she could end her this-is-my-life show. She never liked talking about herself. Talking about her nondescript little life to a rich business mogul like Carlton Harrington III had to be among the most nerve-racking experiences she'd ever had.

Carlton gave her an encouraging smile. It seemed like he wanted to hear more. "That must have been rough. I lost both of my parents when I was fifteen... They died together in a plane crash. Was your dad still around?"

"That's awful. I'm sorry to hear that." Latonya hadn't known that growing up parentless was something they shared. "My father left way before my mother died. And it wasn't so rough. We had Gran and she worked extra hard to take care of us and make sure that we didn't want for anything. When she had the stroke, I had just finished my MBA program and I realized that I had to be there for her. So, I stayed home and took over the mortgage and my sister's tuition."

"That's commendable of you. Most people would have just put their grandmother in a nursing home and let their sibling fend for him or herself."

Latonya just toyed with her food without looking up or responding. She never would have considered any of the options he mentioned, but she often felt overwhelmed by her responsibilities. Even if she did feel as if she were carrying a lot on her shoulders, she certainly wasn't going to admit it to him.

Carlton must have sensed that he'd made her uncomfortable because he suddenly switched the subject. "So tell me how you like working for Harrington Enterprise?"

Her fork fell on the plate with a clang. She glanced up from her meal. Twisting her lips to the side, she gave him her sassiest look. "Well, up until about five months ago, I really liked it."

Smiling the seductive smile that made his eyes sparkle and her stomach flutter, Carlton chuckled before responding. "Okay, I guess I set myself up for that. I know I've haven't been a dream to work for."

She tilted her head and smirked. "Gee, ya think?"

"Okay, okay, enough. Let's eat."

"Yes, let's." She tossed him a saucy grin before digging into her food.

The flavors of the powerfully seasoned dish popped all over her tongue and she couldn't help but compliment the sexy chauvinist on his choices. The garlic and onions melded in her mouth and she momentarily worried about her breath and kissing him later on. As soon as she thought it, she chastised herself.

The last thing you need to be worried about is kissing him again, girl. You need to be concerned with getting away from him this evening with your virginity still intact. Then again, he is fine.... She tried to stop the grin that spread across her face to no avail.

"I knew you'd like it." He flashed the smile that she was sure she'd never get tired of seeing.

"And how did you know that?"

"I just had a feeling. Right now I'm feeling like I know some other things you would like."

Lifting her eyebrows, she gave him a quick glance. "Oh, really?"

"Yes, really."

"And what exactly would that be?"

Smirking, he replied, "Oh, I think if you gave it half a chance you'd find that you really like me. A lot."

She laughed at that. "Oh, really? Not suffering from a lack of confidence, are you? Some might even say you're bordering on arrogant."

He laughed, too, as he refreshed her glass with *mojito*. "I'd say confidence, not arrogance. But I think it would take more than a little convincing for you to agree with that."

Latonya nodded. "Smart man."

"Yes, and as a smart man, I have to say that I am enjoying spending time with you. I'm glad we got away from the office and I really don't want this evening to end."

Picking up her glass, she took a huge swallow. Her throat suddenly became dry while another part of her felt strangely wet.

"Are we back to the 'spend the night with me' conversation?" She voiced the words with an airy lightness that surprised her, given the bolt of nervous energy racing through her body. While she didn't hold any fantasies about the rich playboy falling in love with her, she did find herself wanting, no, needing to examine her attraction to him.

Why not finally try a night of passion with a man who makes my stomach quiver with just a kiss?

Studying him carefully, taking in the hot pulsating masculinity he exuded, she impulsively decided to bargain with the devil.

"If we do this, then I want a transfer out of your department, Harrington."

He wiped his mouth with his napkin as he gazed at her intently. She felt goose bumps trail from the base of her neck to the small of her back.

He smiled when she shivered. "We can talk about a transfer, later." Carlton threw his napkin on the table as if challenging her.

Suddenly feeling as if he had taken over control of the negotiations, she cleared her throat. "Will we do this tonight?"

She managed to maintain a businesslike voice although the strength of her attraction gave her considerable pause.

His eyes narrowed, but not in the angry and irritated way they normally did. This time, they zeroed in on her with a desire that made her heart skip. "I honestly don't think I could wait another night."

Latonya fought the urge to fan herself and she

swallowed before answering. "Should I meet you somewhere?" She figured—like a typical man—he'd want to go to some cheesy hotel to do the deed.

"No, my driver can take us to my place once we've finished dinner. I live close by."

His place? He's taking me to his home? Oh. My. It felt as if a huge cotton ball had lodged itself in her throat, and she could barely force out words. She thought about the huge, extravagant homes they'd passed on the drive from downtown. They were right on the cusp of downtown and Coconut Grove. From what she could see of the bayfront houses they passed, which were all blocked by tall fences and impenetrable foliage, Carlton didn't live in a small home. Between the Italian Renaissance villas, Mediterranean-inspired mansions, and art-deco-styled superhomes, she suddenly felt out of her element. She just hoped that he didn't say he lived on Brickell Avenue, better known as Millionaire's Row. "Your place? You live in *this* neighborhood?"

"Yes. I live on Brickell Avenue. Now, let's share this flan and get out of here. I can't wait to taste *you*." He leaned forward with a spoon in hand and took a mouthful of the dessert all the while keeping his eyes firmly focused on her.

Oh, Peanut, Latonya thought, using her childhood nickname to silently chastise herself, *you are way out of your league, girl.*

Chapter 4

The limousine pulled up to the tall and foreboding wrought-iron gate of Carlton's home. Watching Latonya as she took in the size of the estate, he noticed her give a nervous shudder. Admittedly, it was a lot of house for one man, but he always lived in it when he was in the States. The family estate in the Bahamas was actually much bigger.

Clearly making some sort of mental retreat, Latonya wrapped her arms around herself and held tightly.

When the driver, Paul, opened the door and held out his hand to help her out of the car, she hesitated. Finally, her shaky hand grabbed on to Paul's and she took two uneven steps forward.

Wrapping his arm around her shoulder, Carlton led her into the house.

Jillian, the head maid, who had been with the Harringtons since Carlton's parents were alive, came out to greet them. Her pecan-complexioned smooth skin left people in awe when they found out she was well into her sixties. Only her stylishly coiffed hair with startling streaks of silver gave a small hint of her age. Having her around gave Carlton a sense of stability in his life. Even though the petite woman had an opinionated and somewhat bossy nature, she, like his grandfather, had always been there for him.

"Good evening. You're home early today. And you brought a beautiful young woman home!" Jillian glanced from Carlton to Latonya and smiled brightly.

Carlton noticed a strange expression cross Jillian's face and he cringed as she reached out her hand to Latonya. He could already see the wheels turning in Jillian's head. The woman had a know-it-all aura about her that usually didn't bother him, because he usually didn't have a reason to mind.

"Hello, my name is Jillian. I all but raised this young man. What's your name? And will you be staying for dinner?"

Noting the gleam in Jillian's eye, Carlton realized that he'd never taken a woman to his home before. He took women *out*. Wined them. Dined them. But none had the privilege of seeing the space he once shared with his parents. The way Jillian stood there grinning, he hoped she wasn't getting any crazy ideas. After all, they just happened to be in the neighborhood, he told himself. His bringing Latonya Stevens to his home was no big deal. Right?

Latonya hesitated for a second before answering Jillian, and he feared that she was uncomfortable. He knew for sure that he was.

He jumped in to ease her nervousness and his own. "Jillian, this is Latonya, and we won't be needing dinner this evening."

Both women looked stunned for a moment. Carlton placed his hand firmly on Latonya's back, leading her past the well-meaning but meddlesome Jillian.

Latonya stopped and glared at him. She narrowed her eyes and snapped, "Excuse you!" Then she turned, smiled and spoke to Jillian. "Is he always this rude?"

Jillian laughed. "Not always. He has his moments, though."

"That's what I figured. One minute he's behaving like a pleasant human being and the next he's a complete caveman." Latonya turned and shot him an angry look. "It's not attractive, at all."

Carlton felt himself shrinking under the intense glares the two women shot at him. He didn't like the feeling. "Well, we just had dinner," was all he could think of as a response.

"Right. But that was no reason for us to brush past Jillian as if we're running a marathon." Latonya folded her arms across her chest.

Jillian busted out in a fit of laughter, and the melody of her laugh along with the sharpness of Latonya's tone, left Carlton feeling sufficiently chastised. He definitely didn't like that.

"Anyway, Jillian—as I would have said before we were so rudely interrupted—my name is Latonya

Stevens. And we just had dinner at a wonderful Cuban restaurant, so I'm stuffed. But thanks for offering. It's nice to meet you."

Jillian now held on to her stomach as she laughed. "I'm going to leave you young folk to your business. You're going to be all right, girl. I hope to see you again."

When they reached his suite, Latonya took a step back, put her hands on her hips and narrowed her eyes. "How dare you? Now that nice woman, who could be my grandmother, thinks I'm some kind of whore or call girl here to provide services!"

As he stood in front of a beautiful woman whom he wanted beyond expression, the last thing he felt like doing was having some pointless conversation about what Jillian did or didn't think.

"She doesn't think that," he assured her. "And for the record, I don't care what she thinks, right now. It doesn't matter."

"Well, I suppose it doesn't matter to *you*."

Pulling her into his arms, he kissed her. Resisting the passion she felt, she placed her palms on his chest and tried to push him away. He grabbed her arms and put them behind her back, walking her backward toward the bed, all the while caressing her lips with his.

With a shuddering pant, she broke away. "You really can't see that you were way out of line, can you?"

A rush of feelings blazed through Carlton and none of them were familiar. He wondered how this woman could make him feel things he never felt before. And

then he was able to name at least one of the foreign
feelings, fear. He realized that he was close to ruining
any chance he had at really getting to know Latonya
and figuring out why she had such an impact on him.

Running his hand across his head, he mumbled,
"Okay. I admit it. I was rude a few minutes ago."

She folded her arms across her chest and tilted her
head.

"For the record, I didn't mean to treat you like a call
girl. I just didn't want Jillian to get started. She can be
a bit much at times. And I could see the wheels turning
in her head." He took a step forward and touched her
cheek. "Let's sit down and talk."

He led her over to the sitting area of his suite and
took a seat on the burgundy Queen Anne sofa.

"Your bedroom is bigger than our house," she
mumbled wryly. She turned and looked at him. "This
is all just a little overwhelming. One minute I'm at work
dealing with my ogre of a boss who hates me. The next
minute we're kissing and the ogre seems to be a sweet
prince who likes me. And then I'm dealing with a horny
toad who's rude and revving to jump my bones."

Carlton flinched. "Ogre? Horny toad? Ouch!" He
started laughing, and he couldn't believe he was
laughing when she'd pretty much insulted him. He
didn't usually take insults well. Any other woman
would have been shown the door. *Latonya Stevens is
unlike any other woman*. He let the thought settle in
his mind for a moment as he continued to laugh.

"It's not funny," Latonya said as she struggled to
hold back her own laughter. "I'm being serious."

"I know you are. And I know it's not funny. Okay, so, what can I do to improve your image of me?"

"Tell me who you are. Really. Ogre, toad or prince?" Kicking off her shoes, she turned, got comfortable on the sofa and waited for his answer.

He pondered the question thoughtfully. "None of the above. I'm just a man who is extremely attracted to a woman who makes him feel things he's never felt before. A man who is so out of his realm of reality that he is messing up every chance he gets but hopes that you will have patience with him and allow him a few screwups until he can get it right."

Smiling hesitantly, she said softly, "You know, I feel the same way. It's weird because I'm usually less affected. You know, if you've heard one guy's pickup line, you've heard them all. I've never found myself in this kind of situation before. There is definitely something different about the way you make me feel. You've been under my skin from the first moment I met you. I think I want you out."

"I was thinking the same thing. But now, I'm not so sure." As he stared at the woman in front of him, all of his plans for exorcising Latonya Stevens from his mind went away.

"You're not sure," she mumbled in a hiss of breath as she gazed into his eyes.

Confusion was another one of those feelings that he wasn't typically familiar with. "I'm not sure or I can't be sure until…" He bent his head down and captured her lips. The meeting felt destined and it was all the assurance he needed. *I should have stayed*

far away from Latonya. She was everything he'd
spent his life running from, and having her in his
arms, he realized that he would probably never want
to let her go.

She responded hungrily to his kiss and he felt his
heart swell. Every nerve ending in his body stood at
attention, and he felt more alive than he'd ever felt. He
wanted the feeling to continue and knew the woman
in his arms was the answer.

He lifted his head and took a deep breath. "I'm sure
that I don't want to get away from what I'm feeling for
you. I've been pretty much trying to get away for the
past five months and we see how that turned out."

Latonya laughed and it sounded like music. "You
can say that again." She stopped laughing and he felt
immediately deprived. Her eyes squinted and her
eyebrows came together in serious contemplation. "I
feel so out of my element just giving in a little to my
feelings for you. And that's without even taking in the
fact that we come from two *very* different worlds."

"If you are feeling half of what I'm feeling, then
where we come from won't matter." He had never felt
more certain of anything in his life. The woman sitting
in front of him could have been from outer space. All
he knew was that once he stopped trying to fight his
feelings, they took over. He decided he would let them
and he wanted her to do the same.

He cupped her cheek in his hand. Since he already
felt out of his realm, he figured he might as well go all
the way. "Let's just agree to trust our hearts and our
feelings. Trust that they will lead us where we need to

be." He knew it was a big step for him. But he had a feeling taking the step with Latonya was his destiny.

"I don't know if I can. Things don't usually work out when people let their hearts guide them. My mother died of a broken heart." She fiddled with her thumbs and became suddenly interested in her hands. She nibbled on her lower lip for a moment before continuing. "We didn't have a lot, but for the most part she was happy with her husband and kids. When my father left her...left us, she lost all that happiness. She worked hard to take care of my sister and me. But she stopped taking care of herself. And when she died, the man she loved with all her heart didn't even come back for her funeral."

Carlton felt a sharp pain in his heart, and he thought about his own parents. They, too, had been unlucky in love. He opened his mouth to respond to what she'd shared. He wanted to tell her that they could learn from their parents' mistakes and make it work. He wanted to share his own demons, but he didn't think he was ready.

A nervous laugh escaped her lips and she mumbled, "Wow, I don't think I have ever shared that with anyone before. There must be something special about you. Because I keep telling you all my business!"

Smiling, Carlton pressed his lips against her forehead. "Maybe your heart knows it can trust me even though you're still trying to figure me out."

She slanted her eyes slightly as she considered what he'd said before saying, "Maybe."

He kissed her again, slowly probing her delectable mouth and savoring her sweetness. He let his hands trail her body as he slowly stood, taking her with him.

"Wait." She halted the kiss and ran her hand nervously across her face. She took a deep breath and exhaled. "I need to be up-front about something. I'm not exactly experienced. I've never actually done—"

Watching her lips move, he suddenly got an inkling of what she might be trying to say. "You've never been with a man before?"

She took a deep breath and shook her head. "I understand if you want to change your mind. I—"

Amazed, he cut her off, looking deep into her eyes so there was no misunderstanding between them. "I still want you more than I've ever wanted anything in the world," he said honestly. "I'm just glad you let me know that this is your first time. The last thing I'd ever want to do is hurt you."

He bent his head to take in her mouth again and caressed her succulent body. Every curve on her seemed to be made just for his touch. He'd never felt such a surge of pleasure just from touching a woman, a virgin at that. He had her where he'd wanted her from the moment he first laid eyes on her.

Slowly removing her clothing, he led her to the bed. She started to place her arms over her body in an attempt to cover up. However, he moved her arms, admiring her beauty before he bent his head to take her nipple in his mouth. As he suckled, his hands roamed her generous backside.

Every part of him came to attention as he moved his

lips down her body, finally stopping between her thighs. The salty, sweet taste of her almost made him lose it. He thought that he would gladly continue to please her this way forever because she was just that addictive. Her essence tasted better than he ever could have imagined. When he felt her shake with her first orgasm, he lapped every bit.

Stopping only after he heard her moans followed by soft sighs, he moved to take of his clothes and get a condom.

Pulling her in his arms again, he kissed her as he guided his muscular body between her thighs. Assuring she had no doubts about what was to take place, he spread her legs and penetrated. Feeling her soft heat envelop him, he shuddered and reminded himself that he had to go slow. When he broke her shield, he hesitated again to make sure she was okay.

He noticed her eyes were tightly shut and her top row of teeth bit down hard on her bottom lip. He swore, thinking that she would draw blood if she bit down just a fraction harder. "Baby, did I hurt you?"

She opened her eyes and shook her head.

"Are you sure?"

"Yes. I'm sure." Her husky voice came out in a whisper that he was positive would send him over the edge.

He covered her mouth with his as he completely filled her.

Latonya refused to cry out even though she felt as if she were being spilt in two. The pain of their initial joining was sharper than she'd expected. She marveled at how she could go from feeling such intense orgasmic pleasure to the pain of the penetration.

Just as she thought the pain couldn't get any worse, suddenly she felt the unmistakable pleasure of his sure, slow, soulful strokes. He cupped her behind in his hands, moving her in tune with him.

His lips connected with hers again, and she found herself releasing cries she tried to hold in. He kissed her gently, probing her mouth so that the movements of his tongue matched the movement of his hips.

As he moved his kisses to her neck and then her breasts, she began to move her own hips, tentatively at first, but as he picked up a more vigorous pace so did she.

She let her hands roam his strong back and his solid chest. His muscles felt like slippery steel under her hands as she glided across the sweat-soaked skin. She felt his body shiver at her touch, and his muscles flexed and rippled under her hands.

She'd taken a quick peek at him before he joined her in bed and she couldn't decide which was better, looking at him or touching him. Carlton's muscular body was perfect from the top of his head to his feet, which were big and strong. His naked body was like one of those statues of Greek gods dipped in sweet dark chocolate with just a hint of milk. Letting her hand trail his back, she decided that she liked touching more than looking. *A lot more.*

"Oh, baby, you feel so good. So good, I feel like I could never get enough of you. There is no way I can only have you once," he said, his voice interrupted by grunts and moans.

The accuracy of his statement caused her to close her eyes. She wondered what she was going to do.

Her lids flew open as she felt a tightening in her belly that soon exploded in a release so magnificent it shot from the middle of her thighs to the tips of her toes. Her body writhed and she swore her eyes rolled to the back of her head.

"Oh. My," she heard herself murmur in a voice that was at least two octaves lower than her normal husky voice.

He moved faster and deeper, nibbling on her neck. Soon she felt another explosion more intense than the first two. This time Carlton followed her orgasm with a release of his own.

They remained still wrapped in each other's arms for what seemed like an eternity before he rose from the bed to remove their protection.

While he was in the bathroom an unexpected sense of horror and shame came over Latonya. She never guessed she would feel this way so soon after she had been made love to for the first time. She assumed that it was because she really hadn't been made love to. What they'd shared was probably no more than a romp in the sack for him. But she knew it was so much more for her.

Not wanting to outstay her welcome—or worse, be asked to leave—she slowly got up from the bed and reached for her clothes. She ached between her legs in ways she never thought possible, but she managed to stand. Latonya wondered if the nice maid would be able to call her a cab.

"What are you doing?" The sharp sound of Carlton's voice caused her to jump.

She pulled her shirt over her head. "I'm going home."

"No, you're not. The deal was you spend the night with me."

"What? The deal was we'd have sex. We did. Now I'm going home." No way could she stay the night with him. She didn't think she could take more of his kisses and caresses tonight, and she knew she'd never receive them again.

"Stay the night, Tonya. Please," he almost begged.

"Look, Mr. Harrington—"

"I think we're beyond formalities, Tonya," he countered knowingly.

"Okay, *Carlton*. I can't stay the night here. I have to go home."

"Why can't you stay?"

She couldn't believe that he was badgering her about staying the night. He got what he wanted. So did she. Why couldn't Carlton just let her go? She tried to think of a good reason, anything besides the I-really-liked-making-love-to-you-and-now-I'm-running-scared-before-you-kick-me-to-the-curb excuse running through her head.

"My grandmother, she's recovering from a stroke, remember? I usually spend the weekends at home with her, but I asked Sue, her home-health aide, to stay with her today, because I had to work." She gave him a pointed glare before continuing.

"I have to pay her time and a half under the table

when she does favors like this, and I can't afford to have her spend the night with my grandmother." Grabbing her panties, she started to put them on and winced in pain as she tried to lift her sore leg.

He walked over to capture her hand in his, stilling her movement. "Call her and tell her that you will pay her triple. *I'll* pay for it. You're not leaving here tonight."

She let out a sharp, sarcastic laugh. "Do you even realize how insulting you are? I'm not a whore. You can't pay for me for the evening, *Mr. Harrington!* You can keep your money. I can pay for my own grandmother's care. I'm not going to neglect her for the entire evening so that I can spend the night in your bed!"

His hand moved from her hand to her face. He caressed her cheek. "I'm just not handling this well at all, am I?" He looked almost vulnerable. "What I mean is, I really want to spend the night with you in my arms. We don't have to have sex again. In fact, given the fact that you're sore, we probably shouldn't. I don't want this to end yet. So I'm asking you, please, let me cover your grandmother's care for the evening. Please stay here with me tonight."

She sighed heavily. "Carlton, what am I supposed to tell my grandmother? That I'm spending the night with a man?"

"Tell her that you decided to go out with some girlfriends. I don't know. Just stay with me. Please?" He gave her another one of his soul-stirring kisses and she was lost.

It's only one night, she reasoned. She could allow herself to be loved by him for one night, and then on Monday, she could get transferred to another department and keep the memories of what transpired between them locked away.

When the kiss ended, she had to take two deep breaths just to focus.

"I'll tell you what," he began. He appeared unsure that his kiss had changed her mind. "You use the phone on the nightstand there to call and make arrangements for your grandmother and I'll run you a nice, hot bath. You're probably a little sore and achy and the warmth of the water should help. Is that okay?"

Sighing, she nodded. She had never lied to her grandmother before, but she wanted to spend the night with Carlton more than she wanted anything in a long time. There was no way Latonya was going to tell her grandmother that she was spending the night with a man. Her God-fearing grandmother would think that she had made some kind of mistake raising her. Latonya could hear her grandmother's response, *Peanut, I'm going to pray to Jesus for your soul. What are you thinking staying with some man all night!* No, Gran didn't need to know this.

Latonya picked up the phone and called home. Sue was more than happy to make three times her pay and told her not to worry about her grandmother. Latonya wanted to talk to her, but she was sleeping already. Sometimes, after a frustrating day of relearning how to do things that she at one time had no problem doing for herself, her grandmother took to bed early.

She hung up the phone just as Carlton came strutting out of the bathroom. He was still very naked, and one look at his chiseled form made her glad she decided to stay. She remembered just how each and every one of those muscles felt against her skin, as he held her and stroked her. She let her eyes drink him in. Starting from the top of his wavy black hair to his feet. She stopped there and admired the way each bone, each muscle, each vein seemed perfectly placed. She never knew she had a thing for feet. As her eyes trailed up his muscular thighs, she blinked and realized that hanging around Carlton would no doubt introduce her to many more of her hidden fetishes. *Have. Mercy*, she thought when she met his dark, smoldering eyes again and saw his desire.

He smiled and her heart jumped. "Your bubble bath awaits you."

Why is he being so personable? If she had known that sex would have turned him into a decent human being, she would have put him out of his misery months ago. That would've meant that she would have been subjected to his *sweet, sweet* kisses a long time ago.

Grinning, she walked into the bathroom, took off her shirt and underwear and stepped slowly into the deep bubble bath.

Latonya jumped when Carlton stepped into the tub with her and he had to laugh. The tub was more than big enough to fit the two of them with room to spare. And he was nowhere near ready to be away from her yet.

"I figured I'd join you and help you out," he offered as he poured some of the body-wash liquid into his hands and began to lather her skin. He took a moment to massage her shoulders.

"Umm…that's nice." She leaned back into his arms.

Glad that she had relaxed a little and didn't seem as antsy as she was when she was trying to leave, Carlton exhaled. He realized that she probably felt conflicted about what happened between them. A woman didn't wait until she was twenty-four years old to have sex and take it lightly. The last thing he wanted was for her to feel some sort of guilt about what had happened between them. It had been too special to him and he wanted it to be special for her as well.

"How are you feeling?" he asked.

"I'm feeling okay."

"Really? Better than you were a few minutes ago when you were trying to make your great escape?"

She turned and glanced up at him. "Ha. Ha. Now you've got jokes. Okay. I freaked out for a minute. This is new to me. I've never felt…like this before. I've never done anything like this. And I sort of lost it for a minute and wanted to run."

Latonya's wanting to run from her feelings disturbed him, and he didn't want to put a finger on why. He only knew that if she had left she would have been taking a part of him with her. As new as it all was, he knew that much for certain.

"This is new to me, too. And I can tell you that it was special. What we shared meant more to me than anything. You don't have to be freaked out about it or

feel guilty about it. It was beautiful, and I don't want
it to be a one-night thing. I want more."

Carlton waited for some response from Latonya, but
all he got in return was her even, steady breathing.

Chapter 5

He held her for a moment and marveled over the fact that the one time he decided to pour out his heart to a woman, she fell asleep. He reasoned that maybe that was a good thing. If she almost bolted when they made love, he wondered how fast she would run once she figured out how much he really wanted her.

She looked so peaceful that he almost didn't want to wake her. He had never seen her so rested and content; it made her appear even more beautiful. As if that were possible.

Carlton didn't know what he was going to do with her. He still wanted her, damn it. He knew there was no way he'd be able to work side by side with her each day and pretend they'd never had this night together. The feel of her, look of her, taste of her, would haunt him for the rest of his life. For the first time, he wanted, no, *needed* to have a woman in his life long-term.

"Wake up, sleepyhead," he said, running his hand down a slick arm. "We're going to turn into prunes if we don't get out of this water."

Her eyes fluttered open at the sound of his deep voice as she turned to look up at him and smiled.

Together, they stood and stepped out of the deep bathtub. Stretching her arms, she stopped suddenly, embarrassed by her nakedness. She wrapped her arms around herself, and averted her gaze when she noticed him looking at her with want. He was barely aware of the water dripping down his own body, because he was so caught up in the beads of moisture trailing her shapely form. The way she had her arms wrapped in front of her only made her luscious breasts even more pronounced.

Latonya lifted her head slightly, and Carlton noticed that she was giving him an appraising glance as well.

"Um...can you pass me something to dry off with and then, um..."

He grabbed a towel and wrapped it around his waist, since parts of him suddenly came to attention at the sight of her hot, wet body. "Would you like some privacy?"

"Umm...yeah...if you don't mind."

Letting his eyes drink their fill of the beads of water trickling down her lush toffee skin, he smiled. "Well, it's not as if I haven't seen you already, Tonya."

Since it was obvious Carlton wasn't going to leave, she helped herself from a shelf lined with plush

Egyptian cotton bath sheets. As he watched, she quickly wiped herself dry and then wrapped it around her, covering everything from her breasts to the middle of her thighs. Each stroke of the Egyptian cotton on her body made him think of his own hands caressing her. The bath sheet didn't cover up enough to make him forget what it was like to have her in his arms. He wanted to be the one wrapped around her.

When they returned to the bedroom, she sat down on the bed and then glanced back at him. "Do you have a T-shirt or something I could put on to, um…sleep in?"

He bit back a grumble. He didn't want her in a T-shirt. He wanted as many memories of her beautiful body as his mind could store. But he could tell she was nervous and rather shy about displaying herself, so he dug out one of his plain white T-shirts from a drawer and handed it to her.

She took off the towel, put on the T-shirt, pulled back the comforter and got into his huge brass bed.

She stifled a yawn as her eyes fluttered—he could tell she was tired. She snuggled under the covers and he wasted no time snuggling up behind her. He wrapped his arms around her and pulled her close and tight. She relaxed into his embrace with an ease that surprised him, and soon all he heard was her soft, even breathing.

Latonya didn't know people could go from deep sleep to passionate kissing in a matter of seconds, but Carlton made her a believer when she awoke to his tentative pecks. He seemed almost asleep himself. But all it took was a hint of a response from her to fully awaken his passion. When she opened her mouth to him, he mercilessly plundered it. In her half-sleep state she couldn't tell his tongue from her own. All she knew for sure was that she couldn't get enough of what he offered.

And his hands, they must have memorized every inch of her body and every erogenous zone. First, he caressed her breasts, teasing her nipples with one hand and cupping her behind to press close to his rock-hard erection with the other.

Letting out a soft sigh, she spread her legs and moved her hips so that she could somehow make his erection touch the core of her, which was throbbing uncontrollably. She needed to feel him inside of her again; her body still craved him. She felt as if she couldn't wait to have him fill her.

She didn't have to wait long. Carlton rolled over on his back, using the arm that was cupping her to lift her on top of him. She straddled him and he helped her to ease herself onto his shaft. She stared down at him in momentary shock as she took the length of him inside of her and got used to the size of him in the new position. He sat up, lifting the T-shirt she wore and throwing it to the side.

"I want you to ride me, baby. Can you do that for me?"

Closing her eyes, she caught the rhythm. She moved up and down and back and forth, slowly at first and then with more speed. She shifted her pelvis until she could feel parts of her open, tighten and release around him that she didn't even know could tighten, much less release.

Soon his hands were no longer on her hips, but on her breasts. He reached up and squeezed the heavy flesh with urgency. Her nipples felt tight, straining against her skin. She let her own hands explore his rippled chest as she rode him.

Soon her sex began to tighten and contract in a way that made her sure she had lost all her rhythm. "Oh, oh, oh, Carlton."

"Yes, baby, yes, baby, let it out, baby."

She let out a loud scream before she collapsed against his chest. She only hoped that, since the mansion was so huge, Jillian or any of the other servants hadn't heard her cry out. He gently ran his hands down her back before flipping her over. Still inside her, his strong erection moved slowly. He suckled on her neck as he worked his hips, repeatedly pulling himself all the way out of her and burying himself to the hilt. Each move left her shaking with pleasure. She had never known so much joy.

She lifted her hips to meet each of his thrusts, and she closed her eyes tightly when she felt herself losing it again. She tried not to scream again, but the orgasm that was building ever so slowly was just too intense.

"I will never be able to get enough of you. What are you doing to me?" he grunted in her ear before he took her earlobe into his mouth. "That's right, baby, let it out. Let me know that you like this as much as I do, because I love it."

Just as she could take no more, he bent his head

and caught all her sound with his kiss. She found herself moaning and whimpering instead of kissing. Soon he shook with his own release.

In the aftermath of lovemaking, as he cuddled her in his arms, she wondered how she was ever going to work with him after knowing what he could do to her body, her mind.

He planted kisses on her forehead, cradled her to him and let out a deeply satisfied sigh.

Chapter 6

"Move in with me."

Latonya's eyes, once closed in contentment, opened in shock. "What?"

"Move in with me. I want you. I want you in my bed when I go to sleep and when I wake up. I want you. You're mine."

Insulted, she sat up. "Do you realize how crazy you sound? I'm not a piece of property."

Contrite, he replied, "I didn't say you were."

"Then you're joking, right?"

"I assure you, I am very serious. I want you, Tonya."

She shook her head as if it would help her to gain sanity. She couldn't believe the conversation they were having. "Well, I can't move in with you," she said as if she were talking to a two-year-old. "We hardly know each other and we have only been on one date. It's too soon! And we have to work together, for goodness' sake!"

His hand caressed the small of her back as he spoke. "I realize that it would take more than one night to fully examine what's happening between us. You make me feel things I've never felt before. I know that I want you. And, you know, if you moved in with me, you wouldn't need to work for Harrington Enterprise anymore."

Her head snapped so quickly she felt a sharp pain in her neck. "First of all, I did not get an MBA to become your personal whore! And second, even if I was stupid enough to consider giving up my career to become your bed warmer, I have responsibilities to my grandmother and my sister."

The realization that they hadn't practiced safe sex the second time hit Latonya and she sat stunned for a moment. Her voice went soft, "We didn't use anything."

The longer she silently chastised herself, the more she wanted to just put on her clothing and go home. The fact that Carlton had suddenly turned into Mr. I-can-buy-anything-I-want-even-you made her wish that she had left when she started to the first time.

He let out a deep breath, "I got too caught up in the moment and I wasn't thinking. That has never happened to me before."

"I barely know you," she mumbled. "I don't know the first thing about you, really, and we just had unprotected sex."

"I can assure you that I'm safe. I have been tested.

And like I said, I don't make a habit of going unprotected… Of course if there are any repercussions, I would be there for you." He resumed rubbing his hand down her back in a reassuring manner.

She shook her head in disbelief and mumbled, "I knew no good could come from this…this…little escapade…from losing sight of my goals."

His hand froze and he shot up in the bed. "What the hell do you mean by that?" he asked sharply.

"It's not…it's just I don't want to prolong this. It's bad enough I did it twice. Bad enough I didn't wait for my husband like Gran always told me to. Now you want me to be some kind of live-in call girl?"

"So you were saving yourself for your future husband and big bad me ruined it." His sarcastic tone of voice was not helping the situation.

"That's not what I said," she snapped. "But I don't expect you to get it." She got up and started feeling around for her clothing. What had started out as the sweetness of one night's passion had turned into a big mess.

"This conversation isn't over."

She sucked her teeth and mumbled, "That's what you think." She put on her panties and bra.

"Tonya, we need to figure this out."

"Can your driver take me home or should I call a cab?" she asked as she pulled on her slacks.

"Neither. You're not leaving." He stepped out of bed and walked over to her just as she pulled her shirt over her head. "Please don't leave."

Staring at the naked man standing in front of her,

Latonya almost lost her train of thought. She swallowed and blinked.

"Well, if you're so distraught that you weren't able to save yourself for your husband, you could always marry me."

She let out a short, sarcastic laugh that sounded more like a snort.

"It would be a perfect arrangement," Carlton continued. "You wouldn't have to worry about your job. You wouldn't have to work at all. I could see to it that your family is taken care of. I'd pay off your grandmother's mortgage, your sister's tuition. And I would see to it that your grandmother got the best medical attention available and pay for all of her care." His voice gained more and more momentum as he went along. "Wouldn't it be nice not to have to worry about it?"

She couldn't believe the audacity of the man. He really thought that anything he wanted, even people, could be bought and bartered for. Well, she wasn't for sale.

"I highly doubt that either my sister or my grandmother would want me to sell myself to you for the cost of their care," she said bluntly.

"Then fine, don't do it for them. Do it for yourself. There is something special between us. I know you feel it, too." He reached out and caressed her cheek.

She looked into his eyes, and what she saw unnerved her. As cocky as his words sounded while he professed his wants, his eyes showed a man who was stepping out on a limb and just as overwhelmed and confused as she was about what was happening between them.

"You said it yourself, Carlton. You haven't experienced anything like this before. Neither have I. To me, that's all the more reason to take it slow. We went into this thinking it would be one night of passion to get this out of our systems."

He traced her lips with his fingers and smiled. "It's because I've never experienced anything like this before that I know it's special. I don't want to lose it. I want to start building on it *now*. I want you, Tonya."

She rolled her eyes. "This may be a new concept to you, but you can't have everything you want, especially if your wants interfere with the wills of others. We agreed that one evening would allow us to explore our attraction and then we could move on with our lives."

"Can you tell me that one night is enough for you?" His eyes pierced into her, and she felt as if he could see inside of her soul.

Averting her own gaze, she knew she couldn't face his intense stare and answer his question in the way she had to. Yet she couldn't seem to fix her mouth to say the words.

If she wanted to be free of him and the path of his tenacious will and seductive wants, then she had to tell him that one night was enough for her. She had to lie and make him believe that she would not spend nights in her bed with her arms wrapped tightly around her remembering his touch. She had to say that. But she could not.

All she managed was a mumbled "It doesn't matter what's enough for me or you. It's the right thing to do."

He pulled her close and brushed her forehead with his lips. "Okay, I won't push you on this now. But please come back to bed. I can wait for you to realize how wonderful things can be between us."

Suddenly tired and sufficiently overwhelmed by all of the evening's events, she did exactly that.

Chapter 7

On Monday morning Latonya went to work still reeling over what had transpired that weekend. She managed to talk herself into believing that she and Carlton would be able to continue working together and soon he would give up the outrageous notion that she should move in with him or the even sillier notion that she should marry him.

While the thought of becoming his wife, having his children and waking up each morning in his arms made her want things she never realized she desired, she did not believe in fairy tales.

Her parents' tumultuous relationship had taught her to be cautious when it came to matters of the heart. That didn't mean that she didn't believe in love; she just didn't trust it to last. And she definitely wasn't going to let some spoiled, rich businessman push her into a relationship because he wanted her body. She made up her mind to resist him; it was for the best.

For most of the day, she actually believed that the decision to have sex with Carlton hadn't been a huge mistake. He was being cordial; he didn't yell at her or single her out. And at the joint staff meeting, he even complimented the hard work she'd put in on the Biltmore project.

Everything went along smoothly until the end of the day, when Jeff called her into his office. On her way back from the copy machine, she got a dose of reality.

She laughed and joked with Jeff as he flirted with her. It felt good to let down her guard and laugh with a coworker again. She'd been walking on eggshells at work the past few months.

Giggling lightheartedly, she smiled at Jeff. "Now you know that if I one day decided to take you up on your advances you wouldn't know what to do."

"Like hell I wouldn't. I'd call up the pastor and have him book the chapel." He flashed a dimpled grin as he stood up from his chair and walked around his desk.

"Yeah, right. I'm sure your *Mayflower*–descendent mother would love that."

"Wouldn't matter." Jeff winked at her in a seductive manner, as he crossed his arms and rested himself on the desk directly in front of the chair she sat in.

She was about to tell Jeff what a riot he was when she noticed his puzzled expression. He was staring over her shoulder. She turned, and there in the doorway stood one very agitated Carlton. His eyes were narrowed and Latonya swore she could see veins throbbing at his temples. He appeared ready to explode.

"In my office, Latonya. Now!" He turned and walked away as if he fully expected her to snap and run behind him.

Who does he think he is?

A concerned expression flashed across Jeff's face. "Looks like the boss's reprieve is over now. He's back on your case. Wonder what he has against you?"

Even though her heartbeat sped up a tad bit, she wasn't going to let Carlton's theatrics get to her. And she certainly wasn't going to show the small piece of dread that tried to rear its head in front of her coworker. Her reputation for taking the best the ogre could give was at stake. Carlton needed to learn that he didn't own her just because she'd slept with him.

"I don't know. But I do know that I'm not going to just jump and run to his office because he snaps his fingers. I'm taking my time." Latonya stood and started walking toward the door. She jokingly took slow baby steps to emphasize her point. "I think I'll go put my photocopies down in my office and check my voice mail and e-mail before I see what His Royal Highness wants. Maybe he'll see fit to calm down a bit before I get there."

"Yes, and you can tell me all about it over dinner this evening." Jeff walked with her and put his arm around her shoulder. "A beautiful, brilliant career woman like yourself needs someone she can bring it

all home to. Someone she can vent to and blow off
steam with—"

"Nice try, Jeff. I'll tell you what. Why don't you
settle for a phone call, *if* I don't get too busy?"

Jeff stopped her and briefly let his thumb stroke her
cheek. "Seriously, I just want you to know I'm here for
you if you ever need anything. A shoulder to lean on.
An ear to complain to. A boyfriend. A future husband
and father of your children." He flashed his devilish
smile.

Latonya couldn't help laughing. "You certainly
know how to crack me up. You need to take your show
on the road."

"The show wouldn't work without you. You're my
inspiration."

"How ever do you come up with these? You must
have a pickup line for every occasion," she said as she
suppressed the urge to laugh again. "Okay, I'll call you
later."

Latonya took a calming breath and managed to
make it to Carlton's office.

Carlton told himself to act rational. There was no
reason to be jealous of Latonya sharing a joke with Jeff
Weatherby. No reason except that Carlton *knew* that
Jeff had his eye on Latonya and was trying to woo her.
Still, what Carlton and Latonya shared that weekend
was special, he knew that without a doubt.

But each minute that passed caused more doubt to
seep into his mind. What if she really didn't feel the
same way about him at all? His own mother taught him

at an early age that women *and* their affections were fickle. Watching his mother move from one lover to the next while his father chased after her left an indelible mark on his mind. He'd hoped that Latonya was different.

When she finally came breezing into his office he didn't think before he bit out his angry words. "When I tell you to come to my office, Latonya, you had better make speed getting here. Next time, I would suggest you beat me here if you value this job as much as you say you do."

Folding her arms across her chest, Latonya narrowed her gaze. "I got here as soon as I could. What do you want?" she snapped.

"I want you to stop batting your eyes and grinning in the faces of my staff! Are you tempted to jump from my bed to Jeff's after testing your womanly wiles?"

Her eyes bulged and her mouth fell open. "I don't believe this! How dare you!"

He pounded his hand firmly on his desk. "No, how dare *you?* How dare you think that I would stand idly by and let you prance from one employee to another? The laughing, giggling and flirting with Jeff *and* the others stops today."

Several emotions played across her face, ranging from anger to outrage. "To hell with you and to hell with this. I quit. I refuse to work like this. Consider this my resignation." Latonya hurried out the door and slammed it behind her.

Carlton stared at the door as he tried to process what had just happened. He ran his hand over his head.

Along with all the other emotions Latonya had him experiencing, jealousy was another one. He had never been jealous of anyone in his life. And he had never felt so possessive about anyone. He knew that she probably wouldn't forgive him for acting so irrationally or behaving so badly. He also immediately knew that he had to try to make things better. Watching her walk out the door and seeing it close taught him yet another new thing about himself; he wouldn't be able to take it if he really didn't stand a chance with Latonya.

Storming into her office, Latonya grabbed her purse and briefcase. Harrington Enterprise could keep everything else if it meant she never had to see Carlton again. She almost knocked Jeff and Juan down on her way to the elevator.

"Hey, what got into you? You look like you could kill someone," Juan joked.

"She just met with Harry Tres and I'm sure he was his usual pleasant self," Jeff offered.

Latonya took a deep breath. She knew she couldn't talk about what just happened between her and Carlton with them. She could feel the anger welling up inside of her and she feared that it would come out in tears. She hadn't cried—in front of other people at least—since the day of her mother's funeral. She would be damned if she would start because of Carlton.

She thought that they'd shared an emotional connection. He'd touched something deep in her soul that made her think he could be the one. She'd even let herself imagine what it would be like to be his wife and have his children. Once they dated for a while and got to know each other, of course. If he really believed that she would turn around and have sex with another man, then maybe it was just sex for him, after all.

She rode down in the elevator with Juan and Jeff in steaming silence.

"Hey," Jeff said when they got off on the main floor. "You want to go have a drink with us and get some stuff off your chest?"

"No, Jeff." She sighed. "I'm fine. I just quit my job and I don't have a clue how soon I'll be able to get another, but I'll survive."

She forced a smile and walked briskly away from them.

Chapter 8

When Latonya reached her home, she found her younger sister, Cicely on the sofa. Seeing her sister made Latonya reflect on the gravity of what she had just done. How could she have quit her job when Cee Cee had at least three more years of college left?

"What's up, sis?" Cicely jumped up from the worn blue sofa and gave Latonya a hug at the door.

"What are you doing home?" Latonya asked as she noted that the night she'd planned to spend sulking and eating ice cream would have to be rescheduled due to Cee Cee's unscheduled visit. "Last time I checked FAMU doesn't have any holidays right now and you have Monday classes. Why aren't you on campus?"

"Is that any way to treat your favorite baby sister?"

Cicely faked a pout and plopped back on the sofa pulling Latonya with her.

"You're my only baby sister. And I want to know why you're in Miami instead of Tallahassee."

Sending her sister to the historically black college Florida A&M University, meant a lot to Latonya. She wanted Cicely to get the full college campus experience that she'd missed out on by attending a predominantly white university in Miami. Latonya had been offered a partial tuition scholarship to Howard University and she'd wanted to go. Circumstances and a lack of money required that she stay home and commute.

Cicely had good grades and qualified for some scholarships from the United Negro College Fund, but the bulk of the tuition and housing fees came from Latonya's paycheck. The sacrifice was worth it to see Cicely eventually do things like pledge a black sorority and take part in an active campus life, all the things she had wanted to do herself. Latonya didn't like the idea of Cicely skipping out on classes.

"I got homesick and I wanted to see you and Gran. Plus, I was thinking, it's not fair for me to be all the way in Tallahassee while Gran is recovering and you're working, taking care of her and paying for everything." Cicely folded her arms across her chest. "You went to the University of Miami and commuted while you worked and helped us out. I should do the same thing."

Working in retail ever since she'd been a junior in high school had been a major source of income for Latonya. By the time she'd finished her MBA she was working as a manager in the small clothing store that catered to young women in their teens and twenties. The discount that she had there had come in handy for Cee Cee's school clothes. If push came to shove, she could always go back and work there.

"No. I want you to attend FAMU. You love it there. You're going to pledge Delta. You're involved with the student government association. What's the matter? Did something happen?" Latonya stared at her sister intently. Trying to figure Cee Cee out had always been a struggle. It seemed as if they'd both developed a way to keep the rest of the world ignorant to what they were really feeling inside.

Cicely plastered on a bright smile. "Nothing's wrong. I just missed you and Gran and I needed a break. Don't worry, sis. I just got a little homesick, that's all."

"Well okay. But I hope you aren't missing anything important." Latonya leaned back on the sofa.

"Nope. In fact, I'm ahead in all my classes. So, what's up with you? You look like you've seen better days."

"I'm fine. Couldn't be better." Latonya wasn't about to tell Cee Cee that she had just quit her job. The girl would probably withdraw from college in a heartbeat and move home to help out with the house. Latonya knew she'd be able to find another job with her credentials, even in a tight job market. But when?

"You don't look fine. In fact, if I didn't know any better, I'd say you were having man troubles." Cicely eyed her incredulously.

"Man troubles? What do you know about man

troubles?" The sad fact was, Latonya's sister knew a whole lot more about man troubles than she did. Cicely at least dated during high school and had the occasional steady boyfriend.

Latonya studied Cicely carefully. They shared the same facial features, but Cicely's were a little more angular. Her soft cocoa-brown skin was a couple of shades darker than Latonya's, but they shared the same brown eyes. Cicely's hair, which she currently wore in a long ponytail, was a deep dark brown instead of auburn like her older sister's. Gran always said that Latonya took after their mom in coloring and Cicely took after their dad.

"Spill it, Peanut. Is it that mean old boss you were complaining about? See, that's why you need to let me transfer to the University of Miami and move back home. You wouldn't have to work for that... what do you call him? Oh, yeah, that ogre."

"I'm fine. I don't have man troubles or boss troubles. I'm actually—" Latonya's lies were interrupted by the doorbell. As she watched Cee Cee jump up to answer the door, she figured it had to be one of her sister's friends stopping by to visit her. Cicely must have called them all to tell them she was coming home.

"Woooo! Flowers! For me?" Cicely's high-pitched squeal made Latonya get up and walk to the door.

"No. They're for Latonya. Is she here?"

Latonya felt her jaw drop when she saw Carlton standing in the doorway holding the most beautiful bouquet of tropical flowers she'd every seen.

Cicely looked at her. "Somebody's been keeping

secrets." She turned back to Carlton. "Well, I guess I'd be rude if I didn't invite you in. I'm Latonya's sister, Cicely."

Carlton walked in and Latonya's eyes narrowed. *How dare he just come here with flowers, as if that was going to be enough to get me to forgive him!*

"Hi, Cicely. I'm Carlton. Nice to meet you," he responded as his eyes searched Latonya's face.

"I'll take these. I think we have a vase in here someplace. Although, I doubt we have one big enough for all these flowers. I might have to separate them." Cicely glanced from Latonya to Carlton as she took the flowers. "And, nobody's paying me *any* attention. All righty then…." She walked to the kitchen in the back of the house.

Latonya folded her arms across her chest and gave Carlton a pointed glare. "What are you doing here?"

Carlton took a deep breath and exhaled. "I came to tell you that I was out of line today and I behaved horribly."

She couldn't believe Carlton. The audacity of the man was mind blowing. He probably actually thought he was making a huge gesture! "Oh, so now you're making road trips to the hood in order to state the obvious. Tell me something I don't already now, Carlton!"

Carlton winced. Things weren't going exactly as he'd planned. He hadn't expected her to just leap into his arms and forgive him because he brought flowers, but he'd never done this sort of thing before. Apologizing just wasn't something he did.

"Well, I figured if I admitted I was out of line—"

"I don't need you to admit that you were out of line. I have eyes and ears. I saw it for myself. But thanks for backing up what I already knew. If that is all you came for, then you can leave now." Latonya walked over to the door and started to open it.

"Wait a second, Latonya. Can you just hear me out? Please?"

She turned to face him.

He let out a sigh of relief. "Thank you."

She shook her head in mock amazement. "Wow, he can say please and thank you, but not I'm sorry when he's been a total jerk!"

"I said I was out of line. I brought flowers," was all he could say in his defense. What more did the woman want?

"I want an apology, Carlton, and then I'll decide if I will hear anything else you have to say."

He ran his hand across his head. "Can we sit down somewhere and talk?"

She tilted her head and crossed her arms. Her body posture and stance answered with a resounding no.

"Okay, the flowers are in vases. What did I miss? Why aren't you two sitting down somewhere?" Cicely came breezing back into the entryway.

"Thanks, Cicely, but Carlton won't be—" Latonya started as she made a move for the door.

"Okay, I'm sorry! I acted like a jerk. Will you please forgive me?" The words came out in a mad rush as he struggled to come to terms with the fact that he was experiencing another new emotion with this woman.

The pounding in his chest as he waited for her response was a feeling he *never* wanted to feel again.

Latonya smiled. "That wasn't so hard, was it? Now, if that will be all…" She reached for the door.

"Can we go somewhere to talk? I really want…need to talk to you." He couldn't believe he was begging. Yet another first!

"Do we have anything else to talk about?" Latonya asked hesitantly.

"Oh, come on, sis! Cut the man some slack. He's begging! Plus, he's kinda cute!" Cicely added her two cents, and both Latonya and Carlton turned. He'd actually been so wrapped up in getting Latonya to listen to him that he forgot the younger woman was there.

Latonya's eyes widened. "Cee Cee," she said in a scolding voice.

"Pea-nut," Cicely mimicked Latonya's voice.

"Peanut?" Carlton asked.

"It's her nickname. Everyone calls her that," Cicely replied with a smirk.

Latonya turned and glared at him. "Everyone except for you! And if you tell anyone I'll have to do you bodily harm."

"Hey, it's okay, your secret is safe with me, Peanut. I mean Latonya. I just want to talk to you for a minute," Carlton lied. He wanted to do a whole lot more than talk to Peanut. "Can we go somewhere?"

"You can go, sis. I'm staying in tonight. I'll stay with Gran. She's resting, anyway," Cicely offered.

Latonya glanced at Carlton. "Well, if going to have

a talk with you is the only way I'm going to get you out of my home, then I guess I'll do it." She turned to Cicely. "I'm going to peek in on Gran. Don't tell him any more family secrets before I get back."

Carlton watched Latonya walk down the short hallway and into what he assumed was one of the bedrooms.

"So, what exactly are your intentions with my sister?" Cicely asked.

Carlton turned to see the younger woman studying him carefully. "Only good things, I promise."

Cicely tilted her head and studied him. "Well, judging from that big bouquet of flowers and the fact that she is giving you such a hard time, you aren't off to a very good start."

"I know. I'm working on it," Carlton responded as he nervously ran his hand across his head again.

"Well just so you know, we Stevens girls are tough, but we can still be hurt. You *better not* hurt my sister."

Carlton stared at the young woman and paused to consider her threat. Something in her eyes told him that she had experienced some hurt herself. He took a deep breath. If he had anything to do with it, no one would hurt one of the tough Stevens girls again, especially not him. "Don't worry, Cicely. I got off to a rocky start with Latonya. But I don't plan on messing up again."

"See that you don't."

"Don't what?" Latonya asked as she walked back into the entryway.

"Don't stay out too late. I'm only home for a couple of days and I want to spend as much time as possible with you." Cicely hugged Latonya. "And you have been holding out! I want all the details when you come back. He's cute, by the way. Maybe we can send him over to deal with that mean jerk of a boss of yours." She flounced off.

Cicely was quick on her feet and Carlton decided then and there that he liked the young woman. He understood why Latonya was so devoted to her younger sister.

Latonya's cheeks turned red. "So, I have been complaining about you for the past few months. I had to vent somewhere." She opened the door. "Let's go and get this talk over with. Where are we going?"

"We could go back to my place," Carton responded. He hadn't planned on them actually going anywhere. He thought she would take the flowers, forgive him and they would be on track. He now realized it would take a bit more work. Judging from the way she twisted up her lips when he suggested his home, he reasoned it would take a lot more work.

"We can go grab a bite to eat or a cup of coffee?" he offered. "Or we can just have Paul drive us around the city. It's beautiful at night."

"That sounds good. I have a busy day tomorrow. Job hunting," Latonya responded as she walked out of the house and got into his limousine.

Perplexed, Carlton followed her. Once they were seated in the car and on their way, he asked, "You mean you're still leaving your job?"

Latonya shook her head. "Yes. I think it would be for the best."

"What about us?"

"What about us, Carlton?" She frowned. "I think it's clear that whatever we thought we could share won't work."

"That's not true, Latonya. I know that it can work. I know that I can be hard to deal with sometimes. But I also know that you make me want to be better. I have never felt like this before. Give it a chance. Give *us* a chance." Carlton reached out his hand and clasped hers. "I know you thought I was crazy the other night, but watching you walk out that door today showed me more than ever, I want you. I have to have you."

When he first made the offer to marry her he'd momentarily questioned his sanity. The more he thought about it, however, the more he realized that Latonya was meant to be his wife. No woman had ever made him feel so much and taken him through so many conflicting emotions. He'd started to think that no woman ever could. Watching his mother repeatedly cheat on his father and his father repeatedly run after his mother had hardened him to any emotions as far as the opposite sex was concerned.

Latonya showed him that wasn't the case at all. At first he wanted to run from the feelings. Then he thought he could bed her and get rid of them. Now that he knew for sure that the feelings weren't going anywhere and were instead getting stronger, he needed to embrace them.

Her eyes widened and she stared at him with her mouth open before responding. "You can't seriously still think that I would move in with you?"

"No… I mean yes I want you to move in. But I want you to move in as my wife. I want to marry you. I want to share the rest of my life with you. Will you marry me?"

"Why would you want to marry a woman who you think is primed to jump into another man's bed? You think so very little of me. Why on earth would you want to marry me, Carlton?" Letting out a shuddering breath, she continued, "Why can't you just be satisfied with what we had and move on? All you have to do is give me a letter of reference and let me go."

"Doesn't work for me. I want you. That has not changed. So, what will it be? Marry me, Tonya. Let me take care of you and your family." He pulled her closer to him. A smile briefly crossed his lips, glad when she didn't resist.

Shaking her head incredulously, she said, "And you expect me to just jump into your arms and walk down the aisle at that offer?"

"Things will be good between us. I promise. You're attracted to me. Why are you fighting this?"

Deciding it would be more prudent to show her the benefits of a union between them, he bent his head and took her lush mouth with his.

Her mouth opened, readily accepting the caresses of his tongue. He felt his heart pounding and marveled that every fiber of his being could be impacted by just one sweet kiss from her. Pulling her close, he softly nibbled on her lips.

"I want you so bad I ache. Tell me I'm not wrong, Latonya. I feel like you want me, too. I felt it the first time I kissed you. I have a feeling deep in my gut that if you give us a chance you won't regret it." Carlton had to make her see that things could work. She was The One. His heart wouldn't allow him to let her get away.

"Why are you making this into an all-or-nothing thing? It makes it really hard for me to trust you." She let out a sigh of exasperation and shut her eyes.

"I'm not making it an all-or-nothing. Or at least I don't mean to. I just feel this sense of urgency. You hold my future happiness in your hands. And I want to make sure that we can share it."

Shaking her head, she muttered. "Don't you think it's problematic that you think you deserve to have everything you want? Life doesn't work that way. Sometimes we don't get what we want, Carlton. Sometimes people get disappointed. People get hurt."

"I'm not going to hurt you. I'm not saying that I won't make mistakes, and mess up every now and then. But I swear, I only want to take care of you and make you happy," he offered.

She closed her eyes in contemplation.

"I just want us to be together. Say yes. You felt how good it is. I know you want to be with me. I can feel it when I kiss you." He touched her cheek and willed her to say yes.

She opened her eyes, looked at him for several minutes, and bit her lower lip as she considered what he'd said. She sighed. "Okay, you can cut the sales pitch." She looked at him for what seemed like an eternity before she simply said, "Yes."

* * *

Caught up in a whirlwind of swirling emotions, Latonya could barely believe that the word *yes* had just fallen out of her mouth. The thing she realized as she left Harrington Enterprise earlier that evening was that she cared for Carlton more than she was willing to admit. She had already shared more with him in just a matter of days than she had ever shared with anyone. She looked at the man who had captured her heart before she even knew it was in danger of being lost, and the reality of her situation hit her: playa-proof Latonya had fallen in love. All at once she felt fear and excitement pulsing through her veins. Carlton hadn't said that he loved her. And she hadn't said that she loved him. But when she was with him, she felt as if her heart knew him. She didn't want to lose that feeling. She knew it wouldn't be easy for the two of them, but she also knew she had to move past her fears and give it a try.

It wasn't just the way he made her body feel, either. It was the power he had to make her heart beat faster or even stop with the smallest of acts. It was the way her heart ached when for the few short hours she thought she'd never see him again. She had to say yes, because she couldn't say no.

"Yes!" Carlton shouted as he squeezed her tightly. "You have just made me the happiest man in the world." He brought his lips to hers and kissed her passionately before whispering, "You won't regret this, baby. It's going to be so good between us. You'll see."

Allowing herself to relish the tight squeeze of his

embrace and the soothing touch of his hands, she prayed that he was right. Even though she had no reason to expect good things to last, she didn't want the special stirrings that he'd awakened in her to end yet.

Experience had taught her that even when you tried your best, things didn't always go as planned. She'd tried to be a good girl, help out around the house and take care of her little sister so that her parents wouldn't argue so much. And her father still left them. She stood out in the parking lot of the grocery store helping people carry groceries to their cars to get extra money so her mom wouldn't have to work so hard. And her mother had still worked herself to an early grave. Latonya had even turned down a partial tuition scholarship to a school out of state to stay in Miami and help Gran. And Gran had a stroke, anyway. As she let herself feel the warmth of Carlton's embrace, Latonya figured she was long overdue for a little happiness, even if it didn't last.

"You believe it, don't you, baby? I know you feel it." His hand moved through her hair and her entire body tingled.

"Yes. I do," was all she could say in response, because she did. God help her, she did.

Chapter 9

Married and pregnant in less than three months, Latonya felt as if she'd been swept up in a hurricane— a hurricane named Carlton. So many changes happened in her life in such a short span of time that she couldn't get her bearings. Even though she technically didn't have to worry about her family anymore, or supporting them, she still worried. She worried about them because she wasn't in Miami anymore and couldn't see them every day.

Jillian said she would check in on Gran from time to time, so that made Latonya feel a little better. The older woman was turning out to be a good friend and a much-needed ally as Latonya navigated her new life. Jillian was small in stature but big in personality and will. Latonya adored the way the woman spoke her mind. She only wished that Jillian had come with them to the Bahamas.

As soon as they married, Carlton finished up his restructuring at the Miami office and they moved to the Bahamas, spending their time between Carlton's luxury penthouse apartment in Nassau and the family estate on a private spot in the Berry islands on the weekends. The estate, Marissa, had been named for Carlton's deceased grandmother.

The Harrington estate was only accessible by boat or helicopter. The huge plantation-style mansion forebodingly sat in the middle of the tropical island, and Latonya had never felt more overwhelmed than when she had to spend time there. Just like every day she shared with Carlton in the huge penthouse, she felt sufficiently intimidated by the overstated opulence of the family estate. The expensive furnishings that graced all of the Harrington residences made Latonya feel as if she were living in a museum. Since her grandmother worked in the homes of wealthy people just like the Harringtons, she had a hard time reconciling her present with her past.

The sheer size of her new living arrangements left her head spinning. The properties were enormous, even the penthouse doubled her grandmother's place several times over. Her life changed so drastically in a matter of months that it became harder and harder to get a grip. Moving from entry-level worker to rich, pampered wife took all of her energy, energy that she barely had to spare in the early stages of pregnancy. Even though she had dreamed of one day being rich and being able to take care of her family, she always thought she would do so by working hard and putting her MBA to good use. Her sudden entry into the jet-set lifestyle that Carlton lived put her dreams on the fast track, and she had no idea how she felt about it.

In the space of three months, she'd acquired more clothes, shoes and jewelry than she'd had in her entire life. She outright refused most of the items Carlton insisted she have, but it was to no avail. Finally, she figured that as the wife of a rich and powerful man, she was probably expected to look a certain way. So, she started wearing the designer clothing and fancy jewels. She spent her days shopping in the glitzy boutiques of Nassau while Carlton worked. It seemed to please him when she splurged on some frivolous frock or trinket. And it pleased him even more to see her all dressed up. Nervous about just how much she really wanted to please her new husband, she tried to take the same pleasure that he did out of her transformation. But, she felt as if she wore someone else's life when she put on all the expensive clothing.

She gazed in the mirror at her perfectly made-up face and designer red silk skirt suit. She certainly looked her part. The diamond-and-ruby jewelry that her husband had brought home for her the night before made her feel like she might be able to fake belonging for one more day. And the sophisticated, rich material hugged her curves, which had become just a little fuller in her early months of pregnancy.

When she played her new role and dressed her part, she worried about what the many rich socialites she'd been meeting might think. Did they think her a conniving gold digger obsessed with clothes and jewels? Unfortunately, she didn't have to worry about what the elder Carlton Harrington thought. He made his opinion clear from the moment they told him they were getting married; he wasn't happy about it.

She couldn't blame the old man, either. She, too, would question the motives of some young woman coming out of the blue, pregnant and married so quickly, especially with the amount of money the Harringtons had.

She figured that if she just kept her eyes on her plate during the dinner that night, and let Carlton and his grandfather discuss business, she would escape untouched by the old man's wrath. If only she could have been so lucky.

"So, Latonya, what have you been doing with yourself since you've left Harrington Enterprise?" The elder Harrington's voice sounded pleasant enough.

Looking up from her plate, she tried to ascertain if it was safe, if the old man was really going to play nice. He seemed like he might.

The elder Harrington was handsome, to say the least. He looked like she imagined her Carlton would look in fifty years. His salt-and-pepper hair was short with deep waves. He was still in good physical shape, and the wrinkles in the corner of his eyes gave him a distinguished appearance. Dressed formally, he made quite the imposing picture. The older man peered at her from behind rounded spectacles.

"Well, I've been getting adjusted to the changes that my life has gone through in such a short amount of time, getting used to life here in the Bahamas and not having to work. I've also spent a lot of time going back and forth between Nassau and Miami to see my grandmother and help with her therapy."

"Don't you miss working for a living? Or did you always plan to grab yourself a rich husband to take care of you?" A slight snarl became evident underneath the elder Harrington's pleasant facade.

Not playing nice at all, he instead set her up for the kill and she fell right into his trap. Glancing up at him, she noticed the way his lip curled ruthlessly as he looked at her. Her eyes narrowed and she leaned forward. Before she could respond, Carlton did.

"Grandfather, we're married now. Latonya's having my child, and if you cannot respect that, we don't have to come here and spend time with you. She's my wife, and I won't have anyone disrespecting her. Not even you."

The old man pushed his chair back in shock. "Well. Look at how far she's gotten her paws. She has you disrespecting your grandfather. The man who raised you."

Without breaking a sweat or even raising his voice, Carlton responded, "You raised me to be a man, and I wouldn't be the man you raised if I sat here and let anyone insult my wife."

"You don't even know anything about her. She has your nose wide open. As many women as you've been with, I can't believe that you've let this one—a black American, for Christ's sake—wrap you around her finger." The elder Harrington slammed his hand down on the table and it shook.

Willing her hormones not to take over, Latonya blinked rapidly to hold back the tears. Being pregnant had some drawbacks that she could have done without. Although she couldn't wait for her child to arrive and didn't regret anything as far as the child was concerned, the fact that she broke down crying at the slightest things irritated her. She could not stand for people to see her cry, and she was determined not to let the elder Harrington bring on a bout of tears.

She had no idea that the elder Harrington had issues with her being a black American on top of *all* his other issues. Growing up in Miami, Latonya had been exposed to black people from just about every place in the world, and she appreciated the variety in cultures as well as the things that blacks shared throughout the African diaspora. She remembered being appalled when her best friend in high school told her that her mom said never to date a foreign black man and then proceeded to name just about every island in the Caribbean and several countries in Africa to boot. In Latonya's mind, black was black. Period.

If it were just the class issues that bothered the elder Harrington, she might have been able to deal with it. But how did she deal with ignorant black-on-black prejudice based on cultural and geographical differences? Latonya wondered as she stared at the elder Harrington. The possibility of developing a cordial relationship with the man suddenly seemed insurmountable.

She decided to try to at least initiate a conversation with him about it. "Since I can't do anything about where I was born, Mr. Harrington, what would you have me do? I'm American, African-American. Your great-grandchild is going to be part African-American."

Appalled, the elder Harrington turned and stared at her with wide eyes. The expression on his face showed that he didn't expect her to ask him anything or even stand up for herself.

"*If* he is even the father of that child you're carrying. You are clearly a gold digger and you have gotten yourself pregnant to trap my grandson. Maybe you see it as some sort of a free ticket out of your little ghetto. I don't know. And I don't care. All I know is he shouldn't have married you just because you got yourself knocked up."

Swallowing back all of the curse words that would have surely given the old man ammunition as to just how *ghetto* the little *black American* sitting at his dinner table was, Latonya simply glared at the man. She didn't even look at Carlton. She wanted to go home.

Carlton angrily pushed back his chair and stood. "Not that it's any of your business, but I didn't marry her because she's pregnant. I married her because I wanted to. Now, if you can't deal with my decisions then feel free to let me know. We can leave."

She winced at Carlton's words. He *wanted* to. Not he loved her and couldn't live without her. She wondered if she had gotten in over her head and if she would be able to protect her heart.

An ugly sneer crossed the elder Harrington's lips. "Fine, we can drop the subject. If she is the little gold digger I think she is, then the truth will come out in due time. And I will be the first to say I told you so."

"That's it. Come on, Tonya. Grandfather needs to spend some time thinking about what kind of role he wants to play in our lives and the life of his great-grandchild. You can let us know when you are ready to treat my wife with the respect she deserves and not question her motives or mine." Carlton shot his grandfather an angry glare and motioned for her to follow him.

Latonya wondered if things would ever get better. No amount of dressing up seemed to help with the old man. Even when she wore her fine clothes and jewels, he still looked at her as if she were trash. The beautiful red silk suit suddenly didn't feel so lovely.

The elder Harrington stared after Carlton and his gold-digging trollop of a wife. He never expected Carlton to be so disrespectful and treat him so badly over a piece of tail. *History is repeating itself all over again,* he thought bitterly. He couldn't stand still and let it happen this time. He would not lose another person he cared for because some poor piece of trash decided to set her snares on him.

The elder Harrington loved his grandson more than anything. Carlton was all he had left of his beloved son, and he would be damned if he would stand by and let that American slut come between them. Or worse, do anything to make him lose his grandson for good.

He walked over to the window. As he watched them get into the helicopter, he could feel the blood boiling in his veins. Carlton had chosen the girl over family, over blood. Not good. That meant his feelings for the woman were strong.

When Harrington men fell in love they fell quick and hard. It wouldn't have been so bad if all women were like his Marissa. God rest her soul. But they weren't. For some reason, his son and grandson had chosen gold-digging whores who destroyed everything and everyone they touched.

If Carlton was truly in love with the little American, then the elder Harrington would have to tread carefully, bide his time. He was certain of one thing however: the girl had to go.

The elder Harrington walked away from the window and into his study. He'd already started to quietly spread the word about her upbringing around their inner circle of friends in the Bahamas to make the girl feel anything but welcomed. He'd have to make a few more calls. He had to up the stakes and run her out of the Bahamas while it was still early. Once his grandson saw that the girl couldn't even make enough of a sacrifice to get used to their island, he'd hopefully let her go. And if the child she carried happened to really be a Harrington, they'd just take the child from her. A woman had destroyed his family once. He would not let it happen again.

When they were in the helicopter headed to their penthouse in Nassau, Latonya gazed at the beautiful blue waters below. She swore she could see clear down to the bottom. The Bahamas were breathtaking and she marveled at the white sand beaches and lush green trees underneath. She only wished the tranquil scenery had the calming effect she'd hoped for.

Carlton wrapped her in his strong arms and she felt the calm she yearned. "I'm sorry you had to listen to that, baby. Grandfather was out of line. I married you. He has to deal with that," he said, turning her in his arms. He brushed his lips across her forehead. "Things will work out. He'll come around eventually. But until he does, we will keep our distance. I won't have him upsetting you, especially not in your condition."

She had no idea how to tell him that it wasn't just the elder Harrington. It was hard for her to fit into his world and she didn't think it was going to get any easier.

When she put on the pretty frocks and jewels, she felt like a fairy princess. She saw herself in his eyes and she never felt more beautiful. Then the ball would drop and either his grandfather or someone else would come along and let her know she really didn't belong.

I should have ran and hollered fire, as her grandmother was fond of saying whenever a person encountered someone—usually the opposite sex—who was just a little too much to handle.

"I don't think it would be enough, Carlton. That man is never going to accept me. And I just don't fit in."

"He will eventually. I know how to handle Grandfather. One, he has to see that I won't tolerate his disrespect of you, or he'll lose all my respect. Two, there is no way he is going to let a Harrington heir come into this world without having some input and playing a major part in his or her life. So he'll come around. Now he knows what's at stake. He'll weigh the cost and see that it's easier to treat you with respect than to live the rest of his days without his flesh and blood in his life."

Exhaling a shaky breath, she replied, "I don't think that will happen. But you know the man better than I do."

"I do and I trust that he will see the light." Carlton gave her a reassuring squeeze and she rested her head on his shoulder.

When they finally landed on the helicopter pad that sat on the roof of their penthouse, he turned and stared at her.

Refusing to look at him, even though she could feel his eyes piercing into her, she moved to leave. He reached out and touched her arm.

"I know this is not the exact way you wanted things to go. But the fact is we have a chance to build something really good together. If we're going to build it on our own terms we can't be overly concerned with what other people, and that includes what family—both yours and mine—have to say about our union."

He sounded very convincing, and she turned to face him. He let his arm slide to her growing hint of a stomach.

"I think we have one important reason to at least give it the best try we both can offer." A sweet smile crossed his lips and her heart fluttered.

Thinking of the baby she carried had a strange way of putting things in perspective. A warm feeling overcame her. Carlton was right. They were married and blessedly expecting their first child. She owed it to their family to fight anyone who tried to come between them. "Okay, but this is hard, Carlton."

"Things will be fine. Next month we'll celebrate our first Christmas together. Then our first New Year's. And you'll get to experience the Bahamian tradition of *junkanoo*, and the Junkanoo Ball. I promise it'll get better." He hugged her, helped her out of the helicopter and led her toward the door to their penthouse.

She hoped that would be the case.

Chapter 10

"You look stunning."

Latonya turned to find Carlton watching her in the doorway of the master bedroom. She smiled before turning back to the mirror. The jade-green evening gown she wore left her right shoulder bare and swooped low to reveal the cleavage that seemed to become fuller with each month of pregnancy.

The woman looking back at her in the mirror sported a perfectly made-up face. All her time spent with the personal stylist evidently paid off. She could now "fix" her face in record-breaking time.

At first she'd balked at the idea of having someone help her by telling her how to dress and what kind of makeup to use. But the first time she saw a picture of herself in the society pages with Carlton in the cute to-die-for dress she'd gotten off the rack, she figured she'd better get some guidance from somewhere.

Placing her hand over her small protruding belly, she smiled nervously. "I think you have to say that since you're married to me. I don't think that everyone else at this fancy shindig will agree that a woman five months pregnant in an evening gown is stunning."

"Then they would have to be blind." He took three long strides and stood right in front of her. Placing his hand on top of hers, he caressed her stomach before capturing her lips in a soul-shaking kiss. Her entire body responded to him and when he finally pulled away, she could barely shape words.

"You're glowing, darling. You're going to be the most beautiful woman there." His head tilted down and she could see in his eyes that he was coming back in for the kill.

If she let him, they would never make it to what had been billed Nassau's high-society event of the year. The upper-crust, invite-only celebration of *junkanoo* wouldn't be anything like the delightful parades and carnival celebrations she'd attended earlier in the week. She'd loved the costumes, vibrant music and dancing that went on and found the celebration that originated in slavery to be delightful. It was the one chance she'd had to see and interact with everyday Bahamians, people she felt more connected to than the people that would no doubt be in attendance at the upscale Junkanoo Ball.

She could think of a million better ways to ring in the New Year and none of them had her hobnobbing with a bunch of snooty people pretending to relish their past while the real, sincere, down-home celebrations were going on among the *folk* outside. Because *junkanoo* originated in colonial times when slaves were allowed the holidays to enjoy themselves, Latonya felt that an overly expensive ball in which people stood around and pretended to have fun was simply a waste.

Taking a step back, she waved her finger. "No way. If I let you get started, we will be late and I'll have to fix my hair and makeup all over again."

A devilish grin crossed his face. "I promise I won't mess up your makeup. That much. Just one more kiss for the road."

"No. Now, get out of here so that I can repair the damage you've already done."

Wrapping his arm around her waist, he pulled her close before whispering in her ear. "We aren't staying long. We're just making a polite appearance and then I get to bring you back home to finish what I've started."

A shiver went down her back and she was tempted to say "Let's not go. Let's finish what you started now." But she knew it was important that he attended the gala, and as his wife, she had to be there as well.

From the flashing lights of the cameras as they exited the limousine and walked down the red carpet, to the crystal chandeliers, overflowing fountains of champagne and tuxedo-dressed waiters carrying every delicacy imaginable inside, Latonya felt like she'd stepped onto a movie set. The decorations in the ballroom startled her. They'd given a winter feel to the tropics with the overwhelming presence of crystals and stunning ice sculptures. The silver-and-white-satin tablecloths and seat covers also helped create a winter-wonderland ambience.

Walking around the gathering, where everyone seemed to know one another, and no one seemed willing to allow a new person into the fold, she decided it would be best to stick to herself, anyway. It would have been nice to make some friends in the new country, but she would have enough on her plate adjusting to her new life and being a new mom.

The islands of the Bahamas were breathtakingly lovely, and when she wasn't at one of the high-society functions, she had a wonderful time sightseeing and getting to know the new place. In general, the people were nice. Sometimes she would just walk out to the white sand beaches and gaze at the turquoise-blue water and daydream. It amazed her since she'd never really had the time to daydream before. She'd been too busy working and trying to make something of herself so that she could help her grandmother. Now that she didn't have to worry about working she found herself wanting things that money couldn't buy.

In the fairy tales, when the prince finally came, everyone lived happily ever after. Latonya felt like a fairy princess in the bootleg version of the story. Everything she'd never wanted or dreamed about was at her disposal, and the one thing she never dared to dream for—real love—seemed unattainable.

Walking away from the balcony of the swank ballroom, she decided to rejoin the party. Just as she was about to find a spot to rest her feet, which resisted getting used to strappy dress shoes and longed for her sensible pumps, her overactive bladder pulled rank and she found herself in the ladies' room.

Once done, she prepared to leave the stall, stopping only when she heard the voices of two high-society women, Janice Banks and Sari Underwood. Carlton had introduced her to them at another outing, thinking that since the two women were around her age, they would all become friends. Needless to say, they made it clear not to expect any invites to friendship from them. Having no desire to make small talk with the two snobbish women, Latonya decided to stay in the stall until they left.

"Well, did you see his wife walking around here like she's the Queen of England and butter wouldn't melt in her mouth?" Sari's high nasal voice mocked.

"I know," Janice agreed. "She thinks she can throw on some fancy clothes and we would all forget that she's a scrappy little black American nobody."

Swallowing, Latonya narrowed her eyes behind the bathroom stall. No one had to tell her the two women were talking about her. How many black American nobodies could there possibly be attending the Junkanoo Ball that evening?

"A nobody who snagged one of the wealthiest husbands in the Bahamas. One you had your eyes on yourself," Sari said.

"Like you didn't have dreams of one day marrying Carlton Harrington III," Janice hissed.

"Of course. What little girl in the Bahamas didn't? But like my mother said, history does repeat. Like father, like son. I guess Carlton Harrington II wasn't the only one attracted to poor little nothing girls from the States. Must be in the DNA or something," Sari stated with a nasty snicker.

"Well, I think that the little tramp trapped him and he had to marry her. If he hadn't then she would have probably ended up raising his child in some rat-and-roach-infested ghetto while she collected welfare and tried to hook up with some other rich guy. You know, a rapper or an athlete. I've seen the rap videos. She's what they call a hoochie. And, his mother was *not* from the States. She was from one of the out islands. Very rural, and she was poor for sure, but at least she was from here." Janice's voice trailed off.

Once she was sure that the women were gone, Latonya allowed herself to come out of the stall. Taking a napkin, she patted her face. The tears had certainly done their job. The beautiful makeup was ruined. *Just as well,* she thought. *It hadn't done any good.* She cursed her hormones. Five months ago women like Janice and Sari would have never been able to make her cry or even pay attention to them. She'd known women like them in college, and she didn't desire to be in their circle or want anything they had. *What the hell happened to me?* She repaired her face as swiftly as she could, but she couldn't do a damn thing about the sadness in her eyes.

* * *

The smile that started when he spotted his wife froze when Carlton caught a glimpse of her haunted eyes. Even though she had a dazzling, wide smile on her lips, he could tell she was anything but happy.

After walking over to her and putting his arm around her, he whispered, "You ready to go and finish what we started?"

She took a deep breath and painted on a false smile. "I'm ready to leave, if you are."

Rather than question what was wrong with her right then, he decided it was best they leave. They could ring in the New Year, as he'd wanted to, anyway, with her wrapped in his arms.

"Let's go home."

Back at the penthouse, Latonya still seemed withdrawn. Carlton couldn't understand it. She looked so beautiful and she was clearly the envy of every woman in the room.

Like always, she appeared to be happy when they took off for the evening and more and more dejected as the evening progressed. The only reason he attended the parties and benefits that they were invited to was because he wanted her to make some friends and acquaintances. She didn't know anyone in the Bahamas, and he knew she missed her friends and family in Miami.

She took off her clothes and headed straight for the bathroom. Listening to her shower, he thought it was almost as if she couldn't remove the evening fast enough. What went wrong? Was she really as miserable as she appeared? If they kept going at this rate, would they even make it until their child was born? *We have to,* Carlton thought ruefully.

He knew that he had to find a way to make her happy. He couldn't lose her.

When she returned from the shower, he could have sworn she'd been crying. She joined him in bed but turned her back to him and curled up in her pillow.

"What's wrong, baby? Talk to me," he pleaded.

All he heard was a sniffle and then a mumbled "nothing."

"Something is wrong, Tonya. Look at me. Tell me what happened?"

She sighed but didn't turn around to face him. "It's nothing. I was just thinking I'd go to visit Gran and stay for a little while. She's doing much better now that she's seeing the physical therapist you hired. But I know she must be lonely with Cicely off at college and now me gone as well."

She wanted to leave. Carlton felt a heaviness overcome him. Even though his chest felt constricted and there suddenly didn't seem to be enough air, he managed to speak.

"We can go and visit your grandmother this weekend and even stay for a few extra days if you'd like."

He heard her take a sharp breath before she broke out into hiccupping sobs.

"*I* just want to go back to Miami for a while. I don't really fit in here. I'm trying…but I don't. I know this is your home…*our* home now. And…I will come back. I just really need a break from it all."

The sound of her crying broke his heart. He felt a red haze of anger come over him. "What happened, Tonya? Did someone say something to you? Tell me, baby. I'll kill them. I swear." He'd never had a stronger urge to inflict damage on another person before.

She gulped. "I overheard Sari and Janice saying some things about me in the restroom. Stuff like that doesn't usually get to me. I just need to go home for a while."

"Fine, *we'll* move back to Miami. I can be in Nassau in a half hour by jet. And we don't have to go to any more of these events. I just wanted you to meet some people. But none of these people are worth knowing. You're all that matters to me. Just stop crying, please." He pulled her close. "Would moving make you feel better?"

"But this is your home—"

Cutting her off he said, "I'm just as at home in Miami as I am in the Bahamas. I've always spent my time between the two places."

Didn't she know that she was his home? Couldn't she tell that home was wherever she was?

"Are you sure, because—"

"Positive. We'll go back tomorrow, okay?"

"Okay. I don't want to be a pain in the neck. I'm sure it's just my crazy hormones all out of whack." Turning, she snuggled her head next to his heart and wrapped herself in his arms.

"Trust me, you're not being a pain in the neck. I just want you to be happy."

Yawning, she offered a half-mumbled reply. "I just want *us* to be happy."

He couldn't think of a better way to ring in the New Year. Holding her closely, he closed his eyes in contentment, because they really wanted the same thing: to be happy together.

And for a while, they were.

Chapter 11

Over two years later

The pregnancy and the birth of their child brought Latonya and Carlton closer together, but not nearly as close as she wanted them to be. Moving back to Miami and spending a limited amount of time in the Bahamas made adjusting to married life a little easier. Even though Miami's elite class wasn't all open arms, either, Latonya at least had family and friends there who cared about her. The only time her new lifestyle didn't leave her feeling cold was when she was in Carlton's arms. He had a way of making her melt with just a simple touch.

They still couldn't seem to get enough of each other.

However, she felt as if something was missing and that it could all end as quickly as it started. Didn't her own parents' doomed relationship show her that things really didn't last? Her father left even though she tried to be as good as she possibly could. Even though her mother bent over backward to please him, he still left them.

Carlton's and Latonya's child was two years old and they still had never said they loved each other. In her mind she knew that love was in the actions and Carlton *behaved* like a man happy and in love, at least with the family they'd built together. And it wouldn't have been so bad if she hadn't fallen deeply and completely in love with him.

Was it the sweet tenderness he showed her throughout her pregnancy and when she delivered Carlton Harrington IV? Or was it the way he interacted with their son as if he were the light of his life? If she was honest with herself, she had to acknowledge that it happened the first time he kissed her and it went deeper and deeper each time he did even the smallest thing, like touch her cheek or brush the small of her back.

The chemistry between them felt electric. It ignited the blood in her veins and shot through to her soul. She only hoped that it was enough to last. The realization that she had fallen in so deep made her feel as if she were treading water with a tenuous hold on everything.

Kissing her son lightly on his forehead, Latonya left his bedroom. Before joining her husband in their bedroom, she stopped at the door right next to little Carl's room.

"Hey, Pamela, he's sleeping. I'm going to go to bed now. Let me know if he needs anything or—"

Pamela looked up from the crossword puzzle she was doing and cut Latonya off in her soft Trinidadian-accented voice that had a hint of melody to it. "I will not. If I left it up to you, I'd never have a job to do. Now, go and spend some time with your husband and leave me to do my job," she offered in a mock chastising tone.

Latonya smiled. They had a playful tug-of-war going on when it came to little Carl. Pamela complained that Latonya didn't allow her to do her job enough. And Latonya gave her plenty to complain about and feigned innocence when called on it.

Although in her mid-fifties, Pamela had a youthfulness about her that clearly came from a lifetime devoted to taking care of children. Even though she wore her slightly graying hair pulled back in a harsh bun, there was nothing uptight or stuffy about her. Her honey-complexioned face was always smiling.

At first, Latonya had some hesitations about hiring the Caribbean-born woman. The elder Harrington's issues with African-Americans made Latonya a little wary. She didn't want someone taking care of her child who had problems with American blacks. Luckily, Pamela could care less about things like that. She cared about making children happy and making sure they were well adjusted. She also made the best curry chicken rotis Latonya had ever tasted.

"I know you think I'm crazy, but he's sick," Latonya hedged.

"Who, me? I don't think you're crazy at all. A little obsessive, maybe, but not out of line for a mother with a sick child." Pamela softly chuckled. "But don't worry, sweetie, if he wakes up and it seems like he has a fever or he's not feeling well, I will tend to him and consult you. Deal?"

Realizing that was probably the most she would get from Pamela, Latonya reluctantly acquiesced. "Fine."

She went to join her husband in their bedroom.

Carlton was leaving for a business trip in the morning and would be away for at least two weeks. It would be their first time being apart for such a long period of time since they got married. The achy pang in her chest let her know exactly how much she would miss him.

He looked up when she entered the room and smiled before putting his papers aside. "Is he finally sleeping?"

"Yes, after only five stories. The cold has him so irritable. At least his fever is down." She stood in the mirror and took off her diamond stud earrings. Of all the jewelry she now owned, they were her favorite. Simple and understated, they had a quiet elegance. Carlton had given them to her on their first wedding anniversary.

"Well, that's good. Maybe the two of you can come with me to Barbados, after all."

She turned and glanced at him. It seemed like he really wanted them to join him. Surely he needed a break from his family.

She remembered how her father used to yell at her mother. Screaming that he felt like he was being suffocated. That he needed some space, some time away from her and them.

Latonya didn't think she could handle it if Carlton ever felt that way about her. She reasoned the little break would be good for them. And when he came back the chemistry between them would still be strong.

"I don't know. I think traveling might be a bit much for him at this point. He's not fully recovered and I'd hate for him to relapse. Plus, you'd probably just be distracted with us tagging along."

"Maybe I'd like to be distracted." Getting up from the bed, he walked over, pulled her into his arms and kissed her.

Wrapping her arms around his neck, she leaned closely to his chest. If she didn't do something to steel her heart soon, she would be leaving herself open for a world of hurt once he decided he needed his space or God forbid, wanted a divorce. Slowly and unwillingly, she pulled away.

"Well, I think you should rest for your travels tomorrow."

His hand caressed her cheek. "I can think of lots of things I need to do before my travels, and rest is not even in the top five."

Giving him her best interpretation of a sexy-and-sassy smile, she asked, "Oh, really?"

"Oh, yes, really. Baby, why don't the two of you just join me next week? Two weeks is just too much time away." He let his fingers glide through her hair.

"I know. Maybe this will be good. It's been almost three years. Maybe it would be good for us to spend a little time apart."

He was silent for a second. When he did speak his

voice was strained and he didn't look at her. "So, are you getting tired of me already?"

It was her turn to be silent, because she was so far from being tired of him it scared her, and she didn't know how to tell him that without opening herself up to heartache when he decided to reject her. And he would end up rejecting her. Wouldn't he?

Finally, she decided on being as honest as she could without revealing too much of herself.

"No, I'm not tired of you. I just don't want you to get tired of me. It could happen easily if we keep going at the rate we've been going."

Carlton could only look at his wife in shock. Did she really have no idea how captivated he was by her? Did she really not know that he could never tire of her? That he would eat, sleep, drink and inhale her if he could? That the thought of spending two measly weeks away from her and the beautiful baby boy that she had given him was driving him mad?

She really had no clue of the power she held over him and that amazed him. Sure that he wore his heart on his sleeve as far as she was concerned, he could also tell by the troubled look in her eyes and her apprehensive posture that she really worried he might one day grow tired of her. Suddenly struck with a desire to remove all her worries, he pulled her tight.

"You don't have to worry about me ever getting tired of you."

Considering him thoughtfully, she smiled. "That's sweet of you to say."

"I'm not trying to be sweet. I'm being honest." He tried to think of a way to convey his sincerity. Given the way their relationship got started, it would be difficult to get her to see that his feelings for her went deeper than the sex, even if the sex was pretty damn incredible.

His feelings for her ran so deep that he was afraid to explore them lest he drown in them. He'd seen what that kind of uncontrolled devotion had done to his parents and he grew up without them because of it. He didn't want to relive that legacy with his own wife.

"I will never tire of you." Bending his head, he brushed her lips with his own, resorting to the only form of expression that didn't leave him feeling totally exposed and vulnerable.

The openness with which she accepted his kiss sparked his desire even more than he could have imagined. Her mouth was sweet. A simple kiss from her could bring him to his knees. The feel of her lush body under his hand sent a jolt to his gut. If anyone had told him that she would become even sexier and even more beautiful after giving birth to his son, he would have thought the person crazy.

Pushing her back on the bed, lifting her beige cashmere skirt and pulling down her silk panties, he bent to kiss her in a more intimate way. The subtle moans coming from her urged him on and his tongue took on a life of its own. Once he had positioned her thighs to grant him the exact amount of access he desired, he used his hands for a more pressing and important task. The fingers of one hand spread her folds and allowed his tongue to dart back and forth, sapping up her juices with deft precision. The thumb on his other hand, unwilling to miss out on the action, made circles around her pleasure point until soon the core of her constricted almost violently against his tongue.

She moaned again, but there was nothing soft or fragile about this moan. When she shook with the last bits of her orgasm, he stood and hurriedly disrobed. He joined her in bed just as she was about to curl up into the splendor of her aftermath.

"Not so fast, precious. I'm nowhere near finished with you."

He fought back a laugh as she tried to be helpful, all the while still in her postorgasmic daze. He straightened her and started to take off the rest of her clothing. Her eyes fluttered half open, half shut, and her lips curled into a delicious little smile that made him work all the more diligently.

Trying to help by lifting her hips as he pulled off the skirt, she managed to lift her torso just the few inches that made removing her bra easier. When he was done he examined her for a full minute before the hardened extension of him lurched in protest.

Gazing at Carlton, her eyes fully open, Latonya opened her legs and her arms reached upward toward him. He looked magnificent in his chiseled muscular perfection. Every ripple on his body called out for her to touch it and she could barely wait for him to join her.

He allowed the tip of his penis to tease her folds. She felt her chest constrict and she took a sharp intake of breath as she lifted her legs and wrapped them around his waist. He entered her fully then, quickly with urgency. He felt like heaven.

"Oh, baby, you feel so good. You're so hot and so damn sweet. I don't know what I'm going to do for two weeks without you." Carlton plunged deeper inside of her.

He grabbed her behind and rocked in her. She opened her mouth and let out a sigh just as she felt the soft spasms of her orgasm wrapping tightly around him.

"I love it when you come for me, darling. I've never seen anything more beautiful in my life. Promise that you will only share this with me. Tell me that you're mine."

"Oh, Carlton. Oh, God." Her body quivered and shook with the beginning of another orgasm.

He thrust deeper and harder. His voice, somewhere between a grunt and a growl, demanded, "Say it for me. Tell me that this belongs to me. That you are mine."

Gazing at him with half-open eyes, she swore he was seeing clear into the depths of her soul. She felt as if he was pouring himself into her, all of him.

"Yes, Carlton. I'm yours. I belong to you. All of me belongs to you."

Her words tipped him over the edge. His body shook and she felt him shudder in her arms. When it was over he collapsed, but not before cuddling her closely to him. She never wanted him to let her go.

Chapter 12

After spending a week indoors with her sick child, Latonya was finally coaxed out of the house by Pamela, Jillian and Gran. Pamela had to practically push Latonya out of little Carl's room. And Jillian pulled her the rest of the way out of the house. The older women felt that she didn't get out enough, and that she could at least enjoy lunch and some window-shopping.

Happy that her grandmother could get around almost as well as she used to, Latonya gladly joined them.

Although in her late sixties, the full-figured Evelyn Stevens could give women twenty years her junior a run for their money. In fact, the men who stood in front of the neighborhood liquor store had given Gran the nickname sexy-round-brown. She'd laugh and tell them she was going to pray for their wicked souls before prancing off. She wasn't as round as she used to be due to a doctor-ordered diet plan brought on by the stroke. However she still had what she called meat on her bones. Her flawless brown skin held the slightest makeup. And since she *refused* to go gray, her jet-black hair—compliments of Dark and Lovely—was pinned up in a French twist.

The fact that the Gran and Jillian had become fast friends pleased Latonya, but it also meant that she had to deal with the two of them telling her what to do instead of just one. The two of them together were like a tag team. Adding Gran's tall, full-figured, God-fearing demeanor to Jillian's short, small-framed, sassy persona made for a powerful one-two punch. Latonya just hoped she had the stamina to deal with both of the opinionated women at the same time.

After spending the morning shopping for bargains with them, she treated them both to one of the fancier restaurants in downtown Miami. It pleased her to be able to take them to such an upscale place.

"So, Peanut, tell me what you've been up to and how is my great-grandbaby?" Gran's question seemed innocent enough.

Jillian jumped in and answered before Latonya got a chance to even open her mouth. "Child, you should see how she hovers over that little boy. He didn't have anything but the sniffles, a little bitty cold. She could have gone to Barbados with her husband. But, no, she couldn't trust anyone else to take care of her baby boy."

Latonya glanced at Jillian and noted that the small spitfire was on a roll.

Shaking her head, Gran frowned theatrically before she spoke. "Mmm-hmm, you're going to spoil that baby boy, Peanut. You need to get out more. In fact, now that he's two, you need to go on back to work. You're just sitting home all day waiting for Carlton to come home. You didn't go through all that schooling just to sit home, did you?"

So much for Gran's innocent concern. The lunch date had quickly turned into an inquisition.

"Evelyn, child, I tell her the *same* thing. But I don't think Carlton wants her to work. I can't see why he doesn't. He always was a little controlling. Tell the truth, all them Harrington men are controlling from the senior to the junior—God bless the dead—to the third and, if we're not careful, the little fourth. I'm telling you, Evelyn, you should see how that little baby boy has his mama wrapped right around his little finger." Again, Jillian flooded the air with her thoughts on the matter without being asked.

Latonya studied the two women. They meant well. She knew that without a doubt. Since both women had gone through relationships where the men hadn't stuck around long, they had raised their children by themselves. They were of the don't-sit-around-and-depend-on-no-man school. Gran had always told Latonya to be sure that she could take care of herself. She took their advice in the spirit that it was given. However, she planned to spend a little more time with her child before going back to work. And she refused to believe spending time with her son would do him harm, no matter what the older women said.

Gran frowned as if she'd tasted something bitter. "You're going to spoil him and then he won't be any good for anyone. You should know better, too. You weren't raised with a silver spoon in your mouth. You better be careful with that boy. If he gets too bad, he can't come stay with great-grandmama. Because I don't go in for all that foolishness." Gran took a sip of her tea and shook her head.

"Well, Evelyn—"

Latonya decided it was time to cut Jillian off before she gave her two cents again.

"Um, excuse me, but are you two done talking about me as if I'm not here? Can I get a word in edgewise?" Latonya said jokingly. "Is this how you two get on, when you get together? Telling all my business?" Trying to keep her tone respectful, Latonya thought she'd done a good job. She knew that they were just teasing her and she also understood their reasons. But she couldn't help it if she loved the life she'd built with Carlton and little Carl and she didn't like being away from her son.

"Business? Child, you don't have any business. You're too young to have some business, and truth be told, if I didn't drag you out of the house this morning to be with us, then you would barely have a life outside of that husband and that little boy." Jillian harrumphed before taking a sip from her tea and shot Gran a look that might as well have said, "Do you believe her?"

"Oh, but he is one fine, pretty little boy. My great-grandbaby is a handsome little fellow. Isn't he, Jillian?" Gran sipped her tea, all the while grinning up a storm.

"Evelyn, you know you have *never* lied. The boy is adorable. And just as sweet as he wants to be. You ought to see him come into the kitchen asking me for cookies. 'Miss Dillian,' he says, 'Miss Dillian, may I have cook-cook?' And how can I say no to that precious little face?" Jillian took to grinning, too. One would never know that just a few minutes ago the two women were getting on Latonya's case about spoiling the same little boy.

"Well, who can say no to that precious, sweet little child? I swear he is the most precious little baby." As she puffed up like a peacock, Gran's smile showed every single one of her teeth.

Throwing her hands up in mock frustration, Latonya smiled. "Oh, so, you all can spoil him, but I can't be concerned enough to stay home with him while he has a cold?"

"Girl, please. You have a nanny. Pamela spends more time in the kitchen bugging me because you won't let the woman do her job. Also, I could have taken care of him. Your grandmother and me. And you know old Mr. Harrington looks for any excuse to be around his youngest namesake. You have plenty of people to watch after that little boy." Rolling her eyes at Latonya, Jillian gave Gran another one of her coded looks.

Latonya bristled at the mention of the elder Harrington. Even though he now pretended to at least tolerate her ever since little Carl was born, she knew he would rather see her gone. Any conversation she had with the old man was strained. She still waited for the day that he would give up his animosity toward her.

"Uh-huh, you act like you're selfish or something." Gran noted Jillian's look and chimed in with her agreement.

"Fine. Can we change the subject? I'll bring him over to your place more, Gran." Turning to Jillian, she added, "I'll spend a little more time out of the house so you can give him cookies, Jillian. Is that fine with the two of you?"

"Just so long as you don't start taking advantage. You know how kids are these days. They act like we didn't already raise them." Jillian dashed out another one of her looks and sucked her teeth. "They start dropping off their bundles and expecting us to watch them. That's exactly what happened to what's-her-name. You know, she used to work for the Singletons. Anyway, her daughter just left her kids there and never came back."

"Oh, yes, child. I heard about that. I can't remember her name, either. Bright-skinned woman, right? Bless her heart. How is she going to take care of those children on her social security?" Primed to move onto the next item on their to-gossip-and-cast-their-opinions-about list, Gran chimed right in, not missing a beat.

Latonya excused herself from the table. As she walked to the restroom, she tried to figure out exactly why they even bothered to ask her to join them.

"Hey, beautiful. Long time no see," a male voice called to her just before she reached the restroom door.

Turning, she saw her former colleague and friend Jeff Weatherby. Even though it thrilled her to spend time with her son, she sometimes missed interacting with adults.

"Hi, Jeff. Look at you! It's so good to see you." Giving him a heartfelt hug, she smiled.

Jeff let out a low whistle as he eyed her. "Look at you, girl!"

She glanced down at her smart designer dress and high-fashion stilettos. With her new layered haircut and makeup, she supposed she did look a whole lot different than she did when they worked together at Harrington Enterprise.

Jeff reached out and touched her cheek. "You look fabulous. Like a million bucks," he observed.

She grinned and did a little half spin. The dress—a soft yellow raw-silk number—fit like a dream. It had a simple design, which she'd finally figured out she really liked. She found the dress and others like it at a small boutique named for the owner and designer, Frances. The simple-but-elegant clothing she found there allowed her to be somewhat comfortable in her new life.

Faking a pout, Jeff said, "I can't believe it's you. I feel like I hardly ever get a chance to see you anymore. What happened? You got married and forget about the little people?"

"No. But having a new baby has been work."

"Oh, please, your son is two years old now and I

know Harry Tres has enough money to spring for help. Or are you the only mommy in the neighborhood without a nanny?" Jeff teased.

"Yes. We have a nanny. But I like to spend quality time with my child. He's at an impressionable age." Latonya narrowed her eyes and huffed playfully, "Mind your business! You're worse than Gran and Jillian."

"See, I'm sure even they think you should get out and see old friends. Why don't you come back to work? I'm head of the marketing division now." He let out one of his most flirtatious smiles and stroked her cheek again. "So you wouldn't have to worry about working for your husband. You know I'm too awed by you to give you a hard time."

Smiling, she teased, "Yeah, I heard that you moved on up. You know if I was still on the job that would never have happened. *That would be my job.*"

"Yes, you were good. Then you married the boss's grandson and went into hibernation. It was so quick, too. You broke my heart, beautiful." For a moment he actually appeared somber. Then he let loose one of his fake pouts.

Laughing, Latonya said, "Stop playing. You know you weren't fazed."

"No kidding, I was. But I'll tell you what. If you should ever decide to leave old Harry Tres, don't forget to look me up." Jeff stared at her intensely for a moment before cracking a smile and winking.

"You're such a flirt! Get out of here. We'll do lunch sometime, okay?" She patted her chest because it had

been a long time since she'd laughed so hard. She
didn't realize how much she missed her former coworkers.

"How about next Friday?"

"Are you serious?"

"Yes. I want to catch up." He paused and gazed at
her for a moment before continuing. "I miss you. Next
Friday, you pick the restaurant."

Excited, she agreed. "How about the Tavern at
noon?"

"I'll see you then." Leaning in, Jeff hugged her and
held her tightly before giving her a light peck on the
cheek.

Smiling after him, she turned to continue her walk
into the restroom and ran smack into the elder Carlton
Harrington. *Speak of the devil!* Latonya wasn't super-
stitious. But she knew that no good could have come
from Jillian mentioning the man's name earlier.

"Well. Isn't this interesting. What are you doing
out? Shouldn't you be at home with my great-
grandson? He *is* still sick, isn't he?" The elder Harrington glared at her with thinly veiled contempt.

"No, Mr. Harrington—uh, Grandfather. He is
feeling a lot better, so I came out for a little lunch and
shopping with Gran and Jillian."

"Jillian! Well, who's with the boy?" he snapped.

His harsh tone almost made Latonya feel guilty for
having lunch with her grandmother. It never failed,
whenever she started to feel upbeat and excited in her
new life, the old man showed up to ruin things. She was
convinced he had some sort of radar detector that

beeped every time she got a little too comfortable being Mrs. Carlton Harrington III. Hearing the beep, the old man no doubt jumped in his grumpy-old-man mobile and raced to spoil any notions she had that she belonged and that she'd done the right thing in marrying his grandson.

Taking a deep breath, she mumbled, "Pamela, his nanny."

"Mmm-hmm. Well, don't let me keep you. Go on and continue *whatever* it was you were doing," he sneered. "I'll stop by and check on little Carl this afternoon."

"Yes, sir. I'll see you later, then."

Latonya hurried into the restroom. The old man always made her nervous. Even though he pretended to tolerate her and clearly adored her son, she sensed an undercurrent of dislike and distrust and she didn't know what to do about it.

The elder Harrington watched as the little slut went scurrying off into the restroom. He'd tried to give her the benefit of the doubt, especially when it seemed like Carlton was so smitten with her that he wasn't going to leave anytime soon. The girl even appeared to be a halfway decent mother. But the other one had fooled them all by pretending to care about her child. That is, whenever she hadn't been running off with her newest lover.

He would never forgive himself for standing by while that woman ruined his family. He wasn't going to let it happen this time around.

The way that Jeff Weatherby looked at the girl, it would only be a matter of time before the tramp found her way to his bed.

In a few years he would be handing over even more of the responsibilities for running Harrington Enterprise to Carlton. That would mean Carlton would be traveling more. Leaving the girl to run around with God knows who, while he worked hard to give her diamonds, jewels and designer clothing.

Before the elder Harrington knew it, he had dialed Carlton's cell phone number. If he could stop history from repeating itself, he had to try.

Chapter 13

Even though he was in the middle of a meeting, Carlton answered his cell phone. It had rung several times and he assumed it must have been an emergency. He excused himself to answer his grandfather's call. His voice sounded urgent and upset.

"What's wrong, Grandfather? Is something wrong with Latonya or little Carl?"

"No. But you need to get your tail back to Miami and see about that wife of yours. I just saw that fellow we put in charge of marketing groping and kissing her."

Carlton's heart stopped and dread seeped its way through his body. "What? You saw her kissing Jeff Weatherby? Are you certain? Where?"

"I saw her in public, hugged up and kissing him just now. She must not know how to act when you leave her alone and up to her own devices. I don't know if others saw her or not. But you need to come home and straighten her out. It doesn't look proper, and we have little Carl to think about now." His grandfather's voice sounded foreboding.

"Grandfather, do you realize the gravity of what you're telling me? If there is any way you can be mistaken, then you need to let me know, because you're leading me to believe that you saw my wife in another man's arms. Is that what you're telling me?" Carlton felt as if someone was sucking the air from his lungs. Each word he spoke strained, he tried to take deep, calming breaths.

"That's what I said. Now, delegate the rest of the business affairs. Hell, I'll fly in and finish it myself. You get home and handle your personal life. She cannot be seen making such a public spectacle."

"Fine. I'll be there this evening."

"Good."

Carlton's eyes narrowed as he hung up the phone. His heart raced, and he felt an infusion of heat sparking fire through his veins. Before he realized it he'd broken the small cell phone into two separate parts. Stunned, he looked at the mangled instrument for a second before throwing it against the wall. He didn't bother going back into the meeting to tell the men he'd be leaving. He had to make it back home to his wife.

By the time Carlton made it back to Coconut Grove, it was almost ten in the evening. He found his wife in little Carl's room curled up on the bed. Their son was tucked under the covers; she slept on top with a book on her lap.

Carlton sat in the rocking chair by the bed. Gazing at his wife, he tried to imagine why she would be kissing Jeff Weatherby. The past three years had been better than he would have ever imagined given the way they started out. Happier than he had ever been, he didn't want it to end. She was a great mother. She loved their son beyond measure. He thought she loved him, though she never said it. Her actions were that of a woman in love. Why would she risk ruining everything for a fling with Weatherby?

She must have felt his gaze, because she stirred, opened her eyes and looked at him. She stretched without disturbing their son and sat up in the bed.

Her whole face lit up when she smiled and his heart did a flip-flop. She seemed genuinely thrilled to see him. *Could Grandfather be wrong?*

"You're back early." Her voice was a soft, husky whisper. She slowly got out of the bed in a concerted effort not to wake up little Carl. She walked over to the rocking chair where he sat. "I'm glad you're home."

He took a moment to think before getting up from the rocking chair.

She wrapped her arms around him. "I missed you."

In that moment, a life without Latonya flashed before his eyes and he didn't like the thought of it at all. Deciding not to cast any accusations, he would wait and see if she was really having an affair with Weatherby.

If she were, then he wouldn't have a choice. She

would have to go. He would not relive his father's mistake of trying to hold on to a woman who wanted to be held by others. If she wasn't having an affair and it was just some crazy fluke, a misunderstanding on Grandfather's part, then she wouldn't have to know about his doubts.

He followed her into their bedroom.

Wrapping her arms around him again, she stood on her toes and kissed him.

"So, what makes me so incredibly lucky? Did the negotiations go smoother than you expected, or did you just miss us?" Moving in close, she gazed at him with those beautiful brown eyes.

Letting his fingers run through her silky mass of auburn hair, he thought about how he should answer her.

When it became clear to her that he wasn't going to answer, her gaze faltered a little. He realized by the nervous expression on her face that he must be showing more of his feelings than he intended.

"What's wrong?" She appeared as if she really cared.

"Nothing." Pulling away from her embrace, he walked away, removing his suit jacket and tie as he walked toward the bathroom. "It's been a long day, and a long flight. I'm just tired. I'm going to take a shower and then hit the sack."

He left her standing in the middle of the room, went into the bathroom and closed the door. He leaned against the door for at least five minutes before he finally finished undressing and turned on the shower. It

was all he could do not to go back out there, make love
to his wife and beg her not to throw what they had away
on some silly affair. However, his pride wouldn't let him
do that. Until he figured out exactly what was going on
between her and Jeff Weatherby, he would keep his
distance.

Chapter 14

Latonya woke up yet again to a bed without Carlton in it. She didn't know what was wrong with him. He had come back from his business trip a different man, a colder man. He didn't seem to want anything to do with her. Her worst fears were coming true. *He must be tired of me.*

He wouldn't touch her and would barely talk to her. He stayed late at the office now, and when he did come home, he usually went right to sleep. He seemed to be going to great lengths to avoid her and she couldn't imagine why. Before he left for Barbados, they couldn't get enough of each other. When he returned he couldn't seem to stand her.

He'd been snapping at her for the slightest things. She almost swore the ogre that she knew in the beginning had returned. The one night that she did manage to turn his head long enough for him to quickly make love to her, made him even more irritated and angry.

She'd waited up for him as long as she could the night before because she had news she wanted to share. She'd missed her period and taken a pregnancy test on a whim. The results were positive.

Although they hadn't really discussed having more children, the thought of having another child filled her with joy. She loved being a mommy to little Carl and she wanted him to have a sibling or two. The recent change in Carlton made her a little nervous about telling him.

She kept getting flashes of a memory from her childhood when her mom secretly told her that she would be getting another brother or sister. Her parents had a huge argument that night. Her father screamed that he didn't want to be trapped with another kid on top of a sickly wife. The little brother that she'd hoped that she and Cicely would get never came and her father left soon after that.

Latonya quickly showered and got dressed. Deciding to put the memories of the past away where they belonged, she went to spend time with her child before meeting Jeff for lunch. Carlton and her father were two different people. Carlton would be just as happy about the baby as she was. Whatever had his mood so foul would be handled and she would get her sweet husband back. She had to believe that.

Pamela already had little Carl up, dressed and in his playroom when Latonya walked in.

"Mommy!" Her son came running toward her and latched on to her leg.

Latonya kneeled down and gave him a hug. "Hey! How's my little man this morning? Did you have your breakfast already?"

He giggled and wiggled in her arms. "Yep!"

"Yes," Latonya corrected as she tickled his belly. "Did you eat it all?"

"Yep!" Little Carl rolled out of her arms.

"Yes," Latonya corrected again, and pinched his nose.

"Ye-es," he repeated as he ran toward his blocks.

Pamela smiled as she watched them. "He was a big boy and ate all his oatmeal. Now he's going to show Ms. Pamela how to build a fortress with blocks."

Latonya stood up smoothed her outfit. "I'm going to be out for a bit today. I'm meeting a friend for lunch and I might even do some window-shopping—"

"Good! It's about time you get out of the house and do something fun. We'll be fine, right, Carl?" Pamela's Trinidadian-accented voice chimed. "Go give your mommy a hug and tell her you will see her when she gets back."

He ran over from his blocks and wrapped his arms around Latonya's legs. "Bye, bye, Mommy. See you later. I going to play now." He ran back to his blocks without a care.

Letting out a sigh, Latonya said, "Well, okay. Pamela, you have my cell phone number if you should need anything."

"Yes, I do. Have fun. We'll be fine," Pamela said shooing her out.

* * *

The shopping trip turned out to be a bust. She didn't find anything worth buying. By the time she met Jeff at the Tavern she only had one small bag to represent how she'd spent her morning.

The packed restaurant was filled with the business lunch crowd, and for a minute, Latonya missed her old life. Then she thought about little Carl, the new child she carried and her love for her husband, and realized she wouldn't change a thing.

She scanned the crowded establishment and soon found Jeff sitting alone at a table in the center of the restaurant. She walked over to him and he stood up immediately to greet her.

Jeff embraced her in a hug and squeezed several times before kissing her on the cheek and letting go. "You look fabulous," he complimented her.

She smiled. Even though she would never get used to people commenting on her appearance or the fact that a small part of her took pleasure in the compliments, it felt nice to have someone who knew the old her acknowledge her new look so favorably.

"Okay, now, tell me all about little Harry Cuatro," Jeff teased.

"*Hey,* no silly little nicknames for my son." Latonya pointed her finger in mock admonishment.

"What? You don't like Harry Cuatro? We could make it young and hip. How about *H4?*" A feigned expression of concern crossed his face as he rubbed his chin.

"How about little Carl or Carlton Harrington IV?"

Pretending to think it over, Jeff said, "Nah, those don't work for me. I'll stick to Harry Cuatro. Anyway, how is married life? Are you happy? Because, you know if you aren't, you can always leave him and come to me."

"Stop clowning around, Jeff. Married life is fine. I'm completely and totally enamored with my husband." Smiling even though she felt less and less sure of that statement, Latonya fiddled with her napkin.

"That's too bad."

She lightly kicked him under the table. "Oh, just be happy for us."

"Hey. Ouch. Okay. I am. I always wanted you to be happy. I just figured someday it would be with me."

She had to laugh at that. A real hoot, sometimes Jeff went too far. When she finished laughing, she realized Jeff simply sat there silently. He gazed at her intently, and for the first time she actually saw the want there. She'd always thought he was just a flirt. Studying him carefully, she asked, "Are you serious?"

"Yes, I've always been serious," he replied somberly. "You just never noticed it, or never took me seriously before."

"Well, I can't take you seriously now. *I'm married.* And I am in love with my husband, deeply in love." Taking a breath, she paused. She had never voiced the words out loud to anyone before, and saying them felt like lifting a heavy weight off of her chest.

"Well, I hope old Harry Tres knows what a gem he has in you," Jeff offered ruefully.

Not able to respond because she didn't know what

her husband felt about her or their relationship, she took a sip from her iced tea instead.

Jeff must have sensed her uneasiness because he reached across the table and placed his hand over hers, caressing it tenderly.

Rubbing her hand, he smiled. "He lucked out, beautiful. He got the girl most guys only dream of."

Forcing a smile and laughing, she tried to lighten the mood. "You know, I see why you are such a successful player. You sure know how to say all the right things."

Jeff just laughed. "Fat lotta good it did me with you."

"Boy, shut up."

He simply smiled. "So tell me all about little Harry Cuatro."

Pride pulsed through her veins. No matter what happened between her and Carlton, at least she had her son. No one could take that away from her. "Well, little Carl is the best little boy a mother could ask for. He's smart as a whip."

Nodding his head, Jeff agreed, "Well, of course. Look at his mother."

"He's adorable. I think he's going to be quite the little heartbreaker."

"Well, of course, look at his beautiful mother," he repeated.

"No. Actually, he looks exactly like his father. He doesn't take after me at all. It's weird."

"I'm sure he has more of you in him than you realize." Jeff's voice cracked and a slight cough escaped his mouth. His face started to flush and he covered his mouth as he continued to try to clear his throat. He started to pat his chest as well.

Latonya frowned. She hoped he wasn't choking. But he hadn't taken a bite of his sweet-potato fries or his burger in a while. He also hadn't taken a sip of his iced tea. Yet, he didn't appear well at all.

"What's the matter? You don't look so good."

"I don't know. I think something in this meal didn't agree with me. I have some food allergies and that makes eating out a crapshoot sometimes. Maybe we should cut this lunch short." His voice sounded heavy.

Latonya picked up her napkin from her lap and placed it on the table. Food allergies were nothing to play with. "Okay. Do you carry allergy medicine with you? Do you need me to help you get home? I know you're not going back in to the office today."

"No to all three. I'll just have the host call me a cab and head home. If I need anything, I'll give my mom a call."

The lack of clarity and slight slur in his voice worried her. She knew people's throats sometimes closed up and these kinds of allergic reactions often brought on respiratory failure.

"How about this? *I* help you out of here. *I* take you to the emergency room. *I* call your mom to meet us there. And *you* promise me you will make sure you always have some medicine with you from now on."

She reached in her purse as she stood and dug out the antihistamine she carried with her for whenever her seasonal allergies acted up. "Here, take these." She handed him two. "These should help some until we get you to the hospital."

He took the pills from her and swallowed them along with some water. "There," he said once he had swallowed them, "that should be fine." Barely able to stand, he leaned against the table.

Latonya shook her head. "I'm taking you to the emergency room and that's that." She put her arm around Jeff so that he could lean on her for support as they walked out. She gave him the no-nonsense stare that she usually saved for little Carl when he misbehaved or exhibited the Harrington trademark willfulness.

It didn't take Jeff long to realize that he could be home recuperating sooner if he just took the offer. He left money for the tab, even though she protested, and they left.

Carlton couldn't believe his eyes. First he watched while Weatherby hugged Latonya as if he could barely stand to let her go. Then he watched the man gaze at her the entire time and clutch her hand like a lovesick puppy. The entire time he watched them, he kept thinking of his mother and her many lovers. How they all seemed to be so in love with her and she really didn't care about any of them. The only person she ever cared about was herself.

Carlton told himself that he didn't confront Latonya because he hadn't wanted to make a scene in front of his very important clients. The truth was he didn't want to see with his own eyes the proof that history was cruelly repeating itself. When his clients finally left, he watched his wife walk off with her arms around Jeff. He walked to the front of the restaurant and watched the two of them get into her car and drive off. He had hoped against hope, but it turned out that Grandfather had been right.

Steaming, it took Carlton a few minutes to figure out what to do next. Even if his wife didn't love him, he wasn't going to let Jeff Weatherby ruin his marriage! The thought made him realize that he was just like his own father. It wasn't Weatherby's fault that Latonya was a cheat!

When he made it back to Harrington Enterprise he headed right for Weatherby's office, fully intending to tell him in no uncertain terms to stay the hell away from his wife. However Weatherby wasn't in his office and a quick round of questions gave Carlton information that disturbed him more than seeing his wife leave with Weatherby. Weatherby had taken the rest of the afternoon off, calling in sick to complain of having an allergic reaction to something he ate at lunch.

Not believing that excuse, Carlton had the sudden urge to go home and see if his wife had made it back from her lunch date.

When he got there, Jillian informed him that Latonya wasn't back yet. So, he sat in the front sitting room waiting for her. She showed up at around four-thirty in the afternoon with one small bag in her hands and seemed startled to see him. A warm smile covered her face.

"Hi. I wasn't expecting you here. You're home early today."

"Yes. I am. And where were you?"

"I just did a little shopping."

Eying her small bag, he asked incredulously, "Really? Shopping?"

"Yes. More like window-shopping. I really didn't see a whole lot that I just *had* to have. Although, as always, Frances's Boutique had a few things that tempted me." She flashed a smile.

Taking note that Frances's Boutique was located in the very neighborhood that Jeff Weatherby lived in, Carlton frowned. "Really? Is that all you did today?"

She shrugged. "Pretty much."

His eyes narrowed. That she would stand there and lie to him made the blood boil in his veins. "Well what about your little lunch date with Jeff Weatherby?"

"What?" Her eyes widened.

"You heard me. I know all about your affair with Weatherby. Grandfather saw you with him last week, and today I had the pleasure of seeing it with my own eyes—" Carlton started.

"Mommy!"

The sound of little footsteps followed by adult footsteps halted his speech.

"Walk. Don't run," Pamela scolded as little Carl ran straight to Latonya.

Latonya picked their son up and hugged him close. She planted kisses on his face. "Mommy missed you today. Were you a good boy?"

"Yep!" little Carl answered.

"Yes," Latonya murmured, and her voice cracked a little.

Carlton got a sudden flash of his son going through the same confused childhood he'd gone through, watching as his mother kissed and hugged and spent time with men who weren't his father. She took him with her when she ran off until the last time when he was fifteen and he refused to go with her. He wasn't going to let his son go through the same thing. If Latonya wanted to be with Weatherby and other men, she wasn't going to take his son with her. He refused to allow his son to grow up the way he did.

"Pamela, take my son upstairs, please." Carlton walked over to Latonya and took little Carl out of her hands. She moved for a second as if she was going to try to hold on to little Carl, but she let him go.

Pamela glanced nervously from Carlton to Latonya and took little Carl from Carlton when Latonya nodded. "We'll be upstairs in the playroom until dinner, then," Pamela said.

"I want my mommy now!" little Carl yelled.

"No, no. Let's show mommy and daddy we can be a big boy and they will come up and get you later," Pamela soothed as she walked away with their son.

Latonya watched them climb the stairs and Carlton watched her. She appeared to really care about their child, but Carlton knew from experience appearances were deceiving. His own mother had cried and fought each time she left, demanding that her child come with her. Then as soon as they were on their way she would wipe away her false tears and ignore him for her many lovers.

Latonya turned to him and took a deep breath.

"Carlton, I don't know what you think you saw. Or what your grandfather has told you. But I am not having an affair with Jeff Weatherby. We had lunch today. That's all. It's not what you think, Carlton." She started to walk away.

It's not what you think, Carlton! Those were the exact words his mother said every time his father found proof of a new lover! Carlton grabbed her and yanked her back. "Don't you dare walk away from me! Tell me, did you spend the afternoon in his bed?"

Trying to snatch her arm away from his grasp, she snapped, "Let go of me. I told you I had lunch with Jeff! That's it. I am not having an affair. He had an allergic reaction and I stayed with him in the emergency room until his mother arrived. They used peanut oil to fry his sweet-potato fries. He's allergic to peanuts. All of this is easy enough for you to check! But if you really think that I'm having some kind of an affair, then that's your problem."

"No. Actually, it's your problem. I want you out of here, Latonya. I want you out of my house."

"You're kicking us out?" A shocked look came across her face, and then just like that her face went hard and indignant.

"No. Just you. My son stays here." He let go of her arm.

She rubbed her arm and took a nervous step backward.

"I'm not leaving my baby, Carlton. I can't leave him. I won't leave him. You can't do this to me." Shocked, she widened her eyes and patted her chest.

"You should have thought of that before you decided to bed Weatherby." He bit the words out. Carlton knew what he saw, and *more important,* he'd seen it all before.

"I haven't slept with Jeff. We're friends. I would never jeopardize our relationship like that. Our family means too much to me, Carlton." Her voice pleaded and her eyes joined in as tears started to pool in them.

"What's all this yelling and carrying on about?" Jillian came walking into the room drying her wet hands on her apron.

"Jillian, would you please go and pack up some of Latonya's things. She's leaving. We'll send the rest of her things later."

Latonya narrowed her eyes. "I am not leaving here without my child!"

"You are not taking my son with you. And you are leaving. Jillian, please pack—"

"I don't want any part of this! If you want to throw your wife out on the street, you let that be on your conscience," Jillian snapped.

Carlton turned and glared at Jillian. "Fine, then leave us alone."

"Jillian, help me talk some sense into him! Carlton, I didn't have an affair. I'm not having an affair! Why won't you believe me?"

"Carlton, listen to her. What are you—" Jillian started.

"Save it, Jillian. I know what I saw. Grandfather saw the same thing. He warned me. If you won't do your job and pack up her things then just leave us alone!"

"Your grandfather is lying! He hates me. He always has and you know it," Latonya hissed.

"Get out, Tonya! Save your theatrics. You can't play me anymore." Carlton couldn't stand to look at her. He didn't trust himself not to fold.

"I'm not playing you. Why are you doing this?" Reaching out to touch his arm, she stumbled when he moved out of her grasp. "You won't even listen to me. You've made up your mind and you won't listen. Can't we work this out like adults?" When Carlton didn't respond, her voice soon turned threatening. "I'm not leaving here without my child."

She took off up the stairs and he took off behind her, stopping her just as she got to the door of little Carl's playroom. Grabbing her arm, he dragged her down toward their bedroom.

Latonya planted her feet and struggled the entire way. He had no idea she was so strong. She dug one of her heels into his shin and he almost had to let her go. He was sure she broke skin with the pointy stiletto. But there was no way he was going to let her leave the house with his child.

"Let me go, Carlton. You can't do this." She kicked and struggled, but he continued to pull her along. Her flying arms and legs landed on him sharply. But he didn't let the pain from her hits stop him. The pain in his heart was much worse.

Throwing her on the bed, he snapped, "Get your things and get out, Latonya. I'm not playing. I won't be responsible for my actions if you try to take my son out of here."

Tears streamed down her face and she breathed in soft, shuddering pants. It broke his heart to see her like that. Then the vision of Weatherby's hand on hers followed by an even more troubling image of her spending the afternoon in Weatherby's bed made his heart turn cold even as angry heat covered his flesh.

"Carlton, I didn't do what you are accusing me of. I would never do that. Don't do this." Her sobbing made his heart wrench.

He wished he could take her word for it. But Grandfather's words and what he saw with his own eyes canceled out her pleas.

Her eyes narrowed and she leaped off the bed, heading for the door. He caught her.

"Let go of me! I'm getting my child!" Her nails dug into his hands, slicing into his skin, and he let her go.

She snatched the door open while he inspected the angry red marks on his hand.

Carlton took off down the hall and caught her before she made it to little Carl's playroom. He dragged her back down the stairs.

Latonya reached out and grabbed on to the railing on the way down. Her grip was so tight he had a difficult time pulling her down the stairs.

"I want you out of here. If you ever come within a mile of my son, you'll live to regret it. I'll have him out of the country faster than you could imagine. Stay away from us!" He grabbed her jacket and purse as he passed the sitting room, and when he threw her out the door, he threw them after her.

Momentarily stunned, she lifted herself from the ground.

"Goodbye, Latonya." He slammed the door and leaned against it. His face wet, he realized tears were falling from his eyes.

Chapter 15

Latonya used her old key to enter her grandmother's home. She didn't know where else to go, what to do or whom to turn to. Touching her stomach, she hoped that her struggles with Carlton hadn't done any harm to the baby. She would have a checkup as soon as possible. Right after she found herself a good lawyer. She didn't intend to lose either one of her children.

As soon as she walked in the door, Cicely stepped in front of her.

"Girl, you almost got yourself hurt, walking in here like that. I didn't know who that was jingling keys and coming in the house. What are you doing here?" Cicely asked.

"What are *you* doing here? You're always here when you should be in school." Latonya retorted.

"It's spring break. So, I decided to grace my loving family with my presence. I was going to come see you tomorrow. I just got in a little while ago."

"Hey, Peanut. What are you doing here? Where's my great-grandbaby?" Gran walked down the hall into the entryway. "Well, come on in and close the door. You don't look so good, Peanut. What's wrong with you?"

Latonya followed them into the living room and sat down. "He kicked me out."

"What? Who kicked you out? Carlton? Why would he do that? What happened?" Gran let loose a string of questions as she sat down on the sofa next to Latonya.

Cicely sat on the other side of her. "Where's little Carl?"

"He wouldn't let me take him." Latonya wrapped her arms around herself as if that would help her hold it together.

"He can't just take your child! We have to get a lawyer," Cicely said, and she wrapped her arms around Latonya.

"I don't understand, Peanut. Why would he kick you out and make you leave your baby?" Gran asked.

"He thinks I'm having an affair."

"Why would he think that? You didn't run around on that man, did you—" Gran's face turned concerned and she clutched her heart.

Appalled, Latonya responded before Gran could finish her statement. "Gran! Of course I didn't. Why would you think something like that?"

"Even if she did, that doesn't give him any right to steal her child!" Cicely said.

"I didn't. I had lunch with a colleague. That's all." Latonya took a deep breath. "Carlton's grandfather told him some lies. Now Carlton believes I cheated."

"Why would that man lie on you?" Gran asked.

Latonya had no idea why the old man despised her so much that he would tell an out-and-out lie on her. Even the reasons she could think to give didn't seem like good enough ones to ruin someone's life. "Because he hates me. He has always hated me. He thinks I'm a gold digger and he has issues with African-Americans."

"Oh, Lord. I knew you shouldn't have married in with those foreign folk." Gran clutched her chest again and fanned her face with her other hand. "You should have married a boy from here and then you wouldn't have to worry about this kind of thing."

"Gran!" Cicely scolded. "That's not an appropriate thing to say. Why are African-Americans always tripping when it comes to black folk from other places? We're all black and we all can trace our roots back to Africa! The boat just dropped us off in different spots."

"Well. That man doesn't like African-Americans!" Gran defended herself. "Black folk from other places are always coming here and looking down their noses at black folk from here. They're not better than us because they didn't have to put up with the racism here and they have another home to go to." Gran shook with anger. "Now we have to worry about him taking little Carl off someplace, back to their country. At least if he were from here we wouldn't be worried about that."

The thought that Carlton could very well take their child to the Bahamas and had enough money to make it difficult for her to ever see her child again placed real fear in Latonya's heart. "I won't let that happen." She looked at her grandmother and her sister. "I know that you don't have a lot of extra space, Gran but can I—"

"Don't you insult me by asking can you stay here, Peanut. Of course you can stay here. This is your home," Gran said forcefully.

"Thanks," Latonya replied.

She spent the rest of the evening planning to get her child back.

The lawyer Latonya met with told her that it would be a difficult custody fight given the amount of money the Harringtons had, but he would do his best to get her baby back. The doctor assured her that she hadn't done anything to damage the child she carried. She spent the week with Gran and Cicely, and it felt good knowing that she had their support.

Latonya had to force Cicely to go back to school and finish out the semester. By the time the week was up she'd convinced Cee Cee that there wasn't anything she could really do, anyway. So Cicely got in the car that Carlton had purchased for her and made the drive back to Tallahassee.

After being gone a full week, Latonya missed little Carl fiercely. She knew that she would do whatever she could to get her child. But a part of her didn't want to drag little Carl through a big custody battle over a mis-understanding. She knew that she owed it to herself and her children to at least try once more and get Carlton to see reason. She hoped that the days apart would give him time to calm down and he would at least be open to hear her out. She didn't know if she could forgive him for throwing her out of the house. However, she knew she had to try.

When she reached the house that following Saturday afternoon she fully expected to find him playing in the back yard with their son like he did most Saturdays. Instead, she found the elder Harrington sitting there as if he were waiting for her.

Latonya's eyes narrowed and she could feel bile rising in her throat just looking at him. "Why did you lie on me, old man?"

He turned. "I'll have to get that Jillian to have someone come change the locks. What are you doing back here?"

"I came for my child!"

"You're too late. My grandson figured you'd try something, so he took his son to the Bahamas."

"He what?" Latonya's stomach lurched and a sharp pain darted across her chest. "I have a lawyer. I will fight for my child. Neither you nor Carlton will be able to stop me!"

"You want to bet that I can't stop you? I can and I will. My grandson is done with you, girl. You've out-stayed your welcome. Couldn't keep your hands off the other men and now he sees you for the slut you are. You will not be allowed to ruin the lives of my grandson or my great-grandson." He glared at her.

"That boy is a Harrington and you are *nothing*. You will *never* be allowed to keep him now that my grandson is through with you. So cut your losses and get as far away from here as possible. I will provide you with the money you no doubt think you will miss out on if you leave. But I promise you this, if you come back here after today you'll live to regret it."

Her breath caught and her chest pounded so loud she could feel it in her toes and the tips of her fingers. A cold fear washed over her. The old man had threatened her life, and in doing so, he also threatened the life of her unborn baby.

"Why do you hate me so much? Is it because I'm African-American? Is that a good enough reason to want me gone?"

"I want you gone because you are no good for my grandson. He needs someone who understands where he comes from. Who won't make him leave his home because she's having trouble fitting in. Do I wish that he'd married a nice Bahamian girl from his own class? Yes!" The older man shot her a disparaging look. "You being a black American is only part of it. You being a poor social-climbing slut is the biggest problem I have with you!"

Reaching into his pocket, he pulled out a large envelope that appeared to be stuffed with cash. Handing it to her, he sneered. "Here. I had a feeling that you would come back sniffing around here after a while. Take this and stay the hell away from my boys."

Gasping as he shoved the envelope in her hand, she took the envelope and threw it in his face.

"You can keep your money, old man. I can't be bought. And I am not selling my child to you. I *will* get my child back."

"Really?" He pretended to consider her words before turning a cold gaze on her. "If you don't care about your own life, what about your sister? Hmm? Your grandmother? It would be a shame for her to make such a strong recovery only to have an unfortunate accident. And college campuses aren't as safe as they used to be. Anything could happen to a pretty young lady like your sister. I know people who would do unbelievable things for just a small part of the money you just foolishly threw in my face. Don't test me, young lady. You get out of here and stay away from my grandson and his son. If you don't, you are not only risking your life, but the lives of everyone you claim to care about. Do the smart thing. Leave and don't come back!"

The icy stare that he gave her left her shivering. She realized that if she didn't want to have another child snatched away from her, or worse, murdered along with her before it even got a chance to draw a breath, she had better disappear for good. The coldness in his eyes told her that the elder Harrington would have no problem carrying out his threats on her family. He might even enjoy it.

She picked up her cell phone once she got back into her car and made three phone calls before tossing it. The first two were to her grandmother and sister, telling them that she would be going away and they probably wouldn't hear from her again. The second call went to a friend asking for help to make herself disappear. She knew that if she did this she had to do it all the way. She could never contact her family again, because if anyone found out about the child she carried, then the Harringtons wouldn't waste any time trying to take it away from her. She would miss her baby boy terribly. If the old man were only threatening her, then nothing would make her leave. But the child inside of her deserved a chance to live.

The elder Harrington watched the girl leave and hoped that he'd done enough to scare her off. The fact that Carlton went off that morning looking for her and took the child with him was reason enough to get rid of the girl for good.

He'd tried to talk Carlton out of going after her. The same way he'd tried to talk his son out of going after that other tramp, time after time after time. He wasn't going to lose Carlton, too. He loved his grandson. He loved his great-grandson. He only wanted what was best for them.

In a few years, once Carlton realized that the slut wasn't coming back, he'd be able to find a suitable woman, a nice Bahamian woman to be a wife and mother. It was for the best.

Carlton buckled little Carl into the car seat. They'd spent the day at Gran's house waiting for Latonya to return. At first he didn't think Gran was going to let him in. Luckily she took pity on him and did. He didn't know what he'd hoped. He just knew that little

Carl wanted to see his mother and he wanted to see his wife.

His grandfather tried to talk him out of going, but he knew he had to try to make things right. He'd let a week pass and that was too long. When Gran got up to answer the phone, he had no idea it was Latonya on the other end. Gran came back into the living room shaking. Latonya said she was going away and she wouldn't be in contact again.

He'd made a huge mistake and he couldn't find her to rectify it. He turned and glanced at his son. He was happy that little Carl ended up falling asleep while they were at Gran's. It would have been hell trying to get the boy out of there after promising that he was going to see his mother.

As he drove, he pounded the steering wheel. He'd turned into his father, for Christ's sake, chasing a woman who didn't seem to want to be found. He didn't want to turn into his father. No good could come of that kind of dogged determination to hold on to a woman.

He sighed. If she didn't come back on her own, he would just have to let her go, no matter how much it hurt. He wouldn't chase her. He wouldn't repeat the doomed legacy of the past.

Chapter 16

Three years later

"I don't understand why you feel like you have to run after her. She's been gone for three years. If she really gave a damn about you or the boy, she wouldn't have stayed away so long."

Carlton looked up from the desk in his study and stared at his grandfather. The old man had a point. Carlton had waited and waited for Latonya to return. When it seemed like she would never return, he resigned himself to a life without her. He'd stayed in contact with her family and made sure that they saw little Carl on a regular basis. He'd hoped that one day she would return and little Carl would have his mother again, if nothing else.

"Little Carl wants his mother and I need—"

Grandfather cut Carlton off in an angry rant. "You need what! To go running after her like a lovesick puppy? No good can come from it. Stay here. Let her stay wherever the hell she is. Throw the envelope away." He gripped the front of the desk and spat out his words. "Forget that you know where she is. I can't believe you went and hired a private detective without consulting me, anyway!"

Carlton narrowed his eyes. His grandfather was overstepping his boundaries. Carlton had shared his plans with his grandfather out of courtesy, not for feedback or to be told what to do. No one told him what to do. "I don't need to consult you on my private affairs, Grandfather. I'm going to get my wife and bring her home."

"Why?" Grandfather sneered. "She cheated on you. God knows how many men she's been with in the past three years."

"I told you she hadn't had sex with Weatherby. Her story checked out. He had an allergic—" Carlton started.

"Just because she didn't have sex with him that day doesn't mean she didn't have sex with him ever. If they were having an affair, then they could have had sex numerous times. They could have even been planning to have sex that day. I told you what I saw!"

Carlton gritted his teeth. He wouldn't continue to let his grandfather cut him off so rudely. Even if he meant well, the man was out of line.

In a way his Grandfather was correct. He had no real proof that she had never slept with Weatherby. That she hadn't had plans to have an affair. However, something in Carlton's gut now told him that Latonya wouldn't do that to him. He wished he could have trusted in that back then. He narrowed his eyes on his grandfather. There was nothing that Grandfather could say that would stop Carlton from going to his wife and trying to get her to come home.

"I'm going to get my wife." Carlton slid a picture that the private detective took across the desk. "She has a child."

"So! How do you even know the child is yours?"

"Look at the picture, Grandfather."

His grandfather studied the picture. He pursed his lips in consideration. "You still don't have to go. We can have someone take the child—"

Carlton shook his head in disbelief. He had no idea his grandfather could be so vindictive. He was actually advocating kidnapping! Carlton snapped, "I'm going to get my wife!"

"Fine! Fine! I'm going with you!"

"Knocking hard, Mommy. Won't stop. I'm scared." The tiny mocha-complexioned child rubbed his hands across his face and blinked away tears from his expressive dark brown eyes.

Latonya didn't have the energy to get up from her bed and answer the door. The idiot, who obviously had the wrong door, would not go away. As a result, her two-year-old son Terrence—whom she had just gotten to take a nap while she rested—was awake again and on the verge of tears. He stood in the doorway of the bedroom they shared looking from her to the hall door.

She covered her mouth and let loose a series of coughs. Latonya was having a bad fight with what she'd self-diagnosed as the flu and it was winning by a landslide. Coughs racked her body yet again before she could attempt to soothe her child.

"They'll go away eventually, baby. Come back to bed. Once Mommy gets some rest we can play a game. Would you like that?" The normally soft, husky tone of her voice had a raspy edge due to the rawness in her throat.

The knocking became louder and more rapid. She didn't have any friends or know a lot of people in the small New Jersey town of Lodi. Hiding from her past here seemed like a viable possibility instead of some unattainable hope. She kept to herself and no one there knew her.

The door began to shake and the hinges jingled. Tears trailed down Terrence's face and Latonya realized that if she was going to make any headway against the flu that had her flat out on her back for two days, she was going to have to muster up the strength to go to the door, politely curse whoever it was the hell out and then crawl back into bed to comfort her scared child.

It was probably someone for the young woman across the hall. Her many suitors often mistakenly knocked on Latonya's door. They usually weren't so persistent.

Latonya draped the sweat-soaked sheet around herself and walked the few steps—that felt like a million to her sick legs—it took to get from her bedroom to the front door. It took even longer because Terrence had found a way to latch on to the sheet and was firmly attached to her right leg. Trying to catch her breath by inhaling deeply, she felt the phlegm rattle in her chest.

Wanting to yell, her voice came out in a strained whisper instead. "One second. My goodness!" Her sore throat was tested by even those four words. Leaning against the door for rest before opening it, she realized that she would be lucky to tell the irritating person that they had the wrong apartment, let alone curse him or her out for being so rude and nearly breaking down her door. Her irritation blocked her normal caution of looking through the peephole and putting the chain lock in place. She angrily snatched open the door.

Latonya immediately regretted her haste. A cold chill washed over her as her worst fear materialized. Her husband and his grandfather had found her. She tried to slam the door shut, but the two men were too quick for her weak attempt. They pushed their way inside with little effort and all Latonya could do was squeak a feeble "no."

Her arm instinctively and automatically reached down to pull her child closer to her. Terrence looked up at the men as he grabbed her leg tighter. The two men were fully in her living room and they seemed to overwhelm the small, sparsely decorated space with their presence.

They had stunned expressions on their faces as they studied her child. It was obvious that they were taking in Terrence's rich deep complexion, thick wavy hair and his proud, sturdy features that hinted at a rich Bahamian heritage. They no doubt saw the Harrington-trademark square chin even though it was slightly softened on the small child. To look at Terrence was to *know* whose child he was.

The elder Harrington's face broke out into a wide grin as he studied her son. The younger man simply watched Terrence. His eyes were unreadable when they moved to Latonya.

Her eyes did a quick glance toward the bedroom and then the front door. In her state of illness, making a run for either one seemed pointless. Latonya was too sick to get far, and with Terrence latched on to her leg, she probably wouldn't even make it to the door. A pain that felt like fire shot through her chest and her head throbbed as if someone had used it as a drum.

"Well, I'll be damned." The elder Harrington's voice came out in a low whistle, almost awestruck. He reached out his hand. "Come here, son. Come to your great-grandpop." The older Harrington's once-wavy salt-and-pepper hair had given way to a startlingly white-covered dome that was more straight than wavy. His features proud and pronounced, he still sported very few wrinkles for a man his age.

She instinctively held Terrence closer and thought about denying the words that the old man had spoken. She couldn't. Anyone taking a cursory glance at her child and the two men that had come back to haunt her from the past would be able to see the connection.

She glared at the old man who had made her life a living hell the entire time that she had lived with his grandson as his wife. Holding her head up defiantly, she spat out, "You don't have any claims to my child."

"That boy is a Harrington and you are no better than a common thief. How dare you keep this child from his rightful place in our family!" The elder Harrington's tone took on a sharp edge even as he continued to smile at his great grandson.

She opened her mouth to speak and winced instead. Letting go of her hold on Terrence to cover her mouth and hold her aching chest, she shut her eyes tightly.

It can't be happening. I won't let it happen again.

The elder Harrington knelt beside Terrence and hugged him. "Would you like to come live with your great-grandpop and your daddy?"

"No." She tried to grab Terrence, but the old man had a tight grip. Not wanting to scare her son, she tried to calm down. Her head was spinning and she felt as if she was going to pass out.

Latonya glanced at her husband with pleading eyes, but his face remained expressionless. She figured she probably was the last person in the world that he would help.

Carlton still had a physique that would put most pro athletes to shame. His dark complexion was still flawless and his wavy black hair had some beginnings of gray at the temples. The way the tailor-made, pin-stripe navy ensemble hung on his body, it was clear the man could still wear a suit like nobody's business. The years had been kind to him, and the forty-one-year-old

Carlton looked just as good, if not better than the thirty-five-year-old man she'd married. Latonya felt a familiar fluttering in her stomach as she took in the barreling mass of masculinity that was her husband and silently cursed her *still*-intense reaction to him.

She turned to the man who held her child. He wouldn't harm Terrence, but she knew as sure as she stood that he would take her child away without so much as a backward glance. Tears sprung to her eyes at the thought.

"Please don't do this. I'm begging you. Don't take my child. Can't we work something out?" Even as she spoke, she knew that the elder Harrington was not willing to compromise. Turning back to her husband, "Carlton, please—" was all she managed to get out before her whole world went black.

Carlton sat in the sterile hospital room watching as his wife sleep. Her breathing was finally sounding normal and he thanked God. She was recovering from a bad case of pneumonia. Listening to her struggled breathing the past couple of days had been difficult. She drifted in and out of consciousness, sometimes calling, begging him not to take her child. His heart ached and his mind was consumed with guilt. He didn't know how he would get her to come back with him and give their family another chance. He only knew that he had to try.

Seeing her again after three years looking so different had left him stunned and speechless. Seeing their child, their second son, also had him at a loss for words. He could barely get it together quickly enough to react and catch her when she'd passed out. He'd never known such fear. The thought that he might lose Latonya after finding her again was a reality he didn't want to face. So he did the only thing he could do. He sent his grandfather home with Terrence and stayed by his wife's side.

He rubbed his sleep-deprived eyes just as Latonya woke up. She seemed more lucid than she'd been the previous times, but it was clear she didn't know what to think.

The sun shined startlingly bright through the blinds. Latonya blinked several times to get her bearings. She took a deep breath. Hearing the clarity in her lungs as she did, Carlton again thanked God.

She glanced around the room and her eyes immediately connected with his. She narrowed her eyes and gave him a harsh glare.

"Where is my son, Carlton?"

"Don't you mean *our* son, Tonya?" Carlton wanted to hear her acknowledge that they shared another child.

Latonya inhaled again, clearly readying herself for a showdown. Before she could get one word out Carlton stopped her.

"I know that he is mine and I don't need a test to prove it. Anyone can look at him and tell that he is a Harrington."

"So what if you provided the sperm. He is *my* child," Latonya spat defiantly. "We're no longer together. You kicked me out of our home and I haven't asked you for a dime."

He winced. Every word she'd said was true and he couldn't deny it. He didn't know why the anger in her voice surprised him. She had every reason to be angry with him.

"I'm his mother, Carlton," she bit out before he could respond. "Why can't you be reasonable? Where is he?"

The last thing he wanted was for her to upset herself unnecessarily. She was barely recovered. "Terrence is with family in the Bahamas."

"You took him out of the country! How could you do that? Why are you doing this?" Latonya struggled to sit up, and it was clear that she was going to try to get out of the bed.

"Calm down before you have some kind of relapse." The thought that she could make herself ill again worried him. He leaned forward in his chair. "He's fine, Tonya. He's with family. I couldn't very well keep him here at the hospital."

"I will not calm down! Carlton, surely we can work something out. I'm all he knows. He must be so scared. Can't we come to some sort of deal?" She started coughing and Carlton jumped out of his chair.

"Latonya, listen to me. You aren't going to be any good to Terrence if you don't get better. Please calm down so that you can fully recover." He let his hand rest on her forehead and she eyed him wearily.

The apprehensive expression filled with her lack of trust for him sent a sharp pain through his heart. "Just get some rest. Get better and I will take you to him, okay?"

She took several shaky breaths and soon it became clear to Carlton that her lack of energy had won out. She closed her eyes and he let out a sigh of relief. He hoped that by the time his wife woke up again, he could figure out a way to at least get her to trust him enough to come home with him.

When Latonya opened her eyes in the hospital room again, she found her face wet with tears. Her memories had made her cry in her sleep. She noticed that Carlton hadn't moved from the chair beside her bed.

What is he still doing here? What does he want? Does he want to rub it in that he managed to snatch another child from my arms?

She tried to think of what to do next. Both of her babies were in another country, and the man who put them there sat in the room with her. She'd made a difficult choice when she disappeared and didn't stay to fight for her first son. At the time, she did it because she couldn't risk her unborn child's life. Now it seemed like she would lose them both, after all. However, none of that would stop her from making her way to the Bahamas to fight for them. Far from the pregnant and scared twenty-four-year-old she was when she lived there before, she was certain that the Bahamas had never seen a wrath like the one she intended to bring in order to get both her children back.

Stirring, Carlton opened his eyes. His face was full of stubble. His eyes were bloodshot. He ran his hand across his face and yawned.

"Why are you still here, Carlton? Isn't it enough that you and your grandfather have taken my child out of the country?" Her lips managed to curl into a snarl even as her mouth shook furiously. "I want you to know that I intend to fight you for custody of both my sons. And I'd like you to leave, Carlton."

Carlton seemed to be studying her in deep contemplation. She didn't know what he was trying to figure out. And she didn't care. She wanted her children.

He took a deep breath and sighed before speaking. "No, Latonya. I'm not going anywhere. I came here to find you for a reason and I'm not leaving until I have what I came for."

The thought that something might be wrong with her child ran through her mind. A chill went through her.

Struggling, she sat up in the bed and found that her entire body still ached. "Is there something wrong with my son? Is that why you came looking for me?"

"I came looking for you because our son told me that he didn't want anything for his birthday this year but his mommy. He said that he waited for you to come back to us on your own, but you must be lost or hurt. He wants his mother." Carlton rubbed his eyes and stifled a yawn.

Even though she knew he must have spent the night sleeping in that chair, given the fact that he was there every time she woke up, his yawn irritated her. Her heart ached for her son. Of course little Carl wanted his mother! She wanted him also. Every day she spent away from her child had been filled with want.

Latonya narrowed her eyes. "If you hadn't thrown me out of our home I would be with my son right now! I didn't want to leave my child. You wouldn't let me take him with me. You made me leave him!"

Carlton visibly flinched. For a moment she thought that she glimpsed regret on his face. *That would be the day!* she thought angrily.

He stood and walked over to her bed. "I'm here to take you home, Latonya. Our son needs his mother. I need...I need to try to make things right for my sons' future. Both of our sons need both of their parents in their lives." He hesitated a moment and took a deep breath. "I know it's a lot for me to ask of you and I know that you don't have any reason in the world to trust what I'm saying. But I want to try to put our family back together."

Blinking, Latonya let out a hiss of air. *He actually thinks he can just waltz in talking about his wants like I'm supposed to jump!*

She let her options roll over in her head. With the kids in the Bahamas, they were limited. If she could get them back in the States, then she would be in better shape. "Bring them back to Miami and I'll go with you to Coconut Grove. If I move in, it won't be to live as man and wife. I won't share anything with you but the children."

He stared at her for a moment and then he smiled. A series of emotions crossed his face. Latonya recognized at least two of them, relief and joy. Both puzzled her.

He caressed her cheek with his hand before moving

away from the bed. "Get some rest. Your doctor is discharging you tomorrow and we will fly to Miami as soon as you're released. I'll have Grandfather bring the kids so that they can meet us there. Carl has waited quite some time to see you again, and Terrence has been worried about you since you collapsed. He asks about you every day. They both want to see their mother. They need you."

Swallowing, she willed her heart to stop its rapid palpitations. As long as the boys were in the country, she had a chance of eventually gaining custody. She would fight this time. She just had to make sure they came back to the States. She would tell Carlton anything he wanted to hear, if it meant that he'd bring her children back to the United States.

He walked toward the door. "I'm going to leave for a little while so you can get some rest."

Following him with her eyes, she wondered if she could really live with him again. Could she stay in his home long enough to gain custody? Could her heart take prolonged exposure to the one great love of her life? The man who broke her heart worse than the day her father left? Feeling the hardened shell that covered her heart, she knew that she could. That shell gave her the immunity she needed.

She'd spent a lot of time healing herself after Carlton threw her away like trash. The only thing that had kept her from falling apart was the fact that she had to take care of the child growing inside of her. Thinking about Terrence and Carl with their similar little faces made her smile despite her sadness. She loved her sons with everything inside of her. Thinking of them made her know what she had to do. She couldn't deny her sons any more than their father could. Eventually, she'd find a way to free herself and them.

Chapter 17

Studying Latonya carefully as she sat across from him in the private jet, Carlton noted the way she nervously crossed and uncrossed her legs. In the three years since he'd seen her last, she had changed so much—especially in appearance—so she couldn't be found.

The private detective had had trouble identifying her because she'd taken to wearing green contact lenses, cut her long, wavy auburn hair into one of those pixie cuts that lay flat on her scalp, and dyed it jet-black. Though she was as beautiful as before, he wasn't sure how he felt about that.

When the detective found her and his son, Carlton knew he had to get to her and bring them both home. Beyond that, he hadn't figured out much more. He felt incredibly lucky that he'd convinced her to come home with him. However, Calrton wasn't delusional. He knew her coming back had more to do with the kids than him.

Talking Grandfather into bringing the boys to Miami had been harder than he'd imagined. He almost had to threaten his grandfather with never seeing the children again. He had promised Latonya that the kids would meet them in Miami and he wasn't going to let anything or anyone stop him from keeping that promise. Not even his grandfather.

He wanted his wife back. He had no idea how he was going to get her to give them another chance after the way he ruined things between them. He only knew that he had to try.

Latonya shifted again and sighed. He felt the need to console her, to tell her that everything would be fine. Truthfully, he had no idea how things would be. He only knew that a few months ago when his son told him that he wanted his mother, he felt like he finally had a reason to do something he wanted to do from the moment he'd kicked his wife out.

Finding her after three years had been more difficult than he anticipated. He wondered how she managed to remain so well hidden. He noticed that her wedding rings and diamond earrings were gone. While that would have given her a significant amount of money, it wouldn't have given her enough to disappear so thoroughly. Even the Range Rover she'd been driving, which they never found, couldn't have helped her that much financially if she'd sold it. Not for three years. Certainly not with doctors' bills and the like.

Eyeing her suspiciously, he asked, "Who helped you to disappear?"

She jumped in her seat and opened her eyes. The sound of his voice broke up the hours of silence that they'd nurtured since leaving the hospital and getting on the private jet. When she turned and faced him, her eyes widened in shock for a matter of seconds before she masked it with her cool and icy demeanor.

Arching her eyebrow, she sneered before letting out a hiss of air between her teeth. Her eyes flashed and a flood of emotions passed through them. He registered disgust and anger.

"Why are you so concerned? It didn't bother you when you kicked me out. You didn't care what kind of help I had then. Why the hell are you so concerned now?"

"I was concerned. That's why I never closed any of your accounts. I assumed that you would go to your family and…well…none of that matters now. The fact is you had money and credit at your disposal and you didn't use it. Yet you were able to disappear, take a new name, Dana Dash, and keep my child away from me. Who helped you to do that?"

Narrowing her eyes, she shrugged. "A friend."

"Who?"

Studying him dispassionately for several seconds that felt more like hours, she folded her hands across her chest and crossed her legs. "Jeff Weatherby."

Feeling the heat rise from his chest to his neck and

188 *If Only You Knew*

then his face, he loosened his tie and top shirt button. *Weatherby!* He couldn't say he didn't expect her to say it. He also couldn't say that a part of him hadn't hoped she would name someone else. *Anyone else!*

"Why would Weatherby help you disappear?"

She glared at him. "Because he is my friend. He didn't want to see me lose another child. He cares about what happens to me, unlike my husband, who threw me out on the street!"

Guilt unlike any he'd ever felt ran through Carlton. Latonya was right. She had every right to get help from wherever she could find it. While it hurt him that she had gotten the help from Jeff, it hurt even more that he had been the cause of her needing to turn to the man in the first place. No number of apologies could possibly make up for what he had done. Even as he thought about saying he was sorry, he realized how foolish it would sound. What would *sorry* possibly mean to a woman he had wronged so? She would probably laugh in his face.

No, he had to *act*. He had to show her that he meant to do right by her and their children. He had to take his time and make her trust him with her heart. This time he would do it the right way. He was going to have her heart again and this time he would treasure it for the gift it was.

He'd done a lot of soul-searching while she was away. He knew that he had let his parents' relationship color his marriage to Latonya. He let go of the demons of the past and he refused to allow them to influence him again. If Jeff Weatherby had helped his wife, then he fully intended to thank the man and repay him.

Carlton knew that he wanted a new life with Latonya, a new beginning. He'd rushed her into a relationship and marriage because he hadn't wanted to risk losing her. This time he would take his time and woo her properly. This time, he meant for it to last.

Chapter 18

Entering the Miami home she had once shared with Carlton was something Latonya had dreamed of often. Only in her dreams she came back to get her child, not to live.

She certainly never expected the homecoming that awaited her when she crossed the threshold. In the same front sitting room where Carlton waited for her the day he kicked her out, sat Cicely, Gran, Carlton's grandfather, Jillian, Pamela and Latonya's precious little boys. Her heart had never felt more full.

Little Carl and Terrence stood side by side. Little Carl held Terrence's hand, already protective of his younger brother.

Terrence's eyes grew wide when she entered the

room, and he tugged at his brother's hand. "Mommy! Carl, it's Mommy."

She dropped to her knees as they ran toward her. She wrapped her arms around her sons, and held them as tight as she could without crushing them. She never thought that she would be holding both of her babies in her arms together. After several minutes of holding them close, she let go and just ran her hands over their heads and touched their handsome little faces.

Terrence touched her cheek with his tiny fingers. "No cry, Mommy. No be sad."

Realizing that she must look like a blubbering idiot, she smiled. "I'm not sad, baby. Mommy is just happy to see you and little Carl."

Terrence grinned. "I got a brother and an auntie and a great-granny and great-grandpop and a Ms. Jill and a Miss Pam and a daddy. Mommy, I got a family!"

Latonya kept her gaze on her firstborn child the whole time she spoke to Terrence. "Yes, baby. We have a family. You have a brother."

Smiling at him, she noticed little Carl just stared at her. When he brought his hands to her hair, she wondered if he remembered how she used to wear it, or if he was simply reconciling the real her with pictures he might have seen. He buried his head in her shoulder and she wrapped her arm around him again.

Latonya found herself cuddling the five-year-old and cooing to him the way she did when he was a baby. She inhaled deeply, taking in his scent. "I've missed you so much, baby."

"I love you, Mommy. Please don't leave me again."

Little Carl's voice whimpered as tears trailed down his face.

Her heart broke in two as she looked up and searched for her husband. Catching several visibly moved gazes from other family members before she caught sight of Carlton, she noted the regretful expression on his face.

Forcing a cheerful demeanor, she kissed the top of little Carl's head. "I promise you I'll never be far. I love you, baby. I always intend to be a part of your life." She let him go and wiped the tears from his face.

Puzzled, Terrence proclaimed, "No cry. Be happy. We family."

Latonya smiled and realized how important it was for her sons to have each other, for them to have family. Standing, she took one of each of their hands in hers. She walked carefully toward the women she'd missed almost as much as her sons.

Cicely embraced her without hesitation, as did Jillian and Pamela. Only Gran eyed her with trepidation. Seeing the disappointment in Gran's face, Latonya felt her heart stop. For the second time since she had entered the house, the pain in her chest became almost unbearable.

Mustering all the courage she could, she faced Gran and squeaked out two words. "Gran. Please."

Eying little Carl and Terrence first, Gran seemed to contemplate her words with care. Sighing, she spoke softly. "It's not natural. *No* mother should leave her children without so much as a backward glance," she spat. "I never would have thought that you would leave your flesh and blood just like your father did."

Latonya gasped and took a step back. Did her family think her some kind of animal that carelessly gave birth and then left her child to fend for himself? That Gran held her in the same regard as she did Latonya's father hurt her even more. She wouldn't have left her baby if she thought she had another choice. Tears started to run down her cheek again. "Oh, Gran."

Latonya looked up as she wiped away her tears, and her eyes connected with the elder Harrington. He shifted nervously in her gaze. The man had threatened her life and her family's and she let him run her away. Her eyes narrowed and she did not break her stare. In that moment she knew that she wouldn't allow him to threaten anything or anyone she held dear ever again.

Carlton stepped forward to intervene. It was almost as if he wanted to help alleviate her distress. "Since Latonya is still recovering, maybe it would be best if we gave her a little time to rest, and then we can finish the welcoming a little later this evening over dinner? Tonya, would you like to go upstairs and take a nap?"

She gazed down at her babies as they still held on to her hands. She didn't want to leave them, not yet. She was still recovering, but she wanted to spend every moment she could with her family. "How about I read you two a story first and then I take a little nap?"

"Yeah," the boys screamed in unison.

Latonya cast one more look at the elder Harrington before heading off with her sons. She turned to her grandmother and the others. "I realize that some of you were worried about me. And I'm sorry for that. Just know that I never wanted to leave my child. If I could

have done things differently back then I would have."
She gave the old man a pointed stare before continuing. "But know this, nothing will ever keep me away
from my children again."

The old man bristled, and for the first time ever
Latonya thought she saw real fear in his eyes.

The girl was back and there wasn't anything he
could do about that. The elder Harrington let the
gravity of the situation roll over in his head. She had
even threatened him! He saw it in her eyes. Latonya
would probably tell Carlton everything as soon as she
could and use it to cement her place in his life. And he
wouldn't be able to get Carlton to understand that he'd
done what he did all for him, to save him.

The elder Harrington hadn't done anything to save
his own son until it was too late. He'd even encouraged
the boy to go after the woman the first couple of times
with speeches about the importance of family and
keeping up proper appearances. How was he to know
that the woman wasn't worth the spit it took to say her
name?

Well, if this girl wanted to hand out threats, so be
it! He was a Harrington! He stood by every decision
he'd made. He had simply tried to save his grandson
from the heartache and pain that he hadn't been able
to save his son from. He'd tried to save himself from
the heartache of losing another family member.

If the girl decided to tell Carlton everything, then
he would lose his grandson, anyway. The irony of the
situation didn't miss him. Carlton had all but threat-

ened him when he tried to talk him out of bringing the kids from the Bahamas to Miami. If only he had managed to get Carlton to leave her side and come back to the Bahamas with him and the boy.

He hadn't wanted to leave her. The pain in Carlton's face when the girl collapsed almost broke the elder Harrington's heart. He never wanted to see that kind of pain on his grandson's face. That was the real reason why he wanted the girl gone. The love Carlton felt for the girl was as real as the love that ended up killing his father. The elder Harrington wasn't going to bury another person he loved if he could help it. The little black American girl surely couldn't be worthy of such love.

Once she woke up, Latonya found her Peeping Tom from the hospital still watching her sleep. Carlton sat in the wing chair beside the bed. Warmth that she hadn't expected came over her. Oddly, having him there made her feel secure. That confused her. The way he had treated her made him the last person she should feel safe around. She sighed, not wanting to waste time thinking about Carlton. The only important thing was finding a way to get her children and leave.

"Are you going to watch me sleep all the time?"

Carlton offered a wry grin. "She speaks."

Sitting up in the bed and rubbing her eyes, she glared at him. "Why are you here? What is this sudden fascination with my sleep patterns?" She stopped for a moment, realizing that Carlton had always watched her sleep. She would often wake up to his intense gaze.

Surely he wasn't watching her for the same reasons as he had then? "You stayed in the hospital the entire time watching me. I'm out now. I've been given a clean bill of health. Why are you still doing it?"

He appeared thrown off guard by her question and paused for a moment before responding. "You scared me. Watching you sleep calms me. I can see that you're safe and okay. I guess I don't want to let you out of my sight."

Even though she told herself that it didn't matter in the grand scheme of things, why he watched her, she still found herself asking, "Why not?"

His eyes held her in an intense gaze and he responded, "I don't know. In the hospital, I just didn't want to leave your side because I didn't want to lose you. Now I'm trying to figure out a way to get you to stay. I don't want you to leave again."

"You kicked me out, Carlton. I didn't leave you." Shaking her head incredulously, she continued, "And it took you three years to come find me. So pardon me if I don't buy this song and dance you're selling."

"I went to your grandmother's house a week after throwing you out. Little Carl had been asking for you and I took him to go see you…. I…" Carlton paused and took a shaky breath. "It was the same day you called Gran and told her that you wouldn't be coming back."

Latonya felt the blood freeze in her veins. The old bastard had lied to her. It was on the tip of her tongue to tell Carlton everything that his grandfather had done to keep them apart. Carlton deserved to know the truth.

The fearful expression on the old man's face crossed her mind and she paused. Suddenly, she realized that the fear had always been there masked in his hate. It was the fear, not the hate that caused the old man to threaten her and everyone she loved. She decided she would hold on to her information for the moment.

Neither the old man nor Carlton were important, anyway. The only important thing for Latonya was her children and getting them all out of Carlton's house.

Shrugging with a nonchalance she didn't feel, she stated, "Well, obviously I didn't know at the time that my son was waiting for me at Gran's house."

Leaning forward in his chair, Carlton implored, "Why didn't you come back once you found out that you were pregnant?"

The earnestness in his tone and the confused expression on Carlton's face gave Latonya pause. It seemed as if he really was trying to figure out the past so that they could have some sort of future. The hard shell around her heart let her know there would be no future between her and Carlton. It didn't matter that he had come looking for her. He shouldn't have thrown her out in the first place.

"I knew that I was pregnant when I left. I knew a week before you kicked me out. I was waiting for the right time to tell you. When you came back from your business trip you were so cold and distant. I couldn't find a moment special enough to share the news."

His jaw dropped and his eyes bulged. "You knew that you were pregnant when you left here?"

"When you threw me out. Yes."

Clenching his teeth, he bit out his words in a hiss. "How could you keep Terrence away from me like that?"

A short, sarcastic laugh fell from her mouth. *The nerve of him!* "How could you make me leave little Carl, make me choose between staying and fighting to be a part of his life and keeping my unborn child. No mother should have to make that kind of decision."

"You could have given me time to calm down. My goodness! I saw you with him!" He leaped up from the chair and began to pace the room. "He had his hand on yours. You left the restaurant with your arms around him. Now you tell me that he was the one who financed your disappearance?"

Sucking her teeth, she folded her arms across her chest. "Right, right, and after being married to you for three years, I didn't warrant any trust at all. You wouldn't even listen to me. You just assumed that I was having an affair and you kicked me out."

He stopped mid-pace and stared at her. His face fell and she saw his regret again. It confused her. She could count on one hand the amount of times she had actually seen Carlton Harrington III visibly show remorse for anything he'd done.

"I didn't mean to get you upset. It's just a lot to take in. I know that my actions made it hard for you to do things differently. But I guess I hoped that…I don't know what I hoped back then. I just know that we have a chance to try to make things right now…if you're willing?"

Latonya shook her head. There was no need to feed

him false promises. Even though he realized that he was wrong, he still hadn't apologized. She couldn't stay with a man who couldn't say he was sorry for breaking her heart and separating her from her child. As soon as she could, she was finding a place and she was taking her children with her. "I can't stay here, Carlton. I want to be a part of our sons' lives, but I cannot stay here."

He sighed before sinking down in his chair. "Latonya, you just sat downstairs and told our son that you wouldn't leave him again."

Don't worry. I have no plans to leave either of my sons! "I told him that I would never be far away. I intend to stay in Miami and I intend to be a part of my sons' lives, but I will not remain here. As soon as I can I am finding my own place." She didn't think she could stay under the same roof with him as long as it would take for them to work out a suitable custody situation.

She also didn't know for sure that he would keep the children in the United States if she left. Letting him know her plans to eventually leave was a huge risk on her part. Her heart stopped at the thought of what he could do if he wanted to stop her. He could easily take her children back to the Bahamas. She almost thought it better to lie and feed into his hopes for some sort of reconciliation until she found a way to steal the kids and hide away for good.

Even as she thought it she realized she couldn't keep her sons away from their father. He loved them as much as she did. She had to find a way to get him to see that they could share custody and not be together as a couple.

* * *

Carlton felt as if his heart was being ripped out of his chest. He couldn't lose her again. "Can't we just try to live under the same roof for the moment, for the sake of the children?" He wasn't fazed by the pleading sound in his voice. Even though he couldn't bring himself to actually say it, he wanted Latonya to know that he was sorry.

"Were you thinking about the sake of the children when you kicked me out? Don't try to run a head trip on me, Carlton. How can you really expect me to stay here after everything that has happened?"

He sighed. He didn't want her to leave. He realized that he couldn't force her to stay. She had to do what made her feel comfortable. He had to do what he knew he must. Even if she left, he planned to get his wife back. He would woo her until it became unmistakable that they belonged together. Working at her pace and taking her needs into consideration was all a part of accomplishing that. He knew what he had to do even though he didn't want to do it. "Do what you feel you must, Latonya. The boys will miss you if you go." *I will miss you if you go.* "But if you really must go, then go."

She turned and dropped her arms to her side. "I'm not making any promises, Carlton. I can't say with certainty that I will stay here. But I can say that I won't leave my children."

"Latonya, I have no idea what the future will bring. I know that we both need some time. However, there are two little boys involved and we don't have the luxury of taking that time completely apart." He placed his hands in his pockets. "We're a family. And we should live under the same roof."

"Fine, as long as we're clear on boundaries."

"Oh, I think we're crystal clear." He let out a sigh of relief, happy that she would be staying *for now*.

"Good. Well, I'm going to freshen up for dinner." Getting up from bed, Latonya stood still for a moment.

"Fine. You'll find all of your clothing in the walk-in. We shipped your things from New Jersey. Your old clothing is still here, and I had Frances's Boutique send over some of her latest designs in your size." He hoped he hadn't been too presumptuous. He figured she would need some clothes, even though he had no idea if she would want to stay.

Latonya narrowed her eyes briefly before replying. "Thanks. I guess I'll see you downstairs, then."

As he walked toward the door, he turned and glanced back before he made it out. Carlton smiled a slow, rueful smile as he allowed himself a small measure of hope. "Things are going to be okay, Tonya. I really believe that we're going to be okay."

Chapter 19

The quiet and somber mood of dinner didn't exactly coincide with the supposed celebratory nature of the evening. Conversations were stilted and strained; no one knew what to say to one another. Latonya didn't know what to say to Gran, her sister or Jillian. Glad that Pamela had fed the boys earlier and they didn't have to sit through all the adult tension, she tried not to count down the seconds until she could return to her bedroom and end the forced reunion.

When she could take the silence no longer, she glanced at her sister. "So, Cicely, I hear you've finished graduate school. How did you like it? What are you doing now?"

"Well, I ended up getting a master's in public policy.

Carlton used his connections to get me a nice position in the mayor's office."

Latonya had no idea why Carlton's actions surprised her. She had no idea how she felt about him maintaining a connection to her family and helping her sister. Latonya's shock must have shown on her face, because Gran became more than happy to fill in the silence.

"Carlton has been very kind and very helpful to us in spite of the way you behaved. He didn't hold it against us that you left your child as if you were some wild animal in the jungle. He still let us be a part of little Carl's life so that he would know his family." The clipped and judgmental tone that Gran used cut Latonya to her core.

"Now may not be the best time for this, Evelyn." The elder Harrington, who hadn't even looked up from his plate during the entire tirade, opined, clearly more concerned about the propriety of polite dinner conversation than the attack on Latonya.

Cringing at the sound of his voice, she made a point of glaring at the old man before turning her gaze to Gran. He bristled under her glare and kept his eyes on his plate from then on. *How dare he try to regulate the conversation after his role in the chain of events!*

She cleared her throat and tried taking deep calming breaths before she spoke. She respected her grandmother more than any other person in the world and she never wanted to disappoint the woman.

"I understand you have certain opinions about what happened, about what you think I did, and how I should have behaved. And you are more than entitled to them, Gran." Latonya noticed that the timbre of her voice was shaky and realized that tears were not going to be far behind.

I have to hold it together.

Crying at the dinner table in front of everyone was *not* an option. Steeling herself, she continued, "Gran, you know I love you. I respect you and I would never want to do anything that would shame you or make you think poorly of me. I'm sorry that I disappointed you. I really am. *But* this is truly the last time I will apologize for it and that is the only thing I will apologize to you for. I owe little Carl other apologies, and we will work that out between us. I made a decision three years ago that I felt I had to make at the time—"

Gran's voice broke as she cut Latonya off. "You didn't contact us again. Your sister and I were so worried. If it hadn't been for Carlton and little Carl, I might have had another stroke." Gran's tone softened as she spoke. "I swear, Peanut, when you came through that door, I was torn between dropping to my knees and thanking the Lord, or grabbing you and shaking you for scaring me like that." Glancing up toward the ceiling, she closed her eyes. A single tear came down Gran's cheek, and Latonya knew that her own attempts to get through the conversation without crying were a wash.

She had never seen Gran cry. The woman was the epitome of the strong black women who kept on keeping on. Anger, righteous indignation and steadfast strength were traits that personified Evelyn Stevens, not tears. The fact that she had caused Gran to cry almost made Latonya shed tears of her own.

Seemingly disturbed, Carlton spoke. "Why don't we just table this discussion and just be happy that Latonya is back now and we have time together as a family to make a fresh start."

Although somewhat certain that Carlton was only trying to be helpful, attempting to manage the small situation that had interrupted a staid and calm family dinner at the Harrington residence, Latonya couldn't help but think that he had never been made to take his share of the blame for anything that happened.

She also realized that until he did she would never be able to forgive him and move on. The thought of that made her sad, because she knew that the day Carlton Harrington III apologized would be the day that skiing, ice fishing and ice hockey became leisure-time activities in hell.

Forcing her attention back on Gran, she said, "Gran, you're right. Everything you've said is right. I never wanted to cause you stress. I'm sorry."

Cicely, who had been sitting virtually mortified through the entire discussion, spoke up. "Let's change the subject. I haven't seen my big sister in quite some time and I for one do not want to waste one more moment belaboring to whom and for what she should or should not apologize. She's home and I have a beautiful new nephew to boot. I for one am going to enjoy them both."

"Amen! I agree with you, Cicely." Jillian stood and gave each person in the room with the exception of Cicely and Latonya a harsh, pointed stare. "While I appreciate being included as a part of the family in this welcome-back dinner. I have to say, if you all are going to spend the time attacking Latonya, then I'd rather not be included. She's alive and she's back. Let's just thank the Lord and move on." With that she put her napkin down on the table and walked away.

Before she made it fully out the door, she turned. "Sweetie, I sure am glad to have you back. Your Gran and I made sure your little boy didn't forget you. I'm making cookies with the boys tomorrow afternoon, and I'd love it if you joined us. Good night, all."

"She always was a drama queen." Rolling her eyes at her friend's retreat, Gran turned to Latonya. "Peanut, you know I'm happy to have you back. I love you. You just scared me, that's all. I'm sorry if I was harsh." She rose from her seat and walked to Latonya.

Latonya got up and they embraced the way they should have in the beginning. Not wanting to be left out, Cicely got up and joined in on the hug.

"I love you. Don't forget that. And know that you always have a place to go if you ever have to leave here again. You hear me? You always have a place to go." Gran squeezed her tightly before letting go.

"Yeah, Peanut!" Cicely agreed. "I have my own place now and you and the boys are always welcome."

Latonya's voice choked. "Thanks, Gran and Cicely. I know that and I appreciate it."

"I'm going to go check on that ornery old Jillian before we head out," Gran said. "I'll tell you that mouthy woman needs Jesus!"

"I hope you all aren't leaving yet. I feel like we have so much catching up to do. Cicely, I want to hear all about your new job and the graduations I missed." Latonya surveyed the smart and competent young woman that her sister had become and her heart swelled with pride.

It seemed that Cicely had accomplished everything Latonya had wanted for her. She decided she would at least thank Carlton for all he'd done to help her grandmother and her sister. He didn't have to do that and she knew it.

"Let's go and talk while Gran mends things with Jillian. Then we can go and check on Pamela and the boys. I can't believe how big little Carl has gotten." Latonya grabbed Cicely's hand and together they headed out of the dining room. She glanced back at Carlton before leaving and gave him a hesitant smile. She fully intended to thank him for helping her family later.

Carlton watched his wife leave the room and pondered the smile she'd given him. Was it too much to hope that the smile meant she might one day find it in her heart to forgive him?

"Well, that was a fiasco." Grandfather's gruff voice broke through Carlton's wondering.

The dinner hadn't gone as smoothly as the younger Harrington had planned. But the end result was worth it. Seeing the genuine happiness on Latonya's face once she'd worked out her differences with her grandmother made it all worth it. "Things worked themselves out just fine."

Grandfather harrumphed loudly, causing Carlton to give him a pointed look. Carlton wouldn't tolerate any of the nonsense his grandfather pulled early in their marriage.

"Listen, Grandfather. I know you have never approved of my marriage and you are entitled to your opinions. But you will respect my wife or you won't be welcome in my home. Latonya has graciously decided to remain here for the children's sake. And I fully intend to win back her heart and her trust. I want to make my marriage work and I won't let anything or anyone stop that."

Grandfather's jaw dropped and the older man suddenly looked every bit of his seventy-plus years. "Did she say something...anything about why she left?"

Carlton's eyebrows furrowed. "What do you mean? She left because I kicked her out. I should have trusted in our relationship." He paused and studied the older man. "I don't know what you saw or thought you saw between her and Weatherby. But I do know that my wife didn't have an affair. I know that now in my heart and soul."

Grandfather opened his mouth and shut it quickly. "Well, it would appear you know everything, then. I only hope that you don't end up regretting any of this."

Narrowing his gaze slightly, Carlton responded, "I know that I won't."

After she and Cicely convinced Pamela to allow them to tuck the boys in and read them good-night stories, Latonya sat in the study with her sister.

Cicely was dressed in a classy designer pantsuit

and wore her brown hair in a stylish up-do. She appeared happy and successful, all of the things Latonya had dreamed of for her sister.

"I'm so pleased with the woman you've become, Cicely." Latonya hugged Cicely close. "Look at you, Miss Career Woman living in her own apartment!"

"Well, I had the best role model anyone could ask for," Cicely offered.

"Please, your success is your own. I'm just glad that you are living your dreams." Latonya thought back briefly to when she was Cicely's age, fresh out of graduate school and in her first job. Latonya's life took a detour when she married Carlton and had her children. But she didn't regret any of it. She simply had to find a way to put her life back on track, get her children and move on. "So, I can't wait to see this hot new place of yours. Do you think they have any openings in your apartment complex?"

Perplexed, Cicely responded, "They have openings all the time. Why?"

"I'm thinking it might be best for me to get my own place and set up a secure environment for me and the boys. Hopefully Carlton and I will be able to figure out some sort of shared custody agreement."

"So you don't think that you two will be able to work it out?"

Shaking her head, Latonya replied, "I think that too much has happened and it would be impossible to make our way back from that. He hasn't even apologized yet."

"Peanut, anyone with eyes can see how sorry he is.

As irritated as I was with him when he broke his promise to me and hurt you, I could see that he loved you and he was hurt the entire time you were gone. I can see that he still loves you and he hopes that you two will be able to work it out." The sincerity in Cicely's voice made Latonya do a double take.

Latonya started to ask her sister when Carlton promised he wouldn't hurt her. But Cee Cee's seemingly earnest pleas on Carlton's behalf sidetracked her. "Whose side are you on, anyway?"

"Always yours, Peanut. That's why I don't want you to make any rash decisions." Cicely hugged her. "I knew the man was trouble the day he showed up on Gran's doorstep with flowers. I also knew just from looking at you that you had given him your heart. I'm just hoping that my role model will fight for her heart, fight for her family and fight for her love." Cicely broke out into a wide grin. "Just think about what a bad impression you'd make on your devoted baby sister if you didn't."

Latonya shook her head and laughed. "You are so lucky I haven't seen you in a while. That's the only reason why I'm letting you get away with that crap." Even as she said the words, a part of her let Cicely's words seep in. She realized that she should wait before rushing off to get her own place. She should at least give living under the same roof with Carlton a try.

Cicely joined Latonya in laughter and hugged her. "Besides, what's our favorite line?"

Puzzled, Latonya stared at Cicely.

"Oh, don't act like you don't remember, Lady in

Blue!" Cicely put her had on her hip and struck a pose of mock defiance.

Latonya closed her eyes and smiled. She traveled back to one of those typical summer days when she was in high school and Cee Cee was finishing up the eighth grade. They didn't have any money to go out and do anything, not even catch a matinee. They'd flipped through the channels of the cableless television bored, until they landed on a PBS airing of Ntozake Shange's *For Colored Girls*. They sat glued to the television and the play became a favorite of theirs. Latonya even got tickets to a live version of the play that the University of Miami theater put on and took Cee Cee as a present for her seventeenth birthday. They would often recite lines from the play whenever the mood struck them. But the Lady in Blue's monologue on apologies had been their favorite.

"I remember the Lady in Blue," Latonya responded with a sassy grin.

"Well, then you know that the one thing you don't need is anymore apologies...." Cicely started.

"I got sorry greeting me at my front door. You can keep yours!" They finished in unison and busted out laughing.

Cicely wiped the laugh tears out of her eyes. "Seriously, Peanut. It's not what he says. At the end of the day it's what he does that counts."

If it had been anyone else, Latonya would have been inclined to agree with Cicely. She new that words were often empty. However, Carlton Harrington III needed to own up to his part in this and she wanted to hear an apology!

Realizing that she probably wouldn't be able to influence Latonya, Cicely stood. "I'm going to find Gran and take her home." She paused. "Hey, I was thinking that I would surprise her with a vacation, a Caribbean cruise or something. Do you realize that she has never really had a vacation?"

Latonya smiled. It was wonderful to see her sister taking such good care of Gran. Cicely really had turned out just fine. "I think that's a lovely idea, Cee Cee. But do you really think you're going to be able to get Evelyn Stevens on a boat?"

"I know, right. I can hear her now. 'Child, I'm not getting on no boat. If God wanted me to be in the water he would have made me a fish.'" Cicely did a pretty good impersonation of Gran. "But I'm going to get the tickets, anyway. You can help me convince her. Oh, I'm so glad you're home, Peanut. Let's get together later this week. Okay?" Cicely asked before walking out of the room.

"You bet, Cee Cee." Latonya watched her sister leave.

"Whoa! Oh, snap. You scared me! What are you doing standing out here, Mr. Harrington?" Cicely's startled gasp from outside the door caused Latonya to look up.

"Sorry, I didn't mean to frighten you," the old man apologized gruffly.

"It's okay," Cicely replied.

The elder Harrington walked into the room and Latonya narrowed her eyes.

"Can I talk to you for a moment?" he asked hesitantly.

Latonya pursed her lips. They needed to do more than talk. He had to be made to understand once and for all that she wasn't going to allow him to threaten her family anymore.

Chapter 20

The elder Harrington couldn't believe what he had just heard. The girl was already plotting to leave Carlton. It was the same thing all over again. She might not be an unfaithful, cheating slut. But she clearly didn't love Carlton as much as the man loved her. Not if she were plotting to leave while he was busy planning reconciliation.

Clearing his throat, the elder Harrington took a seat in the sofa across from the one Latonya sat in. "So, you're planning to leave him already, girl."

Her eyes narrowed. "It's rude to eavesdrop, old man. And I would think that you would be happy and helping me pack up my things after all the trouble you went through to get rid of me the last time."

Taken aback, the elder Harrington paused for a

moment. While the girl had never been particularly malleable, she hadn't been this angry and aggressive before. She had at least tried to show respect to him as an elder. He didn't care for the changes in her personality one bit. "I still don't want you here. But clearly my grandson and my great-grandsons do."

The girl rolled her eyes and shrugged as she spat out, "Well you should have thought of that before you told lies that poisoned my marriage, tried to buy me off so that I would leave and threatened the lives of my grandmother and sister."

Yes, he had been right. The girl was definitely on a warpath with him as her main enemy and target. It would only be a matter of time before she dropped her bomb. "Why haven't you told Carlton yet? What are you waiting for? I know you're going to use that to turn him against me. You should know I was only trying to protect him."

"Protect him from what?" she snapped as she glared at him with disdain. "I wasn't going to hurt him. I loved him. I loved our life together. *You* destroyed my family. For what? Because I'm an African-American? Because I grew up poor? What? Why do you hate me so much?"

The forcefulness in her tone and the anger in her eyes took him aback again. He cursed the fact that the girl had the power in her hands to take his grandson away from him for good. He tried to placate her. "*Hate* is a strong word. Yes, I did take issue with the fact that your family apparently hadn't been able to achieve more in this country, especially given the fact that my great-grandfather came here with nothing and was able to build—"

"Oh, cut the crap!" she hissed as she interrupted him. "You are not going to sit here and tell me that you ruined my life over some old black-on-black conflict that doesn't have anything to do with anything! The immigrant experience is different from the experience of black folk who live in and deal with entrenched racism and oppression on a day-to-day basis their entire lives. But you're a smart man. I don't have to tell you that. Because that isn't the real problem you have with me. I realize that now. The cultural differences might have bothered you a little, but that's not really why you had to get rid of me." Her eyes narrowed and he felt as if she could see right into him. He didn't like the feeling at all. "What are you scared of, old man? What did you think I was going to do? Love him too much?"

She knew! The girl really knew what power she held and clearly she took great joy in having him worry about it. The elder Harrington tried to mask the suddenly very real fear he felt. "I wasn't afraid...I'm not afraid. I just... Well, when are you going to tell him what I did? Are you just making me wait because you think you can make me suffer?"

The girl shook her head as if she pitied him. She actually had the nerve to pity him! "You are the one who betrayed your grandson and you should be the one to break his heart and tell him that the man he loved and trusted lied to him."

The elder Harrington flinched before letting out a sigh. "Well, if you're not going to tell him, then we can—"

"*We* can't do anything. *I* want nothing to do with you. I will tolerate you because you seem to love my sons. But that's it. And if anything were to happen to either my grandmother or Cicely, then so help me…" She narrowed her eyes and gritted her teeth. Her threat was certainly more real than the one he had used on her three years ago.

"I wouldn't harm them," the elder Harrington offered. He hadn't meant the women any harm. He was just trying to protect his flesh and blood in a way that he had failed to before.

"Wouldn't harm who?"

Both the elder Harrington and Latonya looked up when Carlton entered the study.

"No one, son." The elder Harrington pretended to look at his watch as he silently thanked God that Carlton hadn't overheard the entire conversation. "It's getting late and I'm going to head out for Coral Gables. I think I'll stay there a few days and then head back to the Bahamas for a while."

"Sure, Grandfather. I'll see you out," Carlton offered.

"No, no. I know the way out." The elder Harrington glanced at the girl and gave her a shaky smile. "Stay put and catch up with your wife."

Carlton watched as his grandfather scurried out of the study. His eyes narrowed. Something had happened. Latonya didn't appear to be upset, but she did seem a little irritated. If his grandfather said anything to upset Latonya, Carlton vowed to get his family as far away from the old man as possible.

"Are you okay?" he asked hesitantly.

"I'm fine," she replied before sighing. "Listen, Carlton, I want to thank you for taking care of Gran and Cicely while I was away. Cicely's job sounds wonderful. And I know that they both appreciated being able to spend time with little Carl."

Stunned, Carlton didn't know what to say. "You don't have to thank me, Latonya. It was the least I could do since I couldn't take care of you. I know how much family means to you."

It struck him that family meant the world to Latonya. That's why she'd been working so hard when he first met her. That's why she gave her all to their marriage. *That's* why he should have trusted in her instead of kicking her out. He felt even more like a heel. Having her thank him for helping her family made him feel even worse.

"Do you think we will ever be able to move past what happened?" He hadn't meant to ask her that, because it was probably too soon. But he had to know if he had a chance.

The change in her demeanor occurred as soon as the words fell from his lips. Latonya's eyes narrowed and she shook her head. "When you threw me out of this house and kept me away from my child, because you thought that I was screwing another man, you hurt me beyond anything words could express. You did so cruelly and callously and without regard for my feelings or my innocence." Biting out the words in a furious rant, she visibly tried to calm herself. Taking several deep breaths, she wrung her hands a few times before continuing.

"I'm willing to get past that eventually for my children's sake. I might even one day forgive you for the way you hurt me. But I really can't say when we will be able to get past it all."

Turning, she left the room.

Stunned, he stared after her. She'd said so much and had spoken with such intense emotion that he didn't quite know what to do with it.

He should have apologized to her when she was in the study with him a moment ago, but he couldn't form the words aloud for some reason. *Saying I'm sorry won't be enough to make it up to her,* he thought ruefully. *Talk about too little too late.* He wanted, no needed, for things to work out between them. Her being in their home again provided an opportunity for him to make things right. And he vowed that he wasn't going to let anything stop him from doing so.

Chapter 21

Within a few days, Latonya and Pamela had worked out a smooth routine for taking care of the boys. Latonya smiled as they worked together to get the boys' breakfast in the kitchen. The Trinidadian woman had finally realized that she wasn't going to be able to stop Latonya from helping out. And Latonya resigned herself to that fact that Pamela loved her job and therefore Latonya needed to get out of the way sometimes and let her actually do it.

"I want juice now," Terrence said with a pout as he pushed away his small bowl of oatmeal.

Latonya eyed the barely touched food. If she let Terrence, he would gladly fill up with juice. "Take a few more bites for Mommy and I'll get you a little more juice."

"I want juice. Don't want more food." Terrence stuck out his lip.

"No oatmeal. No juice," Latonya said firmly.

"I finished my oatmeal. May I have some more juice, Mommy?" little Carl asked.

"Yes, you may." Latonya got up to retrieve the juice, but Pamela headed her off.

"I have it." Pamela poured some more juice in little Carl's cup. Except for a few more gray hairs, Pamela looked the same. She still wore her severe bun and still radiated the same almost contagious joy and happiness.

Terrence eyed the juice for a moment before taking a few more bites of his oatmeal. "See. I eating all, Mommy. Can I please have more juice now?"

Pamela laughed. "Their little personalities are so different. That's why I love working with kids. Each one is so unique and special."

Latonya reached for the juice and poured a little in Terrence's cup. "I know. Are you going to be okay now that there are two of them?"

"Of course! I love children," Pamela responded. "So please tell me you have some place to go today or something to do?"

"Are you trying to get rid of me?" Latonya teased. "Actually now that you mention it, I do have somewhere to go. I'm going to the beauty salon so that I can dye my hair back to its natural color and then I'm going to meet a friend for lunch at Soka's."

"Excellent!" Pamela exclaimed. "We are going to do a little reading, a little playing and, if we are good—" she glanced at the boys before continuing "—we will watch one of our favorite movies."

Latonya left knowing that her boys would be in good hands.

Spending the entire morning in the beauty salon wasn't exactly her idea of fun. But Latonya was happy when she finally left with auburn hair again. She didn't know if she wanted to grow her hair back as long as it had been, but she'd missed her old hair color. Her hair had grown a little. So instead of the flat style Latonya had been wearing, the stylist put flipped curls all over her head.

By the time she breezed into Soka's, the lunch crowd had died down. She was glad she'd told Jeff to meet her for a late lunch. She really wanted to be able to thank him for all he'd done to help her.

"Well, if it isn't the most beautiful girl in the world." Suave as ever and still a flirt, Jeff stood and held his arms open for a hug.

Latonya broke into a grin.

"Give me a hug, girl. And then tell me what the hell are you doing here?"

Entering his embrace, she smiled. "It's a long story. Let's just say it proved impossible to hide forever."

"Are you okay with that?" Although he kept a wide grin on his face, he didn't mask the deep concern in his voice.

They took their seats as Latonya pondered that question. A week ago, she would have said no. The only thing she wanted then was to take her kids and get as far away from Carlton as possible. Now she only knew that she sensed a change in Carlton that she couldn't put her finger on and she had no clear idea how she felt about any of it.

Given her confused state of mind, she felt it best not to answer Jeff's question. "What are you up to now? I heard that you're no longer with Harrington Enterprise?"

"That's right. I finally stopped rebelling and went in with my dad at the family business. To be honest, once your husband came bursting into my town house when I was sick from the allergic reaction, scaring my poor mother half to death, and then I found out what he'd done to you, kicking you out because of some crazy accusations, I decided it was time to move on." Jeff shrugged.

She did a double take. "What do you mean he came to your town house looking for you? He came to see you after he kicked me out?"

Shaking his head, Jeff replied, "The same day. He was shouting and yelling about how I had best stay away from his wife, and he wouldn't leave when my mom told him I was ill. He wouldn't leave until he saw how ill I was for himself."

Stunned and perplexed, she could hardly believe that Carlton had actually gone to confront Jeff after throwing her out. Each and every one of the emotions that ran through her head must have shown on her face.

"I probably should have told you back then. But honestly, after the way he kicked you out, I really thought he didn't deserve you. Are you okay?" Jeff touched her arm reassuringly.

"I'm fine, I'm just...I just hadn't known that Carlton went to your place that day. That he'd seen how sick you were."

"Yeah." Never one for somberness, Jeff teased. "So, how is the newest little *Harry?* I guess I need to think of a nice descriptive name for him, huh?"

"I don't think so. You can call him Terrence," she said in mock admonishment as she playfully wagged her finger at him.

"Hey, *Harry-Terry.* How does that sound?" Jeff rubbed his hand across his chin in mock consideration.

"Sounds like you want a nice pop upside the head," she warned as she smiled at her friend. "You know, I want to pay you back the money you gave to help me. You were a good friend to me and I'll never forget it." She took a sip of her water.

Jeff waved his hand dismissively. "Your money's no good here. Just keep it somewhere safe in case you ever need to make a quick getaway. And know that you've got a friend with deep pockets if you ever need help like that again."

"But, Jeff, that was a lot of money. I have to—"
Cutting her off, he admonished, "No, no, no."
She shook her head. "Fine, but—"
Jeff arched his eyebrow and gave her a weary stare.
Seeing that she was fighting a losing battle, Latonya decided to just enjoy lunch with an old friend.

Carlton glanced at his sister-in-law pleadingly as she sat there with her arms folded across her chest. He had asked Cicely to meet him at Soka's for lunch so that she could help him figure out how to make things right with Latonya. Clearly, Cee Cee wasn't going to help him. He was on his own.

After squirming in his seat the entire meal and making case after case for himself, Cicely just stared at him with that icy glare that the Stevens women must've had a patent on. Just as he was about to say thanks for at least agreeing to see him, Cicely spoke.

"I really shouldn't offer you any advice at all, bro. You messed up big time. And you broke your promise to me." Cicely let out an exaggerated sigh. "But I'm feeling generous. Who knows why? First, I need to know, do you love my big sister?"

Carlton's lip dropped. "Can't you tell? Of course I do."

Sighing in exasperation, Cicely replied, "Sometimes we women need to hear the words, bro. So tell me, do you love her?"

Staring his sister-in-law in the eye so that there would be no misunderstanding, Carlton stated, "Yes, I love Latonya."

Cicely smiled and shook her head. "Well, like I said, I'm feeling generous, but I can't give you any confidential information. Can't break the sister-to-sister code of ethics, you understand. But I will say this. You might want to consider starting with a simple apology."

Carlton couldn't believe that was the advice Cicely offered. "What? That won't work, Cee Cee. Plus, anyone can see that I know I was wrong. That's why I want to make it up to her. That's why I'm here having lunch with you. Hoping you will give me some good advice about how to win your sister's heart again. Trust me, 'I'm sorry' is not a big enough gesture."

Cicely smirked at him and spoke in a tone that suggested she thought he was more than a little dense. "Like I said, bro, sometimes women need to hear the words. *You* need to figure out why you can't say them."

Indignant, Carlton argued, "I can say them!"

Tilting her head defiantly, Cicely challenged, "Say them, then. Go ahead, say them."

"I don't have any reason to say them to you," Carlton mumbled.

"I rest my case," Cicely said gleefully as she took a sip of her iced tea.

"You haven't made a case," Carlton grumbled. He glanced around the slowly emptying restaurant and did a double take. Latonya was there with Jeff Weatherby. *Talk about déjà vu.*

Cicely noticed his stare and asked wryly, "Tell me you're not going to do anything crazy or stupid."

Carlton smiled. "Actually, I'm not. I owe that man a thank-you. He helped my wife when she needed it." He took out some bills and placed them on the table. "Thanks for your help, Cee Cee."

Latonya couldn't believe it when Carlton came waltzing up to their table.

"Hello, Latonya, Jeff," he offered calmly.

"Hi, Carlton," Latonya responded.

"Hello," Jeff added, a slightly startled look crossing his face.

Carlton took a deep breath. If Latonya didn't know any better, she would have thought that he was nervous. But surely Carlton wouldn't have been nervous.

"So, I saw you two having lunch and I wanted to come over and personally thank you, Jeff, for all that you did to help Latonya when she needed it." The sincerity in Carlton's voice caused Latonya's eyes to widen.

Momentarily shocked, Jeff responded, "No problem, man. I was glad to help. That's what friends are for."

Carlton nodded. "Well, I'm just glad that she had someone in her corner during her time of need. I'd like to repay—"

Jeff cut him off. "Like I just told Latonya, you can put it in a trust fund for little Har…Carl and Terrence."

Carlton shook his head as he considered it and smiled. "We'll do that. Thanks, again." He turned to Latonya. "I'll see you later at home. Enjoy the rest of your lunch." He paused. "I love your new hairstyle."

As her husband walked off, Latonya looked around for traces of the pea pod. Surely body snatchers had invaded him. Because there was no way he had just walked up to their table and thanked *Jeff Weatherby* for helping her!

She could barely finish the rest of her lunch as she pondered the implications of Carlton's changes.

Chapter 22

Latonya spent the next few weeks hanging out with both her sons and making up for lost time being a mother to little Carl. They played hide-and-seek. They built things with blocks. They ran around outside and got *really* dirty. And she loved it all.

Pamela had pretty much decided that until Latonya felt securely bonded with both her children again, she would need to get some more crossword puzzles to fill in her time. Latonya didn't have the heart to tell her that she might as well get a lifetime supply. She intended to spend as much time with her sons as possible.

Carlton pretty much kept his distance and let the three of them bond and connect. Both Harrington men seemed to be giving her the space and time she needed to be with her boys. She'd caught the elder Harrington watching her with her sons on several occasions.

She shrugged away the elder Harrington's unusual behavior. However, she'd started to feel a little apprehensive about Carlton's absence. The first couple of weeks, while she still fumed at him, she welcomed his distance, cherished it, even. As time passed by, her temper ebbed and she found herself wanting his company, wanting him to play hide-and-seek with her and the boys.

He needed to make up for as much time with Terrence as she needed to make up for with little Carl. She didn't like the fact that he probably stayed away simply to give her space.

No sooner than she began to contemplate his absence, however, her grace period ended. While she read the boys a story one afternoon, Carlton walked in looking strikingly handsome and behaving in a manner that made him *almost* endearing.

"Daddy!" Barely containing his excitement at seeing his father, Terrence leaped from the sofa and jumped right into Carlton's arms.

Picking up the child and hugging him close, Carlton kissed his small cheeks. "Hello, son."

"Hey, Daddy, come read a story with us. Mommy can finish hers and then you can read us one." Little Carl didn't leave her side, but the high timbre of his voice exhibited his happiness at seeing his dad.

"Okay." Carlton walked over to the sofa and sat down right beside Latonya, holding Terrence on his lap.

So near their bodies touched, Latonya took a deep

breath before continuing *The Little Engine that Could.*
Each time she read the words with Carlton sitting so
close, she thought, *I think I can. I think I can. Stop my
intense reactions to this man.*

The smile on his face, the way he held on to their
son, and the way he responded to the reading with as
much glee as the kids, all made her heart flutter. And
his nearness, the way his muscular thigh and arm
pressed against her own, the smell of his woodsy
cologne, and the way his arm brushed against her chest
when he pointed out one of the illustrations to the
boys, made her so sexually aware of him, she found
herself stuttering at different points just to get the
words out.

Not fairing much better when it came time for him
to read *The Ugly Duckling,* she could barely follow the
story. His deep, rumbling voice had her just as captivated as the kids. However, she was captivated for all
the *wrong* reasons.

When he finally finished reading, she had to pull her
gaze away lest he catch her drooling over him. *That
wouldn't be good at all.* She could not fall for him again.
Even though she had decided not to leave and to remain
under the same roof, she told herself that they were
together for the kids and that was all. Also, she would
never be able to really trust him after what he'd done.

"Can we have snacks now, Mommy?" Little Carl
put on his most angelic face.

Blinking away her momentary daydream, she responded, "I don't want you to spoil your appetites
before you have dinner."

"It won't spoil our appetite. We promise." Already the little negotiator, little Carl pleaded their case.

"Okay. Walk, don't run, into the kitchen and ask Miss Jillian if she will give you and your brother a little bit of fruit to hold you over until dinner." She patted her son's head and smiled.

"I want cookies." Terrence had an aversion to both fruits and vegetables and joined in the negotiations with his own desires.

Turning to her youngest, Latonya smiled. "Well, you will have fruit or you will have nothing and wait until dinner."

Not willing to forgo a snack, little Carl climbed down from the sofa and waited for his brother. "Come on, Terry. Let's go get a snack."

Reluctant, Terrence climbed down from his father's lap and followed his brother.

Once the boys were out of the room, Latonya made a move to get up from the sofa, but Carlton placed his hand on her thigh. She turned to face him.

"I enjoyed that," he murmured.

"Me, too. You know, I feel like I have been hogging the boys all to myself. And…well…if you'd like to spend time with them—you know, father-son time with them—I'm fine with that." Her voice fluttered.

He really needs to remove his hand from my thigh, pronto. "You should be getting to know Terrence. Even though it is clear that he's already smitten with you. He's all, *Daddy! Mommy, who?*"

"Oh, yeah, like little Carl isn't all about his mother. He didn't even bother to get up and give me a hug hello because it would have meant him leaving your side for a minute." Carlton laughed. "But it's good. I'm glad they both know that they have a mother and a father who love them. For the record, I'd love to spend more father-and-son time with them. I would also like for us to spend more times like this, together as a family."

Her breath caught in her throat and she struggled to exhale. Trying to process if she could possibly spend more moments in close proximity to her very sexy, suddenly very sweet husband, she knew without a question she would be a goner if she did. Even though he exhibited all the signs of a changed man, she knew he had a way to go before she would be ready to try again with him. He had to apologize first.

Before she could think of a suitable response, he continued, "If that's going to be a problem for you, then you can just let me know. I don't want to cause you any stress or anything." The sincerity of his words was unmistakable.

Having him sitting so near wreaked havoc on her senses. She didn't know what to say or how to say it. Irritated that he still had the power to affect her in such an overwhelming way, she tried to quickly process the ramifications of that fact. Again, he left little time for her response, eerily in tune with her very conflicted dilemma.

"It's probably too soon for you. I understand. Take your time." Giving her a thigh a soft squeeze, he got up from the sofa.

Only after Carlton had left the room did her breathing return to normal.

Chapter 23

Knowing full well that his wooing-process and therefore his progress with Latonya was moving slowly, Carlton felt no need to rush. He'd rushed things with her before and he didn't want their relationship to end up like it had then.

Often he found himself wishing he had taken more time to court her properly. Maybe then they both would have been a little more secure in their relationship. Back then, he'd felt they had all the time in the world for her feelings to catch up with his, and he didn't want to let her go before that happened. Right now, he found himself in a similar situation, but this time he was determined that her feelings for him be in line with his feelings for her before he pushed the relationship further. There would be no rushing this time.

He felt that the strain was ebbing and Latonya was slowly opening herself up to at least consider the possibility of them starting over again. She hadn't said anything else about leaving. He felt confident that they were on the right track. After the lunch incident with Jeff and their experience reading to the boys, Carlton had a feeling that he might be able to move to the next level soon and ask Latonya out on a date.

That day he'd come home to find Latonya and the children all in the kitchen, covered with flour and making more of a mess than the chocolate-chip-walnut cookies they claimed to be making.

The boys asked him to help out. After searching Latonya's face to make sure she'd be fine with it, he agreed.

Soon covered with flour and gook himself, he stood behind her as she stirred the batter, and he could have sworn he heard her breath catch. Inhaling the smell of her shampoo and perfume made his stomach tighten into a painful knot. She smelled better than the cookies baking in the oven. He quickly moved from behind her when other parts of his body naturally responded to being so close. He'd seen her in some of the finest gowns and jewels imaginable, but she had never looked better to him than she did right then in the pale pink cotton shorts, white T-shirt and cookie dough.

He took a seat at the table with his sons. With the

second batch of cookies mixed, she walked over to the table and they each took turns dropping batter on the metal baking sheet.

He made the boys laugh by placing big blobs of cookie dough on the sheet.

"Yours is going to be ugly, Daddy," little Carl said as he placed his own little round drops on the cookie sheet.

"Yeah, Daddy. You no doing the way Miss Jillian say." Terrence tried to mimic his older brother's perfect balls of dough.

"Well, we'll see what you two say when my nice big delicious cookies come out. I bet you both are going to want them. But, I'm going to say no. They're ugly. You don't want these." Teasing his sons, he plopped another big drop of dough on the sheet.

Smirking, Latonya mumbled something under her breath.

He stopped teasing his sons and turned to his wife. "You have something you want to add, smarty pants?"

She laughed. "Nope. I was just thinking that you'd be lucky if those big blobs of dough even cook all the way through."

"Oh. Now you want to insult the cook. Well, don't you come near my cookies when they're done, either. You're all banned. Just stick to your little nice perfect cookies and leave the original, fantastic cookies to me."

"Fine with us," she said as she took the cookie sheet and placed it in the oven.

He and the boys worked on filling another cookie

sheet with dough while she took the first batch out of the oven and placed them on the rack to cool down.

When she walked back over to pick up the next cookie sheet, she laughed. "Who knew you could make them properly."

Smiling, he shrugged his shoulders. Standing and handing the next cookie sheet to his wife, he said, "Well, I figured you guys weren't ready for my unique style. So, I decided to make cookies the boring way."

"Well, thank goodness. These just might be edible." Laughing, she took the cookie sheet from his hand.

Joining in her laughter, he placed a blob of dough on her cheek.

Putting the cookie sheet down and wiping her face, she gave him a menacing look. "Oh! I know you don't want a food fight, because you won't win. I'll have you know I was queen of the food fight in Mrs. Miller's fifth-grade class."

"Woooo, I'm so scared, I'm shaking," he said before he smeared another piece of dough on her other cheek. Backing away, he admired his artwork.

"Oh! Now it's on!" Grabbing a handful of dough, she approached him.

"Okay. Okay. I was only playing. Can't you take a joke? Ha, ha. Right, boys? Tell Mommy I was only playing." He backed farther away from her slow and calculating approach.

"Oh, no! Mommy's gonna get you, Daddy," little Carl chanted.

"Get Daddy, Mommy, get Daddy," Terrence screamed playfully.

"Hey, you guys are supposed to be on my side. Us Harrington men need to stick together."

"Not today, buddy. You're going down." Taking a giant leap, she raised her dough-filled hand.

As soon as she raised her hand, Carlton grabbed it and the dough plopped on the ground. "Oh, no, food-fight-queen, looks like you've lost your weapon." He let her arm go and pulled her close to him, holding her close by keeping his arm around her waist. Using his free hand, he wiped off the remaining cookie dough from her cheeks.

Something about holding her so close and touching her face made his head tilt, and before he knew it he kissed her.

Her lips felt so soft. Even though he'd vowed to himself to take things slow this time, he couldn't help intensifying the kiss. When her mouth opened, he took that as a welcoming and allowed his tongue to examine her sweetness. It had been *too* long.

He pulled her closer and the moan that escaped her lips made his hands shake.

"Oh-oh, Daddy bite Mommy. Look, Daddy bite Mommy!" Terrence exclaimed, his little eyes wide with disgust.

"He's not biting. He's giving mommy a kiss, a yucky grown-up kiss," little Carl explained.

"No kissy my mommy!" Terrence climbed down from the chair he sat on and grabbed Latonya's leg.

Carlton made a mental note to have a nice long talk with both his sons about interruptions.

Backing away, Latonya was careful not to step on

Terrence, who was still clutching her leg. She softly nibbled her lower lip as she stared at Carlton. Her eyes narrowed and then she pursed her lips ever so slightly.

Carlton swore if she did one more thing with her lips he would kiss her again. He mentally kicked himself for not following his plans to take it slow.

"Something is stinking." Wrinkling up his nose, little Carl frowned.

"Yeah, something stink-stink," Terrence added.

Latonya turned away from him and rushed to the oven to get the burning batch of cookies before the house caught on fire.

Jillian will never allow any of us into the kitchen again, Carlton thought as he walked over to help Latonya get the cookies out of the oven. As he studied the charcoal circles that were supposed to be cookies, he couldn't help but start laughing.

Latonya looked up at him as she tried to pry the cookies off the sheet and rolled her eyes before busting out laughing herself.

Hearing her laugh again made his heart pound with possibility.

As the elder Harrington stood outside the kitchen door watching his grandson and his family laughing and enjoying themselves, he wondered how long it would last. After all, the girl had already so much as admitted that she planned to leave Carlton.

The girl still hadn't told Carlton about his role in making her leave. The elder Harrington knew there had to be a catch. She had to be holding it over him, waiting until the right moment. He knew the day Carlton brought her home that she would be the reason for him losing his grandson. And he had been right.

It didn't even seem worth it to try to break them up again. Carlton was already too taken with the girl. Clearly he would forgive the woman anything. The man was just like his father in that regard.

He had watched her with the boys. She did seem to be a good mother. He couldn't begrudge her that. She clearly loved the children. But it wasn't really the children he worried about. It was Carlton.

"What are you doing out here, Mr. Harrington? Why don't you go in?" The nanny, Pamela, snuck up on him and almost caused him to have a heart attack.

"Why are you sneaking up on people?" the elder Harrington snapped. He was getting tired of these women forgetting their place! "I just stopped by for a visit. They look like they're having a good time. I didn't want to interrupt." He started walking off down the hall.

"Mmm-hmm." Pamela eyed him suspiciously as she followed him.

Taken aback, he turned and faced the woman. She was an attractive woman from the Caribbean who usually knew her place. That she would deign to question him or imply anything about his actions was not acceptable! "What are you mmm-hmming about?"

"Well, I know it's not my place, but I just have to speak my mind. I know you don't care for Latonya. But she really is a lovely woman, a great mother. Before that horrible misunderstanding she was a loving and devoted wife." She hesitated only briefly as she spoke. "I guess I'm saying that if my son were to bring home a woman like Latonya, it wouldn't bother me a bit that she wasn't a Trinidadian. She's a good woman."

Her audacity outraged him. "What are you talking about, woman?"

"Well, I know that she felt like you couldn't really accept her because she is a black American and—"

Indignant, the elder Harrington snapped, "And you should mind your business!" There was a time when the help knew their place! They didn't speak their minds on family issues of no concern to them....

"I care about those boys and they need their mother, even if she barely lets me do the job I'm being paid for." The Trinidadian woman gave him a harsh glare. "And I think that not liking her because she's African-American is just ridiculous."

"Well, I don't care much for Trinidadians, either! Truth be told, most Trinidadians have a penchant for singing their words instead of speaking them," he said lashing out with one of the petty island insults he knew she would take offense to.

Far from backing down the way he intended her to, she narrowed her eyes. She came back with a little insult of her own. "Well, I think most Bahamians are way too conservative and carry all that early British influence way too far, but that's neither here nor there. The little rivalries that islands have against one another have nothing on the way some of us get on when we deal with our brothers and sisters over here."

Since there didn't seem to be any getting away from

the woman or her opinions, he offered, "For the record, my problems with the girl only have a little to do with her being an African-American. I just never thought she was the right woman for my grandson."

Pamela's eyes widened, and she stared at him as if he were senile. "Don't you see the way his eyes light up when she enters a room? Can't you see that even though he broke her heart, she is still here because the vows she took to that man mean something to her? The family she built with him means something to her. You'd have to be a blind old fool not to see that even though their love has been tested they are still trying to make it work."

His shoulders arched up in defiance, but her words had made their mark. There was no way he would admit it to her, however. "You're right. It really isn't your place! Good night." The elder Harrington walked off feeling sufficiently chastised. By the help no less!

Chapter 24

As she worked with Carlton to clean up the kitchen, Latonya thought about the kiss they'd shared. She hadn't been expecting it. And she certainly had no idea that it would affect her so. Her heart still raced, and it was all she could do to appear nonchalant and put away the now-clean bowls and cookie sheets.

That she was working side by side with the enemy floored her. But, then, she didn't feel as if Carlton was the enemy anymore. From his little thank-you speech to Jeff and the way they interacted as a family, Carlton had her feeling unbalanced in a good way. The surprise kiss that would have literally knocked her off her feet had they been alone and in a bedroom was just one example of the way her heart was thawing out and starting to anticipate his next move.

Her body began to tingle as she thought about the way his lips caressed hers and the soft tender draw of his tongue. Latonya found herself biting her lower lip just to keep from moaning again. She wondered if she could trust Carlton enough to give their relationship another chance. Could they really work it out this time?

No sooner than she had the thought, she heard Carlton clear his throat. "Well. I think we've done all we can here. We'll just have to hope that Jillian won't be able to detect the mess that this place was a little while ago."

She laughed. "Well, hopefully the burnt cookie smell will be gone by then."

He sniffed. "I don't think we'll be that lucky."

"Oh, she'll get over it in a couple of weeks and let us back in. Especially once Terrence says, 'Miss Jillian, can we please bake more cookies?' She'll be putty in his hands."

He chuckled. "Yeah, my sons do have the trademark Harrington charm. It's pure Bahamian and potent. Strong. Women can't resist it."

She gazed at him, standing there looking so good and damn it, charming. Her throat suddenly tightened. "Oh, really, is that what they're calling it these days? I guess they'll just have to depend on their mother to teach them how to use their charming powers for good and not evil."

"You can try, but the charm has a mind of its own." He walked over to her.

Blasted charm! Her heart skipped a beat at the same time that his hand reached out and caressed her cheek.

"So, I was wondering how you would feel about us spending some time getting to know each other again.

Possibly going out catching a show, having dinner. You know."

"You mean like dating?"

"I was thinking more along the lines of courtship. But, yes, I mean if you feel that you're ready for something like that."

"I don't think I'm ready. I don't know if I'll ever be ready." *Who knew lying came so easily?*

"Well, your lips tell quite a different story, Tonya," he offered wryly.

Letting out a nervous chuckle, she replied saucily, "My lips? What do they know?"

"They know how to lie. And they know that they want to kiss me." Leaning over, he turned her face to him. "If you don't want me to kiss you then say so, Latonya. Tell me."

The intensity of his gaze made her turn numb. She couldn't move or say a word, not one blasted word. The little word *no* refused to come out. She opened her mouth but no sound came. Her throat suddenly parched—dry as sandpaper—she swallowed.

When he leaned closer, she could feel his breath; she inhaled.

"All you have to say is no. Can't you say it?" He peered at her with hooded eyes. "No. You can't." His lips brushed hers. "Can you?"

As he touched his lips to hers again, she felt him suck in his breath and shudder as his arms reached to grip her shoulders.

"Time's up," he whispered before darting his tongue in her mouth.

She'd known that she could still be floored by his kisses, *but damn*. She leaned into his muscular strength and moaned. Her whole body ignited and came alive as if she'd been waiting for his touch.

"Mmm." Wondering if it was her humming and purring, she wrapped her arm around his neck.

His tongue wrapped around hers and she felt her body tingle. Hands caressed her, brushing lightly across her breast and the small of her back. Each place he touched sent tingling sensations that assaulted her senses and whipped them up into a whirlwind.

Instinctively, she leaned back and braced herself against the kitchen counter and he followed. The weight of his body felt so right pressed up against hers. His lips never left hers. The hands that were once content to brush and lightly touch now feverishly lifted the casual cotton T-shirt she wore. The feel of his hands on her skin sent a trail of goose bumps every place he touched.

Moaning, when she felt his erection press against her inner thigh, she paused momentarily. *What am I doing? I am about to have sex with my husband. In the freaking kitchen! No way can I let this happen.*

As if he sensed her hesitancy, he halted the kiss. Then, drawing a ragged breath that sounded as if he pulled it deep from within his gut, he moved away.

"Well, I know for sure you are not ready for what was about to come next." Inching back, giving her much-needed distance, he leaned against the opposite counter and stared at her, the desire in his eyes unmistakable.

Latonya eyed him and her mind went immediately to the firm muscles that were just within her arms' reach and the broad shoulders that were just perfect for grabbing hold of. She couldn't help but chew on her bottom lip a little as she soaked him in.

"If you keep doing that, I swear I'm going to kiss you again." Carlton's eyes sparkled with passion and need.

Wondering if she was making the right decision while knowing that she couldn't make any other, Latonya tilted her head and bit her lip before speaking. "Okay, Carlton. I'll date you."

Chapter 25

Deciding to go back downstairs later and check on Jillian, Latonya found her in the kitchen sitting at the table having a cup of tea and nibbling on one of the less crispy cookies.

"Hello, Miss Jillian. How was your afternoon with Gran?"

"It was fine. We had a good talk over lunch."

Latonya remembered just how the women spent their time together—discussing everything and everyone. "I bet you did."

"Have a seat, baby. You want me to get you some tea?"

"That's okay, I can get it. Would you like me to refresh your hot water?" Latonya never really got used to having servants, especially since it was work Gran used to do. And she certainly wasn't going to have a woman who could be her grandmother get up and make her a cup of tea.

Jillian gave her a smile. "Oh, that would be lovely. Thank you, baby."

After making the tea, Latonya sat down in the chair at the table and smiled as Jillian turned to look at her.

"Girl, it's so good to have you back here. I missed you something fierce."

"I missed you, too, Miss Jillian. It was hard being away from all of you. At the time, I couldn't think of another way."

Putting down her teacup and placing her hand over Latonya's, Jillian gave her a meaningful stare. "I know, child. You don't have to prove anything to me. I was here that day." Jillian's voice took on a somber tone. "I saw what happened. You did what you had to do at the time." Jillian's normally bright, smiling face dropped, and Latonya could tell that she regretted not being able to help. It must have torn up a feisty woman such as Jillian to think that she hadn't been able to stop what happened.

Latonya reached out and touched Jillian's hand reassuringly. She knew that Jillian had done the best she could.

After spending time with both her children, she'd come to think differently about her own actions, however. "I should have stayed and fought for my child."

"Your world was ripped from under you in a matter of seconds because of something you didn't do."

Clearly Jillian wasn't going to let Latonya feel guilt any more than Latonya was willing to allow Jillian to shoulder any. "You did well to find a way to take care of yourself and Terrence. People who come from where we come from don't think about going up against the rich and powerful." Taking a sip of her tea, Jillian shook her head.

"I've known Carlton almost all his life. He was a sweet little boy. Losing his parents was hard on him. For a while I didn't think he'd ever recover enough to reach out in a real way to another person. But the day he brought you home for the first time, the look on his face, I could tell that he had finally met his match." Jillian reached over and patted Latonya's hand again.

Chuckling, Latonya replied, "I don't know, Miss Jillian. I don't think I'm any match for Carlton Harrington III. And I know for a fact that I was *way* out of my league that first night."

"That's because you didn't know what to look for. The man was so smitten with you he didn't know what to do. He even forgot every lick of home training and manners I tried to teach him." Smiling a knowing smile, Jillian continued, "No I wasn't surprised when you all continued to see each other. The quick wedding and pregnancy didn't even surprise me. When I looked at Carlton that night, I could tell that he wanted you and he meant to have you."

Latonya took a sip of her tea. "Yeah. Well, we see how that turned out."

"Oh, he didn't kick you out because he didn't want you anymore. He kicked you out because he was scared. Scared that what had happened between his mother and father would happen between the two of you." Jillian slapped her hand on the table to emphasize her point. "He threw you out because he thought that he could make you leave and it would hurt less than if you left him on your own."

Intrigued, Latonya looked up from her tea because she'd never heard anything about what Carlton's parents were like. No one in the family ever spoke about what kind of people they were. The only thing she knew was that they'd died in a plane crash. No wonder their marriage didn't work out. They didn't know each other. A sense of sadness overcame her at the realization and she felt an odd lump forming in her throat.

She took a sip of her tea, hoping it would help her to be able to speak without her voice cracking. "What happened between his mother and father? I thought they died together in an airplane crash?"

"They did. But it was the reason that they were together in that plane that haunts Carlton until this day." Jillian then told Latonya the most heartbreaking tale.

Carlton's parents had an awful marriage and it had left him scarred. Latonya's heart automatically ached for the fifteen-year-old Carlton. *No wonder he always felt like a kindred spirit,* Latonya thought ruefully. *We'd both been traumatized by our parents' doomed marriages.*

She felt the lump growing a little bigger in her throat; in fact she could now feel it in her chest. She had shared some of her messed-up childhood with Carlton on their first night together. Yet he had kept his past firmly locked away. No wonder Carlton didn't trust her, he probably couldn't.

"Miss Jillian, this means he will probably never really trust me. So, we'll never be able to work things out between us. Our marriage is as doomed as his parents' was."

"I wouldn't say that, child. Truth be told, his mommy issues are no worse than your daddy issues." Giving her a pointed stare, Jillian continued. "You *both* have some things to work through if you're going to make it last."

Blinking several times, Latonya balked. "Daddy issues? I don't have daddy issues."

Or did she? She just dealt with life as it came. Could she help it if time and time again life proved itself true to course and the men she loved ended up rejecting her love? That wasn't her issue. Was it? How could it be?

"Little girl, Evelyn Stevens has told me all about her no-good son who ran off and left his wife to take care of two little girls." Jillian would have none of Latonya's denial. "Your mama worked so hard to care for you and Cicely that she worked herself into an early grave. And even then your daddy didn't come and see about his children. Left his mama to raise you both!"

Jillian had gotten a little too close for comfort. Everything had been fine when she filled Latonya in on the background of Carlton's life, but Latonya could do without the in-depth psychoanalysis of her own life.

"My goodness, Miss Jillian! What don't you and

Gran talk about? My situation and Carlton's situation are two different things." Trying to bring the subject back to Carlton, Latonya found herself in no way ready or willing to face her own past. "Besides, I trusted him, until he kicked me out and made me leave little Carl. He clearly *never* trusted me and now I know why. It was because of the image he had of women from his mother. He saw her be unfaithful to his father and he figured no woman could remain faithful."

"Oh. And you didn't bring any baggage from your own relationship with your father?" Jillian refused to let her change the focus. "Because from the outside looking in, I saw two people who were too scared to really give their entire selves to each other, both of them holding back because they were afraid of being hurt, of being left alone." She shook her head sadly. "By the looks of things, the two of you haven't learned anything from the past. You still think that because of what happened between your own parents that you have some sort of destiny not to have real love in your lives.

"You're spending your entire time together waiting for the other shoe to drop. You've got to open up your hearts fully, face the fear and learn to trust. Or else you're right that you won't make it. And what kind of legacy will that leave for those two precious little boys?"

Suddenly filled with more hopelessness than she'd ever felt, Latonya felt the ever-growing lump well up. She had agreed to go out with Carlton and spend time getting to know each other again. But they hadn't known each other at all to begin with. How could she have loved him so deeply and not known the pain he carried? Latonya's heart felt as if it were going to explode in her chest. She realized that even though all signs pointed to them not being able to work it out, she wanted their marriage to work. She wanted it, and the thought that she might not be able to have it left her colder than the tea in front of her.

"I think it may be too late already, Jillian. He never trusted me. I can't say, after the way he treated me, that I will ever be able to fully trust him."

"He regretted what he did the minute he did it. I hadn't seen that man cry since he was a toddler. He sobbed serious tears that day. He went looking for you at Evelyn's." Jillian slapped the table again. "He was probably going to beg you to forgive him. You weren't there. And, you never showed up. I think your disappearance was too familiar, felt too much like what used to happen with his mom, so he just stewed in anger for the past three years until little Carl said he didn't want anything for his birthday but his mother."

Latonya couldn't help but smile at the mention of her child. "Yes, Carlton told me that. However, I don't think he would have apologized back then. He *still* hasn't apologized for anything that happened."

Jillian reached over and patted Latonya's hand as she said ruefully, "Well, he *is* a Harrington. We'll have to go through another pot of tea on another night for me to fill you in on the background there, fill you in on what happens when a man bitter about losing his only son has to raise his only grandson."

Taking a sip of tea, she sighed before continuing. "This isn't an easy family you married into, child. If anyone can handle it, you can. The fact is this house has known so much joy since you stepped foot in it, and even when you were gone, you left such a gift in little Carl." Jillian paused for a moment and moved her hand to her chest, patting it lightly.

"You gave Carlton a hope that he couldn't have imagined. That's what I saw on his face the first night that let me know he was a goner. I saw it again when he walked in here with you at his side after three years away. He has hope." Jillian chuckled mischievously. "It's scaring the crap out of him and he will probably mess up a lot before it is all said and done, but he's hoping that the two of you are going to be able to make it work this time. I'd put my life's savings on that fact."

Shrugging, because the years had taught her she couldn't win an argument with self-assured and determined older women like Miss Jillian, Pamela and Gran, Latonya simply said, "Well, I haven't seen it. I guess I'm not as perceptive and wise as you, Gran and Pamela."

"That's right! You're too young to really know it when you see it. Shoot! You don't even know it and you're feeling it yourself! But don't worry. I think the two of you will come around in time."

"If you say so." Latonya took a sip of the now-cold tea.

"I know so." Jillian hit the table with a firm slap as if to reaffirm her point.

Chapter 26

"It's just a date," Latonya mumbled, shaking her head. She'd decided she wasn't going to build up too many expectations for her evening with Carlton.

Sitting in the backyard with Jillian and Pamela, Latonya watched as her sons played together. She also hoped that the two women would stop teasing her about her plans for the evening.

"A date, my behind," Jillian teased. "I can see that this is more than just a date. It's your new beginning with your husband."

"I think it's so romantic," Pamela sighed. "Do you know what you're going to wear? Where is he taking you?"

"I don't know what I'm going to wear. Maybe a dress or something. We're just going to grab a bite to

eat and catch a movie. We want to keep it simple."
Although Latonya hadn't had a lot of experience in
dating before she met and married Carlton, she did
think that dinner and a movie was about as normal a
date as any.

"That sounds nice. Make sure you pick a scary one
so that you can jump into his arms during the fright-
ening scenes," Pamela advised, laughing.

"No, pick a romantic one to set the mood," Jillian
offered with a wink.

"You ladies are too much. We are going to see a new
romantic comedy. So there won't be any jumping into
arms or setting of any moods. Just a nice light evening." Latonya shook her head. She couldn't decide
which pair was worse, double-trouble, as she affection-
ately called the Jillian-and-Gran team or two-for-the-
trouble, the name she'd given the Jillian and Pamela
combination. She decided that pairing the opinionated
Jillian with anyone would probably end up being some
kind of *trouble*. But she liked it. It was good having
people around her who cared.

"Mommy! Terry won't play fair!" little Carl
screamed from across the yard.

Latonya sighed. Most of the time her two boys got
along fabulously. However, there were times when their
strong-willed little personalities surfaced at the same
time and they butted heads. She rose out of her chair to
settle the dispute, but Pamela stayed her with a quick arm.

"Oh, no you don't. I'll handle it. Go get ready for
your date," Pamela advised.

"But I have several hours before then," Latonya

offered. She wanted to stay outside with her sons. Even though the women couldn't seem to stop talking about the date, their company still gave her a reason not to pace the floor, obsessing about it.

"Read a book or something," Jillian offered. "Let us do our jobs."

Latonya almost reminded Jillian that it wasn't her job to watch over the boys, but figured arguing with her would be about as fruitful as trying to stay there when the women clearly felt she should be making better use of her time.

So she let Pamela handle the boys and she went back inside. Deciding to do a little reading to keep her mind off the date, she went into the study and curled up on the plush sofa.

The mystery novel she started with the savvy, hard-hitting sistah-sleuth was just getting good when she heard a slight stir and looked up.

Old man Harrington! Great! She closed her book and studied the elder Harrington carefully as he stood in the doorway. He still hadn't told Carlton the truth. She guessed that he probably never would. She wasn't about to allow him to ruin her day.

"May I speak with you for a moment?" he asked hesitantly.

She offered an exaggerated sigh as she rested her book on the side table. "Since I doubt I'd be able to stop you, sure. What do you want, old man?"

He walked over and sat in the sofa opposite her. "I understand you and Carlton have a date tonight."

"Yes, we do. And I am not canceling it. So, if you have come here to try to warn me away from him, then—"

He cut her off. "No! That's not what I meant. I'm glad that you two are trying to work things out. I think it's for the best."

Latonya did a double take as she tried to figure out what new angle the elder Harrington was clearly trying to work. "Yeah, right! Save it, okay? You know, I really could care less what you think! I know you don't like me and that's fine. Just refrain from threatening my family and trying to ruin my relationship with my sons or their father and we will be cool. You stay in your place and I'll stay in mine."

The elder Harrington appeared as if he were going to get up and leave for minute. But he paused instead. He leaned forward and an earnest expression came across his face. "It wasn't ever really about not liking you. I mean, yes, I do have certain prejudices about black Americans. I am working through those because I have come to realize that it hardly makes sense." He shook his head and continued, "Yes, I had hoped that my grandson would eventually settle with a nice, quiet Bahamian girl from a suitable family. I wanted to be able to control the situation so that I could keep him safe. If he married a girl from home, from a family I picked, then I would have been able to control her through her family.

"If Carlton wasn't as deeply in love with the woman then she couldn't hurt him the way… I could see how much he loved you and I could also see right away that

I wouldn't be able to really control you, or your family. Well, can you imagine anyone trying to control that Evelyn? Or even Cicely? That's a spunky one. You did a good job with her, by the way."

"I didn't raise Cee Cee. Gran raised us—"

"I had you checked out a long time ago, girl. I know that your father left and your mom was sick most of the time. I know that your grandmother worked harder than any woman should have to. You took care of your sister. *You* mothered her. And seeing how she turned out…seeing the way you are with my great-grandsons…I just wanted to let you know that I know you're a good mother. It wasn't about me not thinking you were a good mother. I just didn't want history to repeat itself. The other one…that Anastasia…" He spit out Carlton's mother's name as if it would kill him to voice it. "I just knew that the way Carlton felt about you would leave him open for hurt and I wanted to spare him. I was afraid of losing him."

Latonya's heart softened toward the old man. Carlton's mother had certainly done a number on the Harrington men. "I understand that. But you need to understand that no good can come from mixing fear with love." Latonya had learned that the hard way. She'd spent her entire marriage to Carlton afraid that he was going to leave her the way her father did. Even though she loved Carlton her fear stopped her from having all that their love could have been. "You have to tell Carlton the truth. If you love him, you can't continue the lie."

"If I tell him he will cast me out and have nothing

else to do with me. I can't lose him. I can't lose my great-grandsons. I love those boys." The fearful expression on the elder Harrington's face showed how vulnerable he was.

Latonya knew that the truth had to come out. It was the only way for the entire family to really heal. She also knew that she would not be the one to tell Carlton. It had to come from the old man. "Carlton will be angry. He does have the Harrington temper. But he will eventually forgive you. You have to trust in the relationship you have. You won't lose him."

"I'll think about it. I just want to let you know that I'm sorry." His shoulders slumped and once again he looked every bit of his seventy-plus years. "I didn't really mean to hurt you, girl. I just wanted to try to save my grandson."

"Latonya," Latonya said her name clearly.

"What?" the elder Harrington asked in a perplexed manner.

"Well, if we are going to get off to a new start then you can stop calling me 'girl,' or 'that girl,' or 'the girl' and call me by my name." She tilted her head and smirked at him.

The older man smiled. "Can you see why I had no hopes of controlling you? Fine, Latonya, do you think that you can call me something besides 'old man'?"

Latonya smiled. "Maybe one day."

Latonya tested the knot on the cream silk wraparound dress she'd picked up at Frances's Boutique. It was simply made and hugged her curves nicely. She hoped it was casual enough for the date. While the dress could go either dressy or casual, the strappy little cream sandals she wore might have been a little too much. She debated changing them for some low-heeled pumps.

Her hair had grown a bit more. It still was nowhere near her shoulder-length, wavy mass, which meant she couldn't wear an updo. Soft curls framed her face.

She was just putting the finishing touches on her makeup when Carlton walked into her bedroom. She turned and her mouth dropped. He wore a pair of brown dress slacks and an off-white silk shirt. The first couple of buttons were undone and she could see just a hint of his sexy chest, enough to make her yearn to see more.

He held a red velvet jewelry box in his hand—a big one that looked like it housed a necklace.

"I want you to wear this tonight," he said as he opened the box.

She frowned, a sense of déjà vu overcame her. Lavishing her with clothes and jewels the way he had in the past wouldn't change things. She wouldn't allow herself to be lulled into a reconciliation with costly gifts. However, when she looked in the box, she couldn't contain her reaction as her mouth widened into an O. It was the most beautiful, most simple diamond necklace she had ever seen. Also inside the box was a pair of diamond studs like the ones he'd given her for their first anniversary. She had pawned the others to add to the money she'd needed to disappear.

The small, dainty necklace had three significantly

sized diamonds and a setting that appeared to be antique. She'd never seen anything so precious. "I can't wear that. Oh, my goodness, Carlton, what would make you buy something like that, something so expensive?"

"I didn't buy it. It belonged to my mother. It was the only thing in her collection that I thought you would like. Everything else was a bit much." Shrugging with a nonchalance she knew instinctively he could hardly feel about his mother or her jewelry, he removed the necklace and the earrings from the box and tossed the box on the dresser before walking over to her. "I meant to give it to you a long time ago."

Shaking her head, she gasped, "I can't take your mother's jewelry. This is an heirloom that should stay in the family."

"Are you planning to go somewhere anytime soon? The last time I checked, as my wife, you are a part of the Harrington family."

"I know, but, Carlton—"

Cutting her off, he said, "Just turn around so that I can put the necklace on you."

When he placed the jewelry around her neck, his fingertips trailed her neck. Goose bumps sprang up and she knew her skin must have been flaming red.

He handed her the earrings. "Your ears have been a little bare."

She took a deep breath and put the diamond studs on as he continued to stand behind her and watch her in the mirror. Taking her by the shoulders, he turned her around and took a sharp breath.

Gazing in his eyes, she saw what caused him to inhale so sharply. Desire.

He held her gaze, and she was sure that he wanted her to see how much he desired her. The passion and need held in his stare made her breath catch.

"We'd better go," Carlton said. His slow steps toward the door let Latonya know without a doubt that he was as torn as she was.

She didn't know whether she should pull him into her arms and kiss him or go out on the date that they had agreed on.

As she followed him down the stairs, she gathered they had both decided to stick to the plans and go on the date.

They took one of Carlton's luxury cars instead of having a driver for the night. Twisting her hands the entire ride, she calmed herself by thinking about the boys and how she hoped that the date would be the start of a new beginning for their family.

Even though she felt silly hoping for it, the more she lived under the same roof with Carlton and their children, the more she wanted to be a family, wanted her husband to love her.

After talking with Jillian about Carlton's past and his parents' relationship, she felt less and less confident that they were going to be able to make it.

"Are you as nervous as I am?" Carlton asked.

Latonya laughed. "You would think we were in high school or something, huh?"

Carlton joined her in laughter as he pulled up to

Manny's, the Cuban restaurant that he'd taken her to on their first date. "I figured that this was as good a place as any for us to try to start over."

"Yes. It is, and this time, I'll order," Latonya offered with a smile.

Dinner went well, and Carlton felt himself relaxing just a little bit more with each moment of their date. He had a lot riding on getting it right this time. He planned to court and woo his wife properly. Even if it meant sitting through the latest romantic comedy that he would never have selected on his own. But Cee Cee told him that as hard-core as Latonya pretended to be, she had a soft spot for the lighthearted love stories.

Judging from the way Latonya's eyes stayed glued to the screen, Cicely was right. Oddly, Carlton even found himself being pulled into the story. He shocked Latonya and himself when he found himself talking aloud and coaching the hero in the film, "Oh, come on, man! Go after her!"

The two women sitting in front of them turned around and shushed him. Latonya leaned over and whispered, "Somebody is getting into this little, what did you call it, oh yes, chick flick."

Carlton put his arm around her as he filled his mouth with popcorn and continued to watch the film. He couldn't help it if the guy in the movie was an idiot and was on the verge of losing the love of his life.

They enjoyed the rest of the film in silence until

Latonya shouted out in frustration, "Oh, come on, girl. Forgive him! Can't you see that he loves you? Good grief!"

The women turned around and glared at them again.

"Sorry," Latonya whispered with a soft giggle.

Carlton pulled her close. "Don't worry. She'll forgive him," he whispered in her ear. "I don't know much about chick flicks, but I'm pretty sure these things always have a happy ending."

Chapter 27

Taking off her clothing, Latonya found herself doing a little spin. The date with Carlton had been perfect. She couldn't wait to go on another. In fact, she hadn't wanted the evening to end. When they finally returned from the movie she tried to think of an excuse to prolong the evening. The soft, seductive kiss that he'd given her at the bottom of the stairs just before he said he was going to head into the study to try to do a little work, told her that he'd had just as nice a time as she.

She stared aimlessly at the bed and her nightgown before reaching for the garment. She had to get her mind off of Carlton and his sweet kisses or she would toss and turn the entire night. *If* she got any sleep at all.

As soon as she reached for the gown, she heard the

bedroom door softly open and shut. Naked, she turned to find Carlton in her room. She quickly moved to put her nightgown on.

Carlton inhaled sharply. "Don't…do that." Taking three brisk steps, he stood directly in front of her. Removing the silk garment from her clasped hands, he let it fall to the ground. She turned toward the bed, not able to face the white-hot desire in his eyes when she knew that it matched her own. She also knew that giving into it wouldn't solve any of the problems between them.

His hand trailed her skin from her hips to her arms and shoulders. Bending his head into her neck, he inhaled deeply. His breath sent a shiver down her spine, and she swore she felt her heart skip a beat. She closed her eyes and leaned back into his embrace against her better judgment. Wrapping his arms around her, he caressed the front of her body. One hand found her nipple and the other traveled down her belly, farther still until two of his fingers entered the slick folds of her womanhood. She moaned and instinctively moved her hips in rhythm with his probing fingers.

Rising on her toes and leaning farther into him, she felt his erection pressing into her back. His hands slowly and methodically worked her body, and she felt the beginnings of her explosion working in the pit of her stomach. She sucked in her breath and shook as the tingling release shot from her stomach to her toes. Her knees buckled and her body went limp.

Letting her slide onto the bed, Carlton proceeded to trail soft kisses all over her body. Kisses followed by teasing nips that seemed to go on for hours. His mouth had a mind of its own as it trailed her body. First soft pecks. Then sensuous nibbling. Then torturous tongue flicks. His mouth found her breast, earlobes, wrists, ankles, inner thigh and then the core of her. Her body racked with another orgasm and she screamed.

Even in the middle of the most incredible orgasm she had ever had, her mind was at war with her body and her heart. Two parts of her wanted the man to love her and make love to her more than she wanted anything. And the other part, the thinking part, kept telling her she could have the lovemaking but she would never have the love. That's why her heart ached in the midst of such incredible splendor.

Everything became suddenly too intense, almost as if her body had been waiting for his touch to awaken it. She guessed, but she never really knew how much she missed him touching her and making love to her, until that moment. Every nerve ending in her body stood at full attention. And he, still fully clothed, continued to pay homage to her body with his luscious lips. Closing her eyes, and no longer having the ability to speak, she moaned softly.

He didn't say a word and she couldn't say a word. She realized that she didn't know what she would say. Wanting him so intensely, she willed him to continue licking and kissing and nipping. More than anything, she needed him inside of her with a desire so ferocious it scared her.

When the kisses stopped, the mattress lifted. She opened her eyes, and they immediately locked with his. His hooded gaze probed her as he removed his clothing.

She followed his strong hands with her eyes. Watched as they removed the shirt and gave her a full view of his glorious chest. The ripples beckoned her, and she wanted to run her hands across them.

The kicking off of his shoes and removal of his socks brought her gaze to his feet, and she nibbled on her lips just thinking about how sexy she still found them. She wanted to be his hands as they trailed down his firm washboard stomach before undoing his belt and removing his pants. As he stepped out of them, she relished the muscles in his thighs and imagined grabbing onto the muscular behind that she couldn't see but knew full well was there. Carlton's naked body was a sight to behold. And when she finished letting her eyes drink in every single dark-chocolate-with-a-smidgen-of-milk-covered muscle, she turned her gaze to his sexy, sensual eyes.

His eyes held hers and didn't leave her, even when he moved between her spread legs. She could feel the tip of his erection, but he made no move to penetrate. Remaining still and poised, he simply stared into her eyes.

He still wouldn't speak, and she thought for a frightened second that he wouldn't complete the act and end the sweet torture that he began on her body. She felt simultaneously wanton and panicked.

"Carlton…please."

"Are you sure you want this, Tonya?"

"Carlton—"

"I need you to tell me you want this, Tonya. Do you want me?"

"My, God, Carlton—"

When he inched away slightly, her eyes went wide.

"Okay, Carlton. Yes, I want this. I want you. Damn you!"

Moving forward, his erection teased her. He entered her then, fully, completely. She purred and his lips closed in on hers. With each thrust forward his tongue purged into her mouth, deeper and deeper each time.

Wrapping her legs around his waist, she arched her back, meeting his passion with her own. She circled her arms around him and held on for dear life. They continued without words until they both found release.

Carlton continued to plant soft kisses down her neck and behind her earlobes. He nibbled on her ear a bit before rolling over on his back. Pulling her close, he ran his fingers through her sweat-soaked hair. She felt him gently kiss the bridge of her nose just before she closed her eyes and snuggled into his embrace.

Staring at his wife while she slept peacefully in his arms, Carlton silently chastised himself. He'd done it again, moved too fast, made love to her before getting to a space where they were certain about each other. He'd promised himself that this time he would take greater care, practice restraint.

He'd come in the room because he hadn't wanted their evening to end. He figured they could talk or watch television or something that would have kept her in his presence just a little while longer. But seeing her wearing nothing made him remember all too fully what it had been like to touch her. He swore he felt a piece of heaven each time she was in his arms. He'd just wanted to hold her again and he ended up making love to her instead. He mentally kicked himself for not having the proper patience.

He didn't want to mess things up like he did before, by moving too fast. He'd wanted to woo her the way she deserved to be wooed. He needed her more than he needed air and was determined to do it right this time. Needing time to clear his head, he left the bed before she awoke and returned to the office.

Chapter 28

When Latonya woke up alone in the bed, she didn't know what to think. She'd thought for sure that Carlton would have at least woken her and given her a kiss goodbye before he left for work, the way he used to. Letting out a shuddering breath, she reminded herself that they were far from those days. He had left her in the bed alone just like he'd done the entire week before he kicked her out.

Having no idea where they stood at that moment, she figured she'd have to be a fool to think that just because they'd had sex, they were somehow back on track. Sex alone could not accomplish that.

The sex between them had always been glorious, but she knew that if great sex was all it took to keep a marriage together, they wouldn't have had problems in the first place. By allowing her body its desire, she had foolishly put her heart in peril again.

She loved Carlton, but he did not love her. She had to face that fact, as sobering as it was.

The phone on the nightstand started to ring and she leaped for it, thinking it was Carlton calling to say that he was sorry for leaving without waking her. They needed to talk. She dreaded where the conversation would lead, but she knew it had to happen. Answering the phone hesitantly, she found Gran on the other end of the line.

"Hey, Peanut. How are you?"

"Hi, Gran. I'm doing okay. How are you?"

"I'm fine, baby. I'm more than fine." Excitement pulsed from Gran's voice through the line. "Cicely is taking me on a Caribbean cruise. At first I was a little leery, because I've never been on a boat. But then I spoke to Jillian and she told me I wasn't getting any younger and I'd better start trying some new things. So, I said why not. I called Cicely and told her I'd go. We'll be gone for two weeks. We leave today."

Latonya had forgotten that Cicely had mentioned she wanted to surprise Gran with a cruise. Torn, she didn't know how to respond. On the one hand she felt happy that her sister was treating their grandmother to a much-needed vacation. On the other hand, she wanted to be leaving for the Caribbean with them. She wished she could just take the boys and head off on the cruise. Struck by the urgent need to get as far away from Carlton as she could, she knew that if she stayed she would end up heartbroken again.

But it wasn't her vacation and she didn't want to ruin her sister's and Gran's great time by taking all her problems and baggage on their trip.

She forced pleasantness in her voice and responded, "That's wonderful, Gran. I bet you and Cicely will have a fabulous time."

"Oh, we plan to. We plan to. I tried to call you and tell you the other day, but you must have been out and about with the boys. And Jillian told me that you had a hot date last night with Carlton. So, I didn't even bother to call then."

Not wanting to think about the hot date that ended up with her waking up to an empty bed, Latonya changed the subject. "So what time are you and Cicely leaving? I'd love to bring the boys down so that they could see. They'd get a kick out of seeing the boat leave the dock. Plus, I'd get a chance to say goodbye."

Latonya didn't think her grandmother's voice could become more gleeful, but it did.

"Oh, that's a wonderful idea. Then I can see my precious baby boys before I leave. The cruise docks off at three-thirty this afternoon."

"We'll be there."

"Oh, and one more thing, baby. Would you mind checking up on the house a couple of times while I'm gone? I know it's not much of a house, but it's my home."

"Of course, Gran. Don't worry. I'll be glad to check

on the house for you." A light bulb went off in her head. "Maybe I'll even house-sit until you get back."

"Oh, you don't have to do that. You stay at Carlton's home. No need for you to have to live in my little hovel when you can lay your head in his big home."

"No, Gran. It's my pleasure. You'd be doing me a favor. I need some time and a space to clear my head and think some things through, anyway. If I can't do it on a Caribbean cruise with the two of you, then I might as well do it in the place where I was raised." She smiled ruefully. Two weeks at Gran's house would be perfect.

"Are you and Carlton having problems? You could always come with us on the cruise, Peanut. Do you want us to call the trip off to help you?"

Troubled by the sudden worry in Gran's voice, Latonya forced an upbeat tone into her own. "I know, Gran, and thanks. I just need some time to think things through, and I wouldn't want to put a damper on your vacation."

"Okay, Peanut. Just know you've got family, and we care." Gran sounded hesitant.

Making her own voice more chipper than she felt, she said, "I know, Gran. Listen, let me go get myself and the boys ready so we can meet you at the dock."

"All right, baby. I'll see you then."

Latonya hung up the phone feeling more on edge than she thought she would. She knew that her stay at Gran's house was just the beginning of her separating from Carlton. She would spend two weeks at

Gran's, sleeping there at night and visiting with the boys when Carlton left for work, and she would find a place of her own.

Clearly, things weren't going to change between her and Carlton. The sooner she realized that and moved on, the better.

Chapter 29

Carlton spent the entire day and part of the evening handling one crisis after another at Harrington Enterprise. He regretted that he hadn't even had a spare moment to at least call and check in with Latonya to see how she was feeling. He knew he needed to find a way to get her to see that he was serious about courting her and wasn't going to let his hormones get in the way of them taking it slow.

He was thinking about the best way to go about that when his grandfather walked into his office.

"How's it going, son? What are you still doing at the office?"

"Things have been crazy around here. Are you sure you really need to retire? We could have used you around here today."

"No, Harrington Enterprise is up to you and your boys to run now. I stayed longer than I should have because of what happened with your dad. But I have every confidence that the family business is in good hands now. I plan to spend more time at home in the Bahamas."

Carlton smiled ruefully. His father's share in the corporation officially became his when he turned twenty-one. Knowing that the future of Harrington Enterprise was up to him and his children left him feeling a strange sense of awe. "Well, the boys would certainly miss their great-grandpop if you stayed away too much."

"Speaking of the boys, why aren't you home spending more time with your family?" Grandfather chastised. "I heard you had a date with your wife last night."

Carlton wondered who hadn't heard about his date with Latonya, and he also wondered what his grandfather was up to. Grandfather rarely mentioned Latonya without an agenda. Eyeing the elder Harrington wearily, he responded, "Yes, we had a date."

"Well, what are you doing here? Why aren't you with her? You two are going to try to work it out, aren't you?"

"We are going to try. I just need to take it slow this time. I don't want to mess things up by rushing her."

"Nonsense, she loves you!" Grandfather snapped.

Carlton narrowed his eyes. "What is with you, Grandfather? If I didn't know any better, I'd think you were encouraging me to work things out with my wife."

"I am. I have done you wrong, son, and I need to clear things up." Grandfather's eyes welled up and he took a deep shuddering breath. "I lied to you about Latonya. Son, the kiss I saw between Jeff and Latonya was far from a passionate embrace. It was a peck on the cheek and a quick hug of greeting." Grandfather sighed before he finished in a somber voice. "I told you to come and pay attention to your marriage because of what I saw and sensed in Weatherby, and I thought it would be a good way to make you get rid of her before she caused havoc the way your mother did. I offered her money to leave when she came back to the house after you kicked her out. When she wouldn't take it, I threatened her life and the lives of her grandmother and Cicely."

Grandfather's words came out in a rushed tirade and Carlton felt the air escape from his lungs with each confession.

Carlton's response came out in a series of questions that were just as quick as Grandfather's rant. "She came back? Do you mean to tell me that you never saw her kissing another man? You lied to me? You sowed a seed of doubt where there was none and made me kick my wife out on the street while she was pregnant with my son? You threatened her life?"

"I'm sorry, son. I never would have told you to throw the woman out. She was little Carl's mother and seemed to be a decent one. Once you did throw her out, I used it to get rid of her before she did something that would take you away forever. I was wrong. She loves those boys more than anything. I've watched her with them."

His tone softened. "She's a good mother. She's not like your mother...not like that Anastasia." He hissed the name out. "Latonya loves those boys. Any fool can see that. In spite of everything...I can see now that the woman loves you, too. I'm admitting that I was wrong, not because I hope that you will forgive me, but because I want the two of you to work things out for those boys' sake."

The fact that Grandfather brought up the one woman that the old man hated the most let Carlton know how seriously he wanted to be taken. Grandfather never mentioned Carlton's mother; they never discussed Anastasia, ever.

He'd never allowed himself to think about what it meant that he'd never been able to talk about what happened between his parents to the man entrusted with his care.

As a fifteen-year-old boy who'd suffered the tragedy of losing both parents, who'd grown up listening to them scream at each other, and seen his mother in the passionate embrace of too many men who were not his father, he'd needed to talk with someone. But there had been no one. So, he'd bottled it all in.

Though he felt betrayed, he knew he couldn't entirely blame Grandfather. Carlton was the one who had kicked his wife out. But Carlton knew he would never forgive his grandfather for threatening her life. Threatening her life while she carried his child!

Carlton felt his jaw set harshly. The hardening in his heart toward the elder man standing in front of him felt out of place. But he knew that it would be a long time before it went anywhere. "I think it would be a good idea for you to go back to the Bahamas. I want you to stay away from me and my family."

"Carlton, please, I only wanted to spare you—"

"You wanted to spare yourself! It has always been about sparing you. Do you think that you were the only one hurt by my parents' fiasco of a marriage? I was only a kid. And I hurt, too. I never thought I'd be able to love until I met Latonya. When she came into my life, she made me believe that I could have it all. And you ruined that with your threats and lies. The three years that she was gone were the darkest years of my life. The only thing that held me together was our son. Those three years didn't have to happen because she had come back. You sent her away and made her afraid. I will *never* forgive you for that!"

"I'm sorry you feel that way, son." The elder Harrington turned and left the office.

Carlton watched him go with an angry glare before deciding it was time to go home to his wife.

He finally made it home well after nine in the evening. Carlton planned to once and for all acknowledge his part in their breakup and apologize. He also wanted to tell her that he loved her more than he could ever put into words. He wanted her to be able to look him in the eye while he exposed his soul in order for her to believe him.

Hoping that it wasn't too late for them, he searched the house for her. After the night that they'd shared, he knew that their bodies were still in tune and meant to be together. But how would she react to his love? Could she ever grow to love him? Would she accept his apology? All of his fears and doubts and questions made him search all the more vigorously. When he couldn't find her anywhere else, he looked in her bedroom. Taking a deep breath, he opened the door only to find the bed crisply made and no sign of Latonya.

Carlton made his way to his sons' bedrooms, thinking that she must have gone to sleep while reading to them the way she often did. When he got to Terrence's room, he found the bed empty and his heart dropped; he felt its rapid beating in his gut and bile rose in his throat. A bad feeling started to overcome him.

Racing to little Carl's room, he found his sons sharing a bed. However, Latonya wasn't with them.

Terrence lay sleeping, but little Carl's eyes were still open.

"Hi, Daddy." His son spoke in a hushed voice. "Terry was scared and crying because he thought Mommy wasn't coming back. I told him that Mommy said she was going to see us every day even though she wasn't sleeping here anymore."

Carlton's heart dropped to his feet. Kneeling down by the right side of the bed, closest to his eldest son, he asked, "Where's your mother?"

"We went to see Great-Grandmama and Aunt Cee Cee and the big boat. I wanted to get on the big boat, but Mommy said I couldn't go this time. She'll take me and Terry another time."

Gripping the mattress so tightly he could no longer

feel his own hand, Carlton forced himself to calmly ask, "Did your Mommy get on the boat, Carl?"

His son let out an exasperated sigh. "No, Daddy. Only Aunt Cee Cee and Great-Grandmama this time. We'll go later."

Carlton let out a deep breath he hadn't even realized he'd been holding. "Is Mommy home now?"

"No. She said she needed to go away for a little while. But that she'll be back to see us during the day. To play with us and read us stories. But Terry was sad. I told him not to be sad because Mommy said she wouldn't leave me again. You remember, Daddy, right?"

Carlton patted his son's head and kissed him on the cheek. "I remember. Go to sleep now and I'll see you in the morning."

"Night, night, Daddy."

"Night, night, son." He stood slowly on shaky legs.

She'd left. Stunned, he never thought she would leave the boys. She definitely loved them. He didn't think she would ever willingly leave *without* them. He kicked himself for making love to her. He had pushed her too fast. He should have taken it slow. She probably thought he hadn't changed at all. He needed her to know that he had. He knew he had to get a grip so that he could salvage things.

He went searching for Jillian to see if Latonya had left word about where she was going and when she would be back.

Jillian and Pamela were sitting in the kitchen having tea when he walked in. The icy stares that both women gave him turned the usually toasty room cold.

Carlton felt a foreboding chill in his veins and hoped that whatever had made Latonya leave wasn't unfixable.

"Good evening, ladies. Where's Latonya?" he asked hesitantly. The loud beating came back, and he swore he could feel his heart in his stomach.

Jillian cut her eyes at him and shook her head. "She decided to stay at her grandmother's house for two weeks while Cicely takes Evelyn on a Caribbean cruise. She said she'd be back during the day to spend time with the boys. But she plans to spend her nights there." Sighing, Jillian took a sip of tea. "It didn't sound like she was making any plans to come back here and live once Evelyn gets back. She said she needed time to think things through, to sort out her life."

He flinched. His hand grabbed the edge of the kitchen counter. Why would she just up and leave? How could she do that to the kids? To him? Sure, he had pushed things further than he intended by making love to her, but that wasn't reason enough for her to just up and leave. Was it?

Carlton could feel each heavy, thumping beat of his heart. Fear unlike any he'd ever felt overcame him. It was too late. The mere thought caused a chasm in his chest that felt as large as the Grand Canyon. He stopped and gave the women a meaningful stare. After being the victim of one horrible misunderstanding about Latonya, he refused to make any more rash decisions. "What exactly did my wife say when she left here?"

Jillian narrowed her eyes on him and he felt as if he were a boy again sneaking cookies out of the kitchen.

The normally bubbly and bright Pamela took a sip of her tea. The way her eyes darted back and forth between him and Jillian, it was clear she knew something. Finally Pamela sighed.

"She said that she needed some space and time to sort out her feelings." The nanny paused momentarily as if trying to decide if she should betray Latonya's trust. "And she said that she couldn't stay here any longer. It's too hard for her. She looked like she'd been crying. It didn't seem like an easy decision for her."

Too hard for her? Letting go of the counter, Carlton began to walk out of the kitchen. "I'm going to get my wife and bring her back home. Thanks, ladies."

"Just make sure you do it right this time! Don't mess up," Jillian snapped.

"Jillian," Pamela chided.

Jillian sucked her teeth. "What? The man needs to know that he could lose her, and I know he doesn't want that to happen!"

Carlton froze. The little woman with the big mouth was right. He didn't want that to happen. Couldn't allow it. "Thanks for the advice, Jillian. Anything else?"

"Just don't blow it!" Jillian picked up her teacup and took a sip.

Pamela shook her head. "Jillian!"

"What?" Jillian asked.

Carlton realized that the person he really needed to be reassuring wasn't in the kitchen. "Don't worry, Jillian, I'm going to try not to."

Chapter 30

When Carlton drove up to Gran's home, he was almost tempted to pull the car away. If he truly loved Latonya, he should be willing to set her free, he reasoned. He didn't want to repeat history and keep dragging a woman back home if she clearly didn't want to be there. He'd seen what that had done to his mother and father. It would break his heart if he saw his mother's feelings of trapped misery replicated in his own wife.

As he walked up the stairs, he told himself that he had to let her know how he felt about her. Maybe if she knew how much he cared…

He had to try at least once for the boys' sake. Hell, for his own heart's sake. He needed to get his true feelings out in the open once and for all.

Only when he rang the doorbell did he realize how late it was and wonder if he should have called first. The irony that he had been in the same spot six years earlier, trying to figure out how to get Latonya to listen to him wasn't lost on him. *At least that time I had sense enough to bring flowers,* he mentally chided. His breath caught in his throat when she opened the door. Even in a simple white cotton sleep shirt with big yellow ducks on it and a satin sleep bonnet covering her hair, she looked beautiful.

Covering her mouth as she yawned, she stood between the small crack in the door. "Carlton, what are you doing here? It's late."

Running his hand across his face, he sighed. "Can I come in? We need to talk."

"Can't it wait until a decent hour?" She yawned again and didn't open the door any wider.

"If it could I wouldn't be here, Latonya. Baby, please, just let me come in. I need to talk to you for a moment." He realized that he was pleading, begging even. He knew he would drop to his knees if it would make a difference.

"I don't think that would be a good idea," Latonya said, pushing the door shut a little. "I know we need to talk. But not tonight."

Carlton used his foot as a wedge and winced when she continued to close the heavy door.

Latonya looked down and stopped. "Now, why would you want to put your foot there? I said we could talk at another time. Go home! And move your foot."

"I need to talk to you. You will have to slam that door on my foot to get me out of here. And even then, I would stay planted on this porch until you talked to me."

He watched as she contemplated the very idea and breathed a sigh of relief when she opened the door instead.

"You're lucky. I like your feet way more than I'm liking you right about now. I'll give you five minutes to say whatever it is you feel you need to say."

Trying to figure out the best place to start, the best way to make her know what was going on in his heart, Carlton stepped inside and started pacing the floor instead of sitting on the sofa with her. Finally, he stopped moving and looked at her. She eyed him with suspicion and he could tell that she had her guard up. Latonya didn't trust him. He sat on the sofa, unable to look at the hurt in her eyes anymore, especially knowing that he'd put it there. "I'd hoped that things would work out for us, Tonya—"

She cut him off. "I know, but, Carlton, we can't stay together for the kids' sake. In the end, it would do them more harm than good. You don't love me, Carlton." Her voice faltered and she almost stopped speaking, but she continued. "I thought I could live with you and know that you would probably never love me, but I can't. It hurts too much. You never acknowledged that you were wrong not to trust me. You kicked me out of our home. And you have never even apologized for any of it."

Turning to face her, Carlton lifted her chin. Two

tears trailed down her cheeks. "How can you say I don't love you? I must have loved you from the moment I first saw you. I was so afraid of losing you that I married you before you could get away, married you hoping that one day you would come to love *me*."

Wiping the tears from her cheek one by one, he continued, "Things were going so well between us. I even felt like you had feelings for me, feelings that went beyond the way I made you feel in bed. Then Grandfather called and told me that he saw you kissing Jeff Weatherby." He stopped and let out a shuddering breath at the memory of that moment.

"When I rushed back from Barbados, the first thing I wanted to do was beg you not to throw our marriage away. But my pride made me push you away. When I thought I saw your betrayal with my own eyes, I kicked you out before you could leave me for him. I was trying to protect my heart, but I ended up ripping it out just as surely as if I'd done it with my own hands. When you disappeared, I was miserable. I hurt you and I will *never* be able to apologize to you enough for that. But I am sorry, baby. So very sorry."

"How could you have believed that I would betray you like that? That's what hurt so bad." Latonya bit out the words forcefully and pulled her face away from his caress. "I thought if nothing else, you would have had more faith in me! No matter what your grandfather told you. You should have listened to my side."

Carlton felt as if he was losing his entire world all over again. The hurt and anger in her voice cut him and he felt fear, regret and remorse seeping into the wound her words left behind. "I didn't believe it then. I felt in my heart that you wouldn't do that, but I couldn't trust it. I went into self-preservation mode and ended up losing the best thing that ever happened to me. I ended up losing the only woman I ever loved. I'm sorry. I should have trusted you. I shouldn't have kicked you out."

"You loved me?" she asked tentatively.

"*I still love you.* I understand if you can't forgive me, if you can never grow to love me. I won't try to make you stay somewhere that you don't want to be. As hard as it will be for me to let you go, I will." He knew what he had to do so that his sons wouldn't miss out on their mother's love and attention as an everyday part of their lives. "I love you too much to see the hurt in your eyes, or to break your spirit by making you stay in a marriage you don't want. You can have custody of the boys, all I ask is to be allowed open visitation and that you please don't take them far away."

Latonya folded her arms across her chest. "If you loved me, why didn't you ever say it?"

"I honestly thought you knew. I thought the entire world could see it. And you never said it, either. I figured that given your past with your father, showing you how I felt would mean more in the long run." If he had it to do over again he would tell her *and* show her that he loved her every day.

"You love me? But you're letting me go?" Awe-struck, she whispered the words.

"Yes. It's for the best. You're my heart and I love

you. But if you don't love me, I'll only end up making you miserable."

"How can you love me when you never trusted me and you never told me that you loved me? I loved you so much. I kept thinking that it was only about lust and sex for you and that you were going to get tired of me eventually and move on. I guess my parents' relationship colored my views. I didn't expect what we had to last because their marriage failed. But I thought at least I'd have the memories and our son as a reminder of how much I loved you."

She gritted her teeth and her hands balled up into little fists. "Then you threw me out and kept our son. You broke my heart, but I still loved you. It made me sick when I would lie in bed at night rubbing my pregnant belly and thinking of you, thinking of running back to Miami and begging you to forgive me for something I didn't even do. When I had Terrence and he came out looking so much like the Harrington he was, reminding me of little Carl every time I looked at him, I wanted to hate you. But I couldn't." As she gazed at him, he saw the pain he'd caused her.

"I didn't know that telling you how I felt would have helped. I thought that if you knew that I was in so deep, it would scare you and make you flee. I thought you just married me because you'd been saving yourself for marriage. Women tend to build sentimental attachments to the first man they have sex with…. I knew you loved our child. But I didn't think you could ever really love me. So I never opened my self up enough to let you see my feelings."

He paused and turned away. Although he wished he could have had the conversation with her without bringing his parents up, he knew that he needed to bare all of his soul if she were going to truly understand. He had to come clean about his own demons the way she had about hers.

"You weren't the only one who had a lousy model for relationships to get past. My parents had a very rocky marriage. In spite of everything that went down between my parents, I believe that they loved each other very much. Watching how their love played out, how sick and twisted it became, made me more than a little gun-shy about that emotion." Carlton took a deep breath. The chasm in his chest had turned into a river and he felt emotions pouring out of him that he hadn't even known were there.

He told Latonya about his mother's many infidelities, and what the battle between his parents had done to him, how their deaths had made him feel. "I always thought it was my fault. If I had gone with her, my father would have come for her sooner, before hurricane season…. Their flight might not have run into bad weather. I feel guilty for their deaths and I never felt I could allow myself to fall in love."

He allowed himself to feel the pain, *really* feel it for the first time in decades. Losing his parents, no matter how messed up they were, hurt. He felt a tear running down his cheek. Wiping it away, he turned to Latonya. She appeared to be listening intently, so he continued. He might as well get it all out.

"I didn't like what love did to people. I didn't trust

the emotion at all after they died. That's why, when I
first saw you and felt the sharp piercing in my heart, I
tried everything in my power to push you away. I
actually thought that if I was harsh enough you would
give up and find another place of employment." Remembering how horribly he acted toward her back
then, he paused in shame and glanced at her.

Her silent contemplation showed that she was also
remembering those days.

Carlton wished that he could have found a way to
go back and right all the wrong. He'd almost lost the
love of his life because he'd been too arrogant and
pigheaded to recognize her. The thought that he might
still lose her caused him to finish his story in hopes that
it might make a difference.

Carlton hesitated. Putting everything on the line
was hard. What if it was too little too late? What if she
still rejected him? He knew he had to try.

"You were very determined, and the more I pushed
you the more you pushed back. I can't tell you how
sexy that was. So, I thought if I had sex with you that
would surely free me of the growing feelings I was
starting to have for you. It always worked with women
in the past. But I should have known better, because
my feelings for you were stronger than anything I'd
ever experienced. I mean, I was jealous of your silly,
harmless flirting with Stan, Juan and Jeff, because I
wanted you to flirt with me." Glancing at her again, he
noticed that her eyes narrowed slightly. Carlton closed
his eyes and chided himself over his foolish jealousy.
He knew that he probably didn't deserve Latonya, and

worse, the trip down memory lane was probably confirming that for her. He could lose her! His chest exploded and his stomach suddenly felt queasy. But he knew there was no stopping. She had to know everything.

"But all I did was fall more deeply for you. That's why I asked you to marry me, and I hoped that one day you would grow to love me half as much as I loved you. I wanted you. I needed you. I still do. Can you ever forgive me for not trusting love enough to give you my heart?"

As he turned to face her, readying himself for rejection, his heart stopped when she got up from the sofa. She stood in front of him and studied him carefully. "Love can't survive in fear or if there's no trust."

"I trust you. I'm sorry I ever doubted you. I'm sorry for all I've done, for listening to Grandfather's lies. He admitted it all today. If I had known that you had come back that day, I would have found you much sooner. I will never forgive myself for the three years we lost as a family. And I will *never* forgive my grandfather for threatening your life."

Carlton was certain about that. He would never be able to trust his grandfather again.

Latonya shook her head. She never thought she would see the day when she would make a case for the elder Harrington. But then she never thought she'd see the day when her husband would give such a heartfelt apology, listing all of his faults and wrongdoings. "He did it because he loved you and he was afraid."

Carlton gritted his teeth and his jaw locked defiantly. "I don't want him around you or the children."

"You have a right to be angry with him. But he is family and he is sorry." Standing in front of her husband, she tried to find any of the hardness that had buried itself in her heart since he had kicked her out. She found none.

"Why didn't you tell me what he'd done?" His eyes narrowed slightly and she felt as if she were under a microscope.

She honestly believed that she had made the best decision in that regard. In order for everyone to heal, they had to come to and make their own peace.

"It wasn't my wrong to right." Sitting back down on the sofa, she searched for the strength to confess her own shortcomings. She knew that she had to admit her part in the failure of their marriage if they were truly going to move on.

She put her hand on his hand, held it to her cheek and stared him in the eyes. His gaze was so intense and searing, she couldn't have looked away if she wanted to.

"I have my own faults to confess. I was too scared to trust you not to leave me or throw me away like my father did my mother…like my father did my family. So I never told you how much I loved you. Even today, after the night we shared, I realized that I loved you, and rather than staying and fighting for our marriage, I chickened out and ran instead. I'm sorry. Can you forgive me?" Smiling weakly, she allowed her eyes to plead for understanding.

As if he understood the message she was trying to convey, he said simply, "You never have to plead for my love. I couldn't stop loving you any more than I could stop breathing." He caressed her face, and then he asked, "You want to be with me? You're not leaving me?"

"I will never leave you again. I'm going to give you all the love I have inside so that you will never think not to trust me with your heart." She brought her hand to his face.

Taking a deep breath, he let out a sigh. "She loves me." He bent his head down and his lips claimed hers. "I love you, Latonya. Let's go home."

Leila Owens didn't know
how to love herself let alone
an abandoned baby
but Garret Grayson knew
how to love them both.

She's My Baby

Adrianne Byrd

(Kimani Romance #10)

AVAILABLE SEPTEMBER 2006

FROM KIMANI™ ROMANCE

Love's Ultimate Destination